THE TANGLED WEB OF DECEPTION

For one wild moment as big, handsome Alex Houston took Cynthia in his arms she was lost in a dream of happiness.

Then she awoke. Almost roughly she tore herself from his dear embrace.

For Cynthia knew Alex to be a proud man of highest principles. And she had lied to him about her past.

How could she hope that his love would remain steadfast when he learned her shameful secret?

Books by Emilie Loring

- FOR ALL YOUR LIFE
- WHAT THEN IS LOVE
- I TAKE THIS MAN
- MY DEAREST LOVE
- LOOK TO THE STARS
- BEHIND THE CLOUD
- THE SHADOW OF SUSPICION
- WITH THIS RING
- BEYOND THE SOUND OF GUNS
- HOW CAN THE HEART FORGET
- TO LOVE AND TO HONOR
- LOVE CAME LAUGHING BY
- I HEAR ADVENTURE CALLING

Published by Bantam Books

EMILIE LORING

WITH THIS RING

*This low-priced Bantam Book
has been completely reset in a type face
designed for easy reading, and was printed
from new plates. It contains the complete
text of the original hard-cover edition.*
NOT ONE WORD HAS BEEN OMITTED.

WITH THIS RING
*A Bantam Book / published by arrangement with
Little, Brown and Co., Inc.*

PRINTING HISTORY
*Little, Brown edition published June 1959
2nd printing .... November 1959
Grosset and Dunlap edition published August 1960
Bantam edition published October 1961
2nd printing ..... October 1961
3rd printing .... April 1963
4th printing .... June 1964
5th printing
6th printing
7th printing
8th printing
9th printing
10th printing*

*For information address: Little, Brown and Company, Inc.,
34 Beacon Street, Boston 6, Massachusetts.
Published simultaneously in the United States and Canada.*

---

*Bantam Books are published by Bantam Books, Inc. Its trade-mark,
consisting of the words "Bantam Books" and the portrayal of a
bantam, is registered in the United States Patent Office and in other
countries. Marca Registrada. Printed in the United States of America. Bantam Books, Inc., 271 Madison Ave., New York 16, N. Y.*

All episodes used to develop the plot of this novel are fictitious. Use of a name which is that of a living person is accidental. Newbury Point is a composite of the many charming spots which abound on the New England coast.

I

CYNTHIA's first intimation that something was wrong came from Eric Crane's sharp order, "Let go, I'll take over!" He turned from peering out the window and his tanned hands flashed to the wheel of the little plane. There were two sets of controls, so she needed only to release her own grip and shift her feet from the pedals to give him command. At the same moment she glanced at Eric beside her; his face was white and tight-lipped.

How had she blundered this time, she wondered. Taking off, as she'd done dozens of times before, what stupid mistake caused her fiancé to suddenly take over? Of course, there was that jolt and twist of the plane just before the landing wheels left the ground. But that was not unusual in *her* take-offs. Eric criticized her often for driving an airplane like a snowplow.

Could it be something else? She remembered being startled by his unexpected demand for a speedier wedding than they planned, but the argument which followed had been perfectly amicable and she was secretly rather flattered. All that was half an hour ago, so why this abrupt action which was anything but flattering? Puzzled, she looked down as they swept back over the field.

The lump which always jumped into her throat at the first sputtering throb of the plane's motor and subsided when they took to the air now swelled to mammoth proportions. On the sunlit field men were running, waving their arms. One of them was holding something over his head, making wide sweeping motions to attract their attention to it. A wheel! She knew too well what that signal meant—a landing wheel of their plane was missing. Had it spun away as they left the ground, or just dropped off on this practice flight? As if that made any difference!

Was this to be her last flight? The end of the rigid self-discipline she had administered during all of her two month's engagement to Eric Crane, forcing herself to *endure* flying because flying seemed to be his whole life? What a satiric ending!

She clasped her hands tightly together in her lap and shook her head.

"Don't be a cry-baby—yet, Cynthia Farley!" she mentally reproved herself, and dragged her fascinated eyes away from the field.

How clear the mountains showed, sun-drenched except for the purple shadows of the clouds along their sides. Nearer, and higher still, a big silvery airplane floated, seemingly almost motionless. A black speck dropped from it, shot downward for a long breathless moment until a dazzling white flower opened wide above it and drifted slowly earthward. Parachute jumping. The girl set her teeth tight on her lower lip and shivered. Would Eric order her to try that next?

And if he does, I suppose I'll jump, she thought bitterly. What Eric says, Cynthia does. Why Cynthia? Why had Eric Crane, youngest son of an English nobleman and an American mother, test pilot for a world-renowned British firm and hero of more than one spectacular flight abroad, come to California and immediately singled her out from among all the girls who set their caps for him? Beauties, some of them, and some with far more social standing than she had.

Never mind *why,* the fact remained that he *had* chosen her. And she, dazzled by his reputation, thrilled by his devotion, not only accepted his proposal of marriage, but took a mental oath to please him by becoming as air-minded as he—or perish in the attempt. At the moment, she thought with a shudder, it looked as if it might be *perish.*

Crane noticed her shiver, for he spoke impatiently.

"We're in trouble! You must have hit something back there in the field because we're minus a landing wheel on my side, but I'm going in anyway. Stop squirming around and brace yourself." He settled lower into his seat and stared at the instrument panel.

"A control tower would help, but there isn't one, so we're on our own. Look at your landing wheel—seem all right?" When she nodded he flashed her a white-lipped smile. "We may take a nasty bump, but there is no real danger, Cynthia. I've landed on one wheel before."

She tried to speak, to answer his reassurance with confidence, but her throat was paralyzed. It didn't help to notice beads of perspiration forming just below his blond crew cut.

Crane eyed her again and spoke harshly.

"Did you hear me? Snap out of it and check your safety belt! Cover your face with your arms and keep low. Come on—*move!*"

With the sensation of watching her double perform in slow motion, Cynthia at last obeyed. Crouched forward with face covered, she felt the plane sink slowly, tilt and then bound upward. That must have been the single landing wheel touching the runway. Now—

A siren wailed faintly in the distance. An ambulance? Had they called an ambulance? Not so good—The plane sank abruptly, steadied, but at an alarming angle, touched ground, sped onward. Good old runway! Blessed solid earth! Safe? Of course. Hadn't Eric landed minus a wheel before? He was slowing now, cutting the throttle. How silly to be afraid with an expert handling the plane—

A sudden, sickening face-about whirl—a grinding, crunching jumble of noise tearing at her eardrums. Crash! The plane whipped over like a giant cartwheel . . . darkness.

A bright light dazzled Cynthia, seared her eyes. Then smothering blackness again. Clinging desperately to something warm and throbbing she felt her body rise, float, and begin to sink.

"Don't—don't let me go! Hold me!" she cried wildly.

"I am holding you, my dear."

The voice was strange but calming. She felt safe; terribly tired; she tried to smile. Here came the black cloud again! She must fight it off! She opened her eyes.

"Hello there!" The same voice, gruff but soothing. She looked up at the gray, smiling man. His hands gripped hers. "I am Doctor Barnes. You will be all right now. Here, drink this."

Something deliciously cool, slightly salty, slipped down her throat. The leaden weights which had pressed against her lids were gone; it wasn't nearly so much effort to open her eyes.

Twin lamps of wrought iron, twisted vines with tiny lights set among the leaves, like the ones on her dressing table. What in the world were they doing here? With a superhuman effort she turned her head and stared. Leaf-green plaster walls, deeper green hangings at the windows. Her own room! But the plane was landing—there'd been a crack-up.

She forced her shoulders up from the pillow, caught the doctor's arm, whispered, "Eric?"

Dr. Barnes patted the hand on his sleeve, peered over his rimless glasses.

"Your friend? He's all right, my dear. It was quite a smash, but nothing seems badly damaged except the plane. The young man suffered a lot of bruises, including a black eye and a mean twist to his knee, which may keep him in bed for a few days. You were both very lucky."

The girl sank back on the pillow but her spirits soared. Eric would be out of action for a few days! No flying! She would take her car and get out into the country, far from this air-minded atmosphere. No more jittery dread of take-offs and landings! How wonderful! Then a shattering thought—

"Am I—much—much scratched?" she whispered.

Dr. Barnes studied her for a moment, then smiled.

"Neither scratched nor broken."

"Then why—why am I—in bed?"

His big hand gently restrained her when she attempted to sit up.

"Lie still," he ordered. "You've had a severe shaking up and I want you to be quiet for a while. Tomorrow, if you look all right to me, you may get up."

There was finality enough in his voice to impress her. She attempted a cheerful smile and nod of acquiescence, but her heavy lids drooped.

When next she opened her eyes twilight was stealing into the room. She heard the far-off drone of a plane and shivered. Somewhere in the house a door slammed. Aunt Julia coming in or going out with her customary energy. Cynthia felt far from energetic but ravenously hungry. As though in answer to the thought a velvet-footed shadow appeared in the room and advanced to the bed.

"Sara, you angel!" Cynthia greeted the Filipino maid with real enthusiasm. "Can that possibly be a tray of food in your hands? I am starving!"

"Yes'm, Miss Farley, it is and you generally are," chuckled the girl. "I'm sure glad *you* aren't an angel tonight! They say it was awful, the way your plane—"

"Spare me the details, Sara, I was there."

"Yes'm. That doctor said you can have anything you want to eat. So I fixed you a nice supper." She set the tray on a bedside table. "I'll twist this around so's you can get at it easy. It sure must have been kind of scary when you found that wheel had fallen off."

"The understatement of the year," Cynthia agreed cheerfully. "I was petrified. Please hand me the mirror from my dressing table." Restraining the almost overpowering urge to look at herself, she slid the mirror under the covers. "Thank you for everything, Sara, you're precious."

"Yes'm, I knows it. If you want anything else, just yell." The maid took a last look about the room and tiptoed out.

Cynthia whipped up the hand mirror. Doctor Barnes was an honest man; not a scratch or bruise. Breathlessly she inventoried the almost black hair, heavily lashed brown eyes and lips now set in a wistful curve. Not much color, but otherwise none the worse for the adventure. Relieved, she turned to her meal.

There would be no need to "yell" for Sara, she thought, surveying the laden tray. Cream of tomato soup, avocado salad with wafer-thin but luscious toasted cheese sandwiches, a mouth-watering ice of raspberry hue. She enjoyed every mouthful. How nice it was to be alive!

Leisurely sipping her coffee she leaned back against the pillows and regarded the diamond on her finger. With more than a slight twinge of conscience she wondered at her reaction to the news that Eric would be out of circulation for a day or so. Relief—not that he was safe, but that she would not have to fly again until he recovered. Was this love?

For the first time in months she had the desire and the opportunity to think things through. That terrible accident which took both her father and mother had left her stunned. In a stupor of agony she closed their home and while her two older brothers went their separate ways she came here to California to live with Uncle Joe Darcy and his second wife, Julia.

"Julia!" She groaned as she set her cup down and pushed the table away. "Aunt Julia, the world's champion pain-in-the-neck, self-centered, nagging and so madly socially ambitious that you shame me a dozen times a day!" She repressed a shudder as she remembered Julia's broadcasting of every detail of Cynthia's inheritance. A million dollars when she was twenty-three—or married.

Had she accepted Eric as a refuge from life with the demon aunt? From the day of her arrival Julia had persistently condemned Cynthia's likes, ridiculed her dislikes. It seemed, Cynthia thought bitterly, as though she seizes every occasion to call me "odd"! Because I'm not a social climber, I'm *odd*. Because I don't enjoy going out with the pawing, over-drinking sons of her friends, I'm *odd*.

Her thoughts raced as she studied the diamond ring. At last she had done something which met with her aunt's approval—probably because Eric might some day come into a title, a glittering prospect to a social climber. Cynthia had been jubilant, too, at least in the beginning. Why? Because she loved him, of course. Well—she did love him, didn't she? He was so attractive—although a bit more chin and a trifle less nose would improve him. But that, according to Julia, was typical of English nobility. And he seemed so unspoiled by fame that she forgave him his faults, although they did trouble her.

He was easy to get along with—when he had his own

way, she added ruefully. Not very considerate, and to be honest, downright domineering at times. Unambitious, content to drift along. She wondered, not for the first time, what he did when he wasn't with her and her friends at the Club. He made frequent visits to big airplane plants and factories in the vicinity, but he never mentioned their purpose and changed the subject when she inquired. Oh well, what if he didn't have a regular job? That didn't matter; when they married she would come into her inheritance—plenty for both of them.

She had met him at the Country Club where he was staying after a solo flight from England and a cross-country tour in his own plane. She burned with shame when she recalled her aunt's palpitant introduction with its thinly veiled hints of her niece's financial prospects. If Eric was embarrassed at Julia's crude approach his suave courtesy had concealed the feeling while he put himself out to be charming to Cynthia.

Before she realized it she had succumbed to that charm, so completely in fact that in a few weeks she was learning to pilot a plane under his tuition. A mistake. She enjoyed flying as a passenger, but this do-it-yourself routine was something else again—and something that frightened her. Every moment at the controls was an hour of tense foreboding, although Eric never seemed to realize this. Heart in mouth she dived and zoomed, raced ahead of a storm, stonily regarded the red-hot skeleton of a crashed plane, never betraying her inward turmoil. Why endure such torture? Because Eric had set his heart on making a pilot of her!

Idly she pleated the edge of the mint green sheet while she wondered if he appreciated what she was going through for him. He had never said so; in fact, now that she searched her memory, he had never praised her for anything she did in the air. Could she be as bad as all that?

At the beginning of their romance he had been generous with compliments. Since their engagement had been announced she could not remember one nice thing Eric had said about her. Now that he was sure of her, did he take too much for granted?

Could she be, deep down, the same snob which Julia was so brazenly portraying? Was she thrilled by the nobly connected visitor from England, the test pilot who made headlines, and flattered when he selected her from the crowd of eager girls who surrounded him at the Club? Was it that which had drawn her to him—and not true love? Was the thrill beginning to wear off and—

Cynthia's heart tripped, then raced on. "Of course it isn't

that!" she whispered, relaxing her clenched hands. "I do love Eric and that crack-up has me all shook up!"

Into her reverie burst Aunt Julia, talking as she came. "Don't tell me it wasn't all your fault, Cynthia Farley! Eric is being very chivalrous, swearing that *he* was at the controls. Could anything be more ridiculous! An experienced pilot such as he, smashing up a plane—!"

"There was a wheel off, remember?" Cynthia informed her crisply. Then changed the subject hastily, anxious to plunge at once into what she knew would be a nerve-racking scene. The sooner begun, the sooner ended. "I have some exciting news for you, Aunt Julia. Eric doesn't want to wait for the June wedding we planned. In spite of all the arrangements you've made he wants to be married at once."

II

THE ORGAN lifted its muted voice in the first soaring notes of the wedding march. Cynthia dug her fingers into Uncle Joe Darcy's solid arm and drew a long breath to quiet her fluttering heart. Good grief! If she was as nervous as this at a mere rehearsal, what would be her mental state tomorrow during the ceremony?

For a moment she wondered if she were tempting fate by ignoring the age-old taboo against a bride's taking part in the rehearsal. But Aunt Julia scoffed at such an antiquated idea; the latest authorities agreed that girls no longer cared, and Aunt Julia was running this wedding. Deprived of the social splendor of the huge June ceremony she had planned, Julia threatened hysterics until Cynthia agreed to cater to every whim in this abbreviated version.

The bridesmaids and ushers began their measured march toward the chancel. Uncle Joe, perspiring and puffing with nervousness, started to follow too soon, shuffled back and performed a little soft-shoe dance of impatience while he waited. Cynthia patted his hand comfortingly, staring ahead into the dim tunnel-like church.

More friends than she expected had chosen to watch the rehearsal, the pews lining the aisle were dotted with pale blotches of staring faces. Cynthia didn't mind. The more now, the less awe-inspiring the crowd tomorrow would seem. Except that she did wish Debbie Winfield could have had a previous engagement to keep her away. Debbie had never forgiven her for snaring the desirable Eric Crane, probably never would forgive her. That was Debbie's way, with her face of a cherub and tongue of a serpent—

Uncle Joe stepped forward, sure of himself this time, and dragged Cynthia with him. Far down the aisle she saw the commanding figure of Aunt Julia overshadowing the short and rotund clergyman as she beat ponderous time with upraised purse. Cynthia's impulse to laugh was short-lived; beside Doctor Gresham stood Eric Crane and her brother, Alonzo. Bless Lon, she thought devoutly, for smothering his disapproval and agreeing to act as best man when Eric's selection came down with the flu.

She was near enough now to see Eric's slightly bored smile and Alonzo's mask of repressed disgust. Poor Lon, best man, after all his storming against the match—"How dumb can you be, tying up for life with a man you hardly know, a loafer and a rounder, unstable as a weathercock when it comes to liquor and women? How do I know? I have ears, haven't I? If you weren't slap-happy with what you think is love you would have found out for yourself!"

Cynthia thrust the disturbing memory into the farthest recess of her mind as she and her uncle stopped before Dr. Gresham. Afternoon sunlight slanting through the stained-glass window colored them all. The organ's soft notes fell to a rhythmic murmur. The clergyman opened his book to describe the service he would read and point out the proper responses and actions for the participants. The soberly intent bridesmaids nudged the ushers into line, Uncle Joe stepped back, Eric stepped forward . . .

A shrill voice slashed through the church's hush, *"Stop it, Eric Crane!"*

Cynthia stood frozen, unable even to turn her head, while ice water feathered through her veins. Behind her a rustle like leaves presaging the onrush of a storm stirred through the pews as the onlookers turned to face this interruption.

"Eric, you belong to me!" the same strident voice screamed. "You have to marry *me!"*

Cynthia's groping hand found Eric's arm. Brown eyes wide with horror, she pleaded:

"I don't believe her, Eric! I *don't!"*

Now she was able to turn, to see the crowd around a sobbing woman near the entrance. Only a close-fitting hat showed between the shoulders of the men who urged her out of the church as she shrilled:

"You can't get away with this, Eric Crane! I'll never let you go! You—"

Mercifully the closing door shut out the tirade.

Cynthia whirled to Eric, passionate entreaty in her eyes. "Tell me she lies—" Agony clamped her throat, dried her lips as she saw his chalk-white face—saw at last his real self peering in desperation from between narrowed lids.

"Later," he muttered, shaking off her clinging hand. "I'll straighten everything out—"

Cynthia backed away, felt her brother's arm around her.

"Take me out of here, Lon!" she gasped. "Quick, before Aunt Julia—comes!"

As though in the numbing grip of delirium she felt cool outside air on her face as they went down the back steps to the parking lot. She was in a car—her own convertible. It swayed as her brother lurched into the driver's seat and his hard shoulder pressed against her. Voices shouting to them—hurrying footsteps crunching on the gravel. She buried her face in the rough tweed of his coat, heard the door slam, the wheels spurn gravel. The car shot out into the street, merged with the traffic. She heard the beat of motors on every side.

Cynthia straightened and sat with clenched hands, pale and still as a ghost girl, while Lon wove his way through the late afternoon rush. At a red light on an intersection he pulled over, switching his directional signal for the turn.

"Not home! *Please*, Lon, not home!" she entreated. "I just couldn't bear it!"

He nodded and dropped a reassuring hand on hers. The light turned green and he drove straight on. Mile after mile, through suburban business centers, onto expressways, off them to open country.

It was Cynthia who broke the silence at last.

"Eric didn't—didn't say that it wasn't true." Her voice was hoarse, almost inaudible. "He couldn't! I—I knew it from his expression."

Her brother grunted and nodded violently.

"You are *so* right, Cynthy!"

She studied his face. White—as white as hers must be—lips clamped in a line as unyielding as granite. Her own were quivering. As shudder after shudder shook her she huddled against him for comfort.

The car swerved to the side of the road and stopped.

"Sorry, dear," he apologized. "I didn't realize that the wind was so strong with the top down." He raised it, slipped out of his jacket. "Here, wrap this around you. You've caught a chill and are shaking like a leaf."

"I—I'm not—not cold." She set her teeth hard on her

lip to stop their chattering. When her brother eyed her anxiously she managed a wan smile. "Don't be afraid I'm going to have hysterics, but—but—Oh, *Lonny!*"

"Take it easy, Sis," he soothed. He drove on stolidly. "Crane will probably fix everything up."

"Never!" With the explosive gasp her self-control crashed. She pounded a tight clenched fist on her knee. Words tumbled out pell-mell.

"If you believe he can explain away that girl—you didn't see his face! He was scared! You can't tell me that she didn't really have something on him, Lon. I'll never believe that he wasn't—wasn't mixed up with her—if she swore to it herself."

She stared at him wildly and wrung her hands. She felt the ring and tore it off.

"Here!" She thrust it at Lon, who pocketed it without comment.

Cynthia relaxed and felt an unbearable relief.

"I've been thinking while you drove," she admitted. "Thinking harder than I ever did in my life. Now I realize that I drifted along, willfully shut my eyes to facts—doped my instinct. Things like this don't bolt from a clear sky. Little clouds show which way the wind blows—or are they straws?"

"Straws, usually," Alonzo advised dryly. "And plenty of them, if you'd had your eyes open."

"That is what I am saying!" she cried. "Of course I knew his reputation—a little wild, and drinking more than he should—but I thought that he would change when we were married. *Married!*"

Cynthia snapped erect to stare at her brother. Almost hysterically she demanded:

"I'm not married, am I? That hideous nightmare happened *before* the wedding, didn't it? Pinch me, Lon! Shake me! Tell me—"

"Pipe down!" It was the familiar bullying big brother who barked the command. "You'll fly off the handle if you keep that up!" Then with an obvious effort he softened his tone. "You are still Cynthia Farley, spinster." He took one hand from the wheel to pat her knee. "Chin up, mite, you are as free as the air."

The childhood nickname and the gentle touch melted a little of the ice around Cynthia's heart, and she clung to his hand.

He let her hold it, steering easily with the other while he went on quietly:

"This has been a terrible shock, I know, but try to pull

yourself together. This isn't the right time to say 'I told you so' and I—"

"There never is a right time for that, Lon," she interrupted.

He pulled back his hand and grunted.

"If you didn't sound like Mother then! Okay, I didn't intend to rub it in. Just put your mind to believing that what has happened is for the best. That it has saved you from a lot more unhappiness later on. Nothing I can say will help you, only time will do that, but I know you well enough to be sure that you will ride over this."

The girl's laugh was bitter. She rubbed her cheeks roughly and let her hands fall back in her lap.

"I've heard that the first fifty years are the hardest," she said. "Lon, I'm never going back there! I don't know what I *will* do, but I won't go back. I couldn't stand Aunt Julia after this—it was perpetual torture before. Uncle Joe tries to be kind, when she'll let him—but they were both relieved to have me taken off their hands."

Her voice sank to a husky whisper. "And I couldn't face anyone I know around home after this—I simply couldn't! What Debbie Winfield will have to say—!" She shivered. "I don't suppose that dreadful answer to the heart-stopping command, 'If anyone can show just cause why these two should not be joined together—' happens once in a hundred years—but it happened to me!"

"That is enough of that," her brother advised curtly. "Anyway, it was a switch, wasn't it, to have the wronged woman bust up a *rehearsal?*"

They rode in silence then, until the sun had set and a haze of twilight veiled the world. Ahead shone the colorful lights of a roadside stand flanked by overnight cabins shining with fresh white paint. Alonzo turned into the small parking area and drew up before the stand.

"Let's try for coffee and sandwiches here, mite," he suggested. "It looks new and clean."

"I—I couldn't swallow a mouthful!"

"You'd better—you're all shot. Besides, I'm starved. I'll bring you out something, if you don't feel like going in."

Cynthia's smile was contrite. "Oh, Lon, of course you are hungry. You've been a lamb, and I'm just thoughtless. Bring out whatever looks good and I'll try to eat it."

Through the broad front window she watched him confer with a lank, round-shouldered woman with flying red hair. Then he disappeared and the woman turned to fling two hamburgers on the griddle and wield a gleaming spatula.

Cynthia fixed her attention on the cook, following every move. Anything to keep from thinking! As though *anything* could still the furious whirlpool of memories, regrets and shame.

It seemed an hour before Alonzo returned empty-handed. He slid behind the wheel and sat staring through the windshield.

"We are going to eat in a minute," he advised. "While we were riding all over the country I did some heavy thinking. You say you don't want to go home—" An upraised finger stopped her as she started to speak—"and you don't have to. I've taken a cabin for you here—bedroom, bath, and a living room with a fireplace. We are going there now. Mrs. Mandley, the boss, will bring sandwiches and coffee there, also her daughter's new set of pajamas which has never been used. Okay so far?"

"Oh, yes, Lon, it sounds wonderful. I can't thank you enough."

An hour later, after Lon had devoured both hamburgers, two long slices of green pickle, a basket of potato chips, a bowl of coleslaw, and a huge wedge of frosted lemon pie, Cynthia sat holding a cup of coffee which she had scarcely tasted. Her wide eyes were fixed on the whispering, flickering flames in the little fireplace. She looked up with a start when her brother cleared his throat with a warning rasp.

"I telephoned Uncle Joe," he announced woodenly. "Told him that you were with me. He wants you to come right home—says that everything is fixed up so that you can be married."

"You mean he wants me to go on with it, after—after what has happened?" she demanded incredulously. "I won't—and I never want to see any of them again!" In sudden terror, "They can't *make* me, can they?"

Her brother stared at her in surprise.

"Of course not! You are twenty-one and can do just as you darn please. Nobody can *make* you do anything you don't want to." He shook his head. "Unfortunately!"

They sat silently for a few moments and then he asked:

"What do you want to do, Cynthy?"

"I want to go away! Hide—hide from everyone I ever knew," she muttered.

Lon rose, rested his elbow on the mantel and rubbed his chin in perplexity.

"That is what I expected," he admitted. "It will take some heavy planning, and you know I haven't much time. My plane leaves San Francisco for Japan and way stations tomorrow night. I figured on ducking out right after the ceremony to make it, so if I'm to help you we'll have to work fast."

"Must you go, Lon? Or could I go with you?"

"Yes to the first, no to the other, mite. You know that when Dad left the plant to me and the money to you—in trust till you are twenty-three—he left me the responsibility of keeping several hundred men employed. Japanese competition is hurting us, but if I can arrange to buy parts over there and assemble them at our factory, I think we can keep going.

"As to your second question," his tone sharpened with annoyance, "you know you got yourself into this mess in spite of what I said. Now for Pete's sake don't start hanging around my neck, but *take* my advice this time and get yourself out of it!"

The transition from a worried and sympathetic Alonzo to the more familiar domineering big brother helped to calm Cynthia.

"I'll try," she agreed, "but I don't know which way to turn. I have no clothes, no money, and no place to go. If I go home to pick up anything, Aunt Julia will get me in her clutches—"

"No she won't!" Lon promised sharply. "I've figured that out. You stay here tonight, I'll go back to town and come out again for you in the morning."

"I wish you'd stay here, too," she said forlornly.

He shook his head and paced back and forth across the room.

"Too much to arrange. I plan to call Joe and Julia in the morning, tell them to meet us at my hotel to discuss this affair. And I must—"

Cynthia jumped to her feet and confronted him.

"I won't see them! I couldn't—"

He placed his hands on her shoulders and forced her back into her chair. Then he stepped back and leveled a rigid finger at her.

"Quiet, now, and listen!" he ordered. "You won't have to see them at all. I just want to get them out of the house. I'll tell them to wait in the lobby until I come for them—while we go out and pick up your things."

"Sara will be there," Cynthia objected.

"Good thought." Lon snapped his fingers. "So I go out to the kitchen and keep her talking while you pack. You blow the horn when you get back to the car and I'll come out. Then to the bank—how much have you in your checking account? In case you have the faintest idea!" he added with masculine superiority.

"Certainly I know my balance!" Cynthia protested indignantly. "Two hundred and ninety dollars."

"Okay, that's a start. Then we sell your car to the first dealer that will buy it. It ought to bring eleven hundred from anybody, and that will give you a good enough stake to go away with. And listen to this—if you get strapped, shoot a collect telegram to the plant, I'll write them to send you some cash if you call for it."

"You've thought of everything, Lon, except where I'm to go," Cynthia complained.

"It should be away from everybody you've ever known," he argued. "A fresh start with a clean slate. Not back to Chicago, you'd be bound to run into friends there. Umm! I know—better head east—Boston would be good. We've never been there, no relatives in that town that I ever heard of. That covers it, I think."

He stared at her thoughtfully for a moment and then nodded.

"Okay, all set. I will be here early for you, so try and get some sleep, mite, and be ready. And remember the old Farley slogan when things look rough—'Tomorrow is another day!' "

"I'll remember, Lon." A tremulous smile lightened the despair on her pale face. "This time I promise to do everything that you advise."

III

Lying in an upper berth, Cynthia listened to the myriad sounds of the busy Chicago station while she mentally urged the train to pull out without more delay. The cramped quarters were uncomfortable, but bearable, and she had gladly taken this only available reservation rather than wait hours for a compartment on a later train. Chicago was no place for Cynthia Farley to linger.

How shrewd Alonzo had proved to be when he advised against lingering in this city; merely in changing trains she had narrowly escaped a face-to-face meeting with Uncle Joe's sister, Anne Darcy. Catastrophe, that would have been! She and Julia were bosom buddies; surely by this time good old Aunty must have poured out her woes by phone or air mail. Dodging in panic Cynthia had fled to her Pullman and to bed, there to silently pray that the sister was not taking the same train.

It was the worst shock to Cynthia's frazzled nerves since

that dreadful moment in the San Francisco terminal when she turned from the ticket window to find Debbie Winfield's startled eyes on her. Darn the luck! She *must* have overheard Cynthia asking the fare to Boston, seen her tuck the ticket in her purse. That news would be all over town by now, unless some miracle suddenly wiped all the mischief from Debbie's active tongue. A miracle indeed!

Cynthia heaved a resigned sigh. If only she had obeyed Lon in every way, as she had promised. As long as she did, everything went as he planned it, smoothly and swiftly. Collecting her things at home—at Uncle Joe's rather, for never could she consider that "home"—was a harrowing experience; she kept brushing a mist from her eyes while she selected the few clothes she could carry.

Better wear the opal gray "going away" suit, in spite of the aching knowledge of how different was this going away from what she had anticipated. Take only the clothes she had collected for a trousseau, leave everything else behind—make this a clean, sharp break with the past, no matter how it hurt.

But the maroon leather traveling clock was a must, a gift from her mother when she went away to college, and the little framed snapshot of her family which always held a place of honor on the bureau. She avoided looking at the picture while she tucked it in the suitcase, those smiling faces would surely bring on a flood of tears.

She turned over impatiently in the narrow berth, still with that day's doings flickering across the screen of her mind. Yes, just as long as she followed Alonzo blindly her path was smooth; visiting the bank, selling her car—the dealer had tried to take advantage of her, but Lon had bullied a fair price out of him. There certainly was a lot to be said for having a man to look after you! Would Eric have been as understanding and—?

That was a perilous line of thought, better switch to another channel. Back to Alonzo, whose very efficiency and continued success with the plans he made increased his dictatorial manner until at last Cynthia rebelled. When he announced that she was to take the next plane east the prospect of flying conjured too many bitter memories and she insisted on going by train. The argument, as acrimonious as any of their childhood battles, was won by Cynthia. A victory she now regretted. By plane she would have missed Debbie Winfield, avoided the jolt of almost meeting Anne Darcy, and would now be settled in her new home, whatever that turned out to be. Drowsily she wondered . . .

Cynthia gave a muffled scream as a crushing weight pinned

her legs to the berth. Terrified she struggled to sit up. The curtains of her section were swept apart and a man's face appeared between them, the dim light from the aisle revealing gray eyes, black with astonishment, in a strong, clean-cut face. Speechless with surprise the girl glared at the suitcase reposing on her knees and tried to push it off. It was huge, heavy as lead, and wouldn't budge a fraction of an inch.

The intruding face whitened.

"I *beg* your pardon!" the man exclaimed, anxiety furrowing his brow. "Did it hurt you?" He growled irritably as he lifted the case and swung it to the floor. "Trust me to ask a silly question! Hope no bones are broken. That fool of a ticket agent said he was giving me the whole section, so I heaved my bag up here without looking. I am on my knees in apology!"

The voice was deep, pleasant and completely convincing. Cynthia felt a stir of excitement as she studied the serious face and what she could see of his tall lithe figure. Tentatively she flexed her knees and admitted with a smile:

"I seem to be perfectly all right. As long as this wasn't an attempted pick-up, you are forgiven."

"A pick-up!" He recovered enough to return the smile. "Using a suitcase instead of the caveman's club? Honestly, that sort of thing is out of my line. It was just plain dumb carelessness; I ought to be shot! You are sure you aren't hurt?"

"Positive. I was half-asleep and when that thing landed I thought I had been atom-bombed," she confided with a shaky laugh. Reading interest and admiration in the steady gray eyes she suddenly realized that she was sitting up in her filmiest pajamas and with a convulsive motion whisked the curtains together and buried herself under the bedclothes.

She caught a smothered laugh from beyond the curtains, then his voice berating the porter and curtly ordering him to stow his damn bag in the lower berth, with angry emphasis on the adjectives. It wasn't the porter's fault, Cynthia thought defensively; but give a man a fright, Mother used to say, and he'll take it out on anyone within reach. Perhaps now I can go to sleep in peace—and store up strength to face a new life in Boston.

How long she slept she had no idea, but she woke at a dizzying lurch of the car and a shattering, grinding crash that stunned her.

"Oh, not *again!*" she muttered, then came fully awake to find herself canted at an alarming angle and the car in darkness, the darkness filled with shrieks and startled swearing.

"A wreck! What next?" she wondered hysterically. She

fumbled on the light switch but nothing happened. Her groping hands found her dress and she struggled into it with difficulty in the cramped quarters. Where were her shoes—her handbag? A swirl of smoke drifted across her face, choked her. In panic she swung her legs over the edge, still groping for her belongings. There was an angry glow of flames lightening the blackness now, and more screaming. She found her purse—

Hands fastened on her arms and swung her clear of the berth.

"Don't stop for anything—I'll get you out!" The commanding voice of the bag-thrower. Gratefully she relaxed, clutching the purse with one hand and his hard-muscled arm with the other. He carried her through the crowded aisle, edging his way slowly and carefully. Down the car steps they went into chill misty night among flashing lanterns and clusters of half-clad frightened train passengers.

Cynthia could see him more clearly now, the brown hair mussed, a smudge of soot on his cheek, but the strong face calm and unworried. Her jumping nerves quieted magically.

"How did you get dressed so quickly?" she asked as he set her gently down on a wooden platform under a sheltering roof. "I couldn't find my shoes or—"

He rubbed the beads of moisture from his face and smiled.

"I was in the club car. You stay here and I'll get your things. Is your bag under my berth?"

"Yes—and a small case in the upper, please. And oh, *my shoes!*" she called after him. He waved without turning.

The damp planking became unpleasantly cold. She stood on one foot and then the other shivering, until she discovered that backing into an angle of the little unlighted station cut off most of the wind.

The man hurried to her laden with bags and tumbled clothing, and dumped the load beside her.

"Hope I got everything for both of us," he exclaimed, breathing hard. "It was pretty difficult to see much in our car with the smoke and only my cigarette lighter. Here!" He upended a suitcase. "Sit on this and get dressed. You have your two bags, shoes and stockings, and coat, but I couldn't find any hat. Oh, you've got it on!"

Cynthia put a hand to her head.

"So I have. When did I do that, I wonder? I certainly must look a mess!"

"Not to me you don't!" He flashed his attractive smile. "Wish *I* could come out of a wreck looking like a fashion model." He glanced back at the train. "You put your things on while I go see if I can help over there."

Perched on the bag Cynthia put on her stockings and shoes. Beside her two trainmen were tinkering with a floodlight, talking while they worked.

"—Sideswiped a box car on the siding. Somebody's going to get it hot for not hauling his train clear of the main line."

"You can say that again. See anyone hurt bad?"

"Nothing serious. It was that flare-up of fire and smoke that panicked 'em, I guess. The track is sure a mess and we won't get away for hours."

"Plenty of hours, chum!"

Cynthia glanced toward the people milling around the stalled cars and her heart thumped with foreboding. An elderly woman was being assisted down the steps of the nearest Pullman, one hand clutching a hat jammed over her eyes, the other gripping the railing. It just couldn't be—it was! Uncle Joe's sister! Miss Darcy reached the platform and stood trying to straighten her hat. Quickly Cynthia averted her face and turned up her coat collar.

A thin, stooping man in a chauffeur's cap sidled up to her. "This train's going to be here all night, ma'am," he announced. "I got a taxi over there, three women in it, room for one more. Take you over to the junction for five bucks. You can catch a local there and pick up the Boston train on the other line—the one that goes through Detroit. Make it easy."

Cynthia hesitated. The workman, too, had said that it would be hours before this train could proceed. Hours, with Anne Darcy to be met at any instant. She hadn't thanked her rescuer properly, hadn't thanked him at all, as a matter of fact. Where was he now? Somewhere in the crowd around the cars? Out of her reach for the moment anyway.

"Make up your mind, lady," urged the taxi driver. "There's plenty other fares."

"I'll go," the girl decided, jumping to her feet. The man snatched up the luggage and hustled her around the building and into his car.

The station at the junction, while no larger than the other, appeared more cheerful. There were lights and unexcited people, anyway. The driver tumbled armfuls of baggage on the sidewalk before the front door, collected his four fares and departed with a rush, probably eager to harvest more five-dollar bills from other stranded passengers.

The three women who had ridden on the back seat picked suitcases and bags from the jumbled pile and disappeared into the station, leaving Cynthia to stare in perplexity at what remained. Her blue and gray striped overnight case, the matching suitcase—and an oversized pigskin bag with the gold initials "A. H." on the end. With a stab of horror she recognized the suitcase that she'd sat on while she finished dressing—*his!*

Where was that officious taxi driver? Gone, of course. No chance to send it back by him. She couldn't leave it unattended, unidentified, at this way station in the wilderness. Since she was responsible for its presence, although unintentionally, it was up to her to take care of it. Perhaps she could think of some solution on the train. She carried her own things into the waiting room, came back to tug the heavy pigskin case to rest beside them, and sat down to get her breath. What a night of mishaps this had been!

The local was not crowded, so Cynthia had room to heave the big bag up onto the opposite seat. She snapped open the catches and began to search for some identification.

"A. H. is going to *love* me," she muttered. "He risks his life—at least, he takes the trouble—to rescue a damsel in distress who repays him by absconding with all his worldly goods!"

Possibly that was an exaggeration, but not by very much, she decided while she gingerly probed the contents. A neatly folded dinner jacket and trousers, shirts, a tan pullover and slacks, from their fabric obviously in the luxury class. Dress shoes and golf shoes at the bottom on one side, something smooth and hard on the other. An electric razor in its case. There was a halfsheet of note paper fastened around it with an elastic.

Hopefully Cynthia removed it and read the few words scrawled in an impressively masculine hand: "Better call Ober."

"Oh, dear!" she exclaimed.

She replaced the note carefully. It must be very important, she thought. He had put it where it would remind him first thing in the morning. And now he *wouldn't* be reminded! That was her fault, too. Why did he have to call Ober? Could there be a suggestion of danger in those admonitory words—'Better call Ober"?

There seemed to be nothing helpful among the miscellany of the unknown man's possessions. Cynthia felt desperation mounting in an oppressive tide. Was she to be saddled forever with this pigskin burden, her own Old Man of the Sea?

And then, in a flat sidepocket of the bag, she discovered a thin packet of letters held by another elastic. The name Archibald Holme on the first meant nothing to her, but it and the address in Philadelphia were plainly typewritten.

Riffling through the bundle she could see that the others bore the same name and address.

Archibald Holme, his initials matched those on the suitcase. What more was needed to identify the owner of the bag?

"Elementary, Watson!" she chuckled, very much pleased with herself. "Thank goodness, I can ship this off by express while I wait for my train, if there is time. Otherwise I'll get the porter to do it at the first long stop. Mr. Holme ought to receive it without too much delay."

Satisfied, she replaced the letters and closed the bag. Only one thing disturbed her. He wouldn't see the reminder that he had strapped around his razor tomorrow morning, or whenever it was that he decided to shave.

She drummed her fingers on the seat arm and stared out the window at a huddle of passing lights. The train was certainly hitting the high spots, she ought to be in plenty of time to make her connection.

"I wonder if I should send him a telegram, 'Better call Ober'?" she mused. "But I can't, can I! He's on his way to Boston or way stations!"

IV

NINE o'clock of a beautiful late May morning, but Cynthia still sat in her room at the small Boston hotel and dutifully scanned the help wanted ads in the newspaper. No matter how urgently the sunshine called she made it an inflexible rule to go through the advertisements before she stirred out. Sometime, somehow, something would *have* to give; someone, somewhere would break down and offer employment to an "inexperienced girl typist."

She couldn't regret the two weeks she had spent in exploring this quaint city, in acquiring a complete wardrobe to replace what she had abandoned at Uncle Joe's, while her capital dwindled. Brother Alonzo would have been infuriated at such extravagance. Fortunately he was thousands of miles away and need never know.

Of course there was no imminent danger of starvation, but her bank balance had become the warning handwriting on the wall. She must begin earning money soon or face the necessity of appealing to Lon's company for funds—an admission of defeat that she would not contemplate.

Having concluded the fruitless examination of the newspaper she tucked her purse under her arm and went forth to haunt the employment office where she had registered.

Her favorite bellboy was doubling as elevator operator at the moment, and his cheerful greeting lifted her spirits. He paused in closing the door long enough to eye her newly purchased pink tweed suit and flowered hat and emit a politely muted wolf whistle.

"What is that for, Ted?" Cynthia asked smiling. "The hat or the business girl's costume?"

"The—er—the toot ensemble," he assured, one corner of his crooked mouth twitching in a friendly grin. Then he sobered. 'Want to buy a little good luck, Miss Farley?" He held out his hand. Something tiny glittered on his not too clean palm.

"Good luck? I could use some!" She peered at the bit of gilded metal, poked it with a gloved finger. It was a miniature star.

"It's a lucky star, see?" the budding salesman recommended. "Sure to bring you all kinds of good breaks."

Cynthia picked up the trinket. A lucky piece? If it could bring her one break she wouldn't ask for more—at present. And it might; even holding it sent fresh determination surging through her veins.

"How much, Ted?"

"A buck."

As she picked a dollar bill from her purse she asked, "If this lucky piece is such a sure bet why are you selling it?"

"Got two." The crooked grin again. "Figured I'd cash in on one, and you looked like you could use it."

Leaving the hotel Cynthia wondered why she had been such an easy mark, paying a dollar for a doodad which probably sold for a quarter at any five-and-ten. But a lucky star! With the thought there came again that curious lift of her spirits, as though the way ahead had suddenly become clear, as though good fortune waited to meet her when she turned the next corner. The feeling was well worth a dollar.

Perhaps Fortune had been testing her to see of what stuff she was made. The last few weeks of unsuccessful search were wearing—but what were a few weeks? Even without business experience or training, except for the meager typing skill she had picked up in junior college, sooner or later someone could use her. Only it must be a woman, she had had enough *man* in her life for a while!

She slipped the gold star into her left glove. With the lucky piece on location a break was bound to come her way. The sense of impending good fortune accompanied her as she crossed the Common and headed for the employment agency.

Even thinking of that office, and how she had found it, cheered her. On the day when the coldly impersonal statement of her bank balance first shocked her to action she had seized the classified telephone book, opened it to "Employment Agencies" and stared in helpless confusion at columns and columns of names. How could she know which was the best? At random she ran her finger down a column—and stopped with an indrawn breath of amazement. A shiver of superstitious awe tickled her shoulder blades as she read, "Ober Employment Service."

Through her brain like an incantation ran that mysterious message in the pigskin suitcase, "Better call Ober." Of course there was no connection, that man on the train came from Philadelphia. But just the same—

"Ober's an omen," she murmured, noted the address and closed the book.

Omen or not, the agency had been a disappointment so far. Nurses seemed to be in constant demand, "trained technicians, female" and "secretaries, experienced," were snapped up by avid employers the moment they appeared. But not Cynthia, inexperienced.

"Today it will be different," she asserted stoutly as she approached the agency's door. She pressed her fingers against the charm in her glove. "Ready, lucky star? Then do your stuff!"

The absurdity of the appeal lighted little flares of laughter in her eyes as she walked through the waiting room, peopled at the moment with only the ghosts of eager hopes and lost jobs. In the manager's office she smiled down at the thin, polka-dotted woman who drooped behind a desk crammed in among ancient filing cabinets and stacked wire baskets of letters.

"Greetings, Miss Ober! Anyone in that crowd in the waiting room clamoring for my services?"

Ruth Ober's harassed eyes glared through thick lenses, her colorless lips pursed in disapproval.

"Crowd! You wouldn't bounce in here sparkling with fun if you had my job, Miss Farley. Business needs girls so badly that they will take on anyone who isn't hopeless—"

"Like me?"

"I didn't say that—you didn't let me finish!" A faint flush of annoyance tinted the thin cheeks as the little woman explained, "It's the typing, you know; I am afraid that you might not be able to satisfy them. Then of course, it would reflect on the agency, you see."

"I understand perfectly, Miss Ober," Cynthia soothed her. "But you must have *some* hopeless ones, as you call them.

Let's say that I fall in that category—what would you advise?"

"I'd tell you just what I tell them." The reply was acid. "Not to camp in here and plague me about getting them jobs—which is impossible, or practically. That I will telephone them if I do find something. It gets on my nerves to see the same ones sitting in the waiting room day after day, eying some of my clients who come in for someone *special.*"

She wrung her hands and shook her head.

"I just can't stand it!" she sighed. "Why, Miss, I haven't had but one call for an inexperienced secretary since—" She stopped with her mouth open and peered at the girl through the thick glasses. "Why, good gracious, my dear! I—you might—" Her excitement died, her voice lapsed into the toneless despair brought on by twenty years of attempting to fit employee to employer. She shook her head. "No, you wouldn't."

"What do you mean?" Cynthia prodded, " 'You might—no, you wouldn't.' "

The older woman tilted back in her chair and shook her head again.

"I have a place for an inexperienced secretary, but she must be married."

"Married?" Cynthia echoed. "I thought that was a liability. Who in the world would specify that?"

"Miss Eva Shaw, real Old Boston. She is writing some sort of a book and I've supplied her with girls for some time, but they don't seem to last."

Miss Ober plunged into a wire basket and came up with a letter. When she smoothed it out on the desk the heavy paper crackled luxuriously.

"This will give you an idea of *why* they don't last," she muttered as she ran her eyes down the page. "This first part is bawling me out for being so slow. Here, this is it—'I repeat, inexperienced. The experienced women know so much that they feel called upon to correct my phraseology and my grammar. They drive me to distraction. And no more single girls, Ober. They moon and roll calf eyes at Cousin Alexander because he happens to be well off, and since he, as my lawyer, is often here, that means they neglect their work. A pesky nuisance!' "

Cynthia laughed. "She seems to have her troubles."

"So do I," Miss Ober groaned. "She is so impatient—and imperious! Listen—'Get busy, Ober! Find me someone who can type but knows nothing about being a secretary—I will train her *my* way. Someone who at least looks like a lady, knows how to wear evening clothes—and has them—and is married.' That word," Miss Ober announced, looking up round-eyed over her glasses, "is underlined twice!"

"I get quite a picture of Miss Shaw," Cynthia said, drawing down the corners of her mouth. "Any more screwball specifications?"

"No, that covers it. She only adds, 'Don't dare send another misfit or she will go packing like the rest. And I must have someone at once, my work is at a standstill.' How do you like that, Miss Farley? *At once!* Just as if I could pick one out of the air and shoot her down to Newbury Point!"

"Where?"

"Newbury Point. Miss Shaw is at a hotel there, for the summer."

"What was that about evening clothes?" Cynthia wondered.

"Oh, she expects her secretary to fill in when she needs an extra at dinner or bridge."

Cynthia heaved a dramatic sigh. "I have some dreamy outfits that I've never worn, because—" She quickly shifted conversational gears. "Do you suppose that I could get the job if I signed an affidavit promising not to fall for her priceless lawyer cousin?" She laughed. "I can see him trotting in with his toupee askew and his green bag clutched in gnarled fingers!"

"Lawyers don't carry green bags any more."

"Oh dear! Another cherished notion of Boston destroyed!"

"And please don't make fun of anything to do with my best customer!" Miss Ober protested with a worried frown. "If I lost her and a few others, I don't know what I'd do."

"Perish the thought that I would spoil your business!" Cynthia tucked her purse under her arm. "I will now follow your advice to the hopeless ones and leave you alone."

"I will call you if anything—"

"Spare me! I know that line by heart. I will fare forth and try to find some sightseer's Mecca that I haven't seen yet. And believe me, that will be hard."

Instead Cynthia frittered away two hours at a morning movie and ate a bowl of clam chowder in a one-armed lunchroom near Faneuil Hall. Then she wandered restlessly along Washington Street, studying the resort dresses in the windows, dropping in at two five-and-tens to scan their "jewelry" displays. She still felt uneasily that her lucky piece might have come from one of their counters, but when she saw nothing remotely like it, she was reassured.

Passing a jewelry store she caught a glimpse of a black velvet panel set with a dozen wedding rings of gold and platinum. Some impulse halted her, drew her closer to the window. She stared at the rings and the gold star in her glove nudged her palm gently. Was its magic working so soon? What else could have prompted the daring idea which set her pulses racing and shot prickles of excitement along her nerves?

She shook her head in self-reproof. It was unthinkable to stoop to deceit for a mere job. Firmly she walked away and for want of better amusement returned to the hotel. Crossing the lobby she looked toward the clock over the reception desk and with a muffled gasp of alarm shrank behind the magazine stand. A hatless man, hands thrust into the pockets of a tan trenchcoat, stood talking to the desk clerk. There was no mistaking that straw-colored crew cut or the arrogant tilt of the chin. Eric Crane!

So Debbie *had* broadcast Cynthia's destination after their unlucky meeting at the ticket window! That was no surprise, but Eric's pursuit was unnerving. He must be checking every hotel in the city. Despair numbed her spirits.

With no other emotion, as though he were a perfect stranger, she watched him accept a sheet of paper from the clerk and write a few lines. The helpful employee supplied an envelope. Eric enclosed the note, sealed the flap and handed it back with some inaudible instructions. Then, hands in pockets and shoulders squared, he walked whistling to the front door and went out.

"Not a care in the world, now that he has found me!" Cynthia muttered bitterly.

She started to cross the lobby when she noticed that he was still visible on the sidewalk and retreated again. He was talking to a shorter, thick-bodied man, whose red face was partially shadowed by the sagging brim of his stained felt hat. Not an appealing character, Cynthia decided, even in this distant view. After a moment the two climbed into a car at the curb, the stranger taking the wheel.

Allowing them time to get well on their way she approached the desk. Her palms were damp as she braced them against the counter and asked the needless question:

"Any messages for me, Mr. Frost?"

"Yes, Miss Farley. Too bad you missed the gentleman, he just left." The smiling clerk handed over her key and the envelope.

Going up in the elevator Cynthia congratulated her inner self because she felt neither pang of regret nor thrill of anticipation while she opened the note. Definitely Eric Crane was a closed chapter in her emotional life.

Cynthia, I must talk to you, the message ran. *Let me explain that unfortunate incident at our rehearsal.*

Unfortunate incident! Would that, she wondered, be typical British understatement or equally typical Eric Crane insensibility? She read on:

Everything is all right now. I love you. Will see you at six tonight. Eric.

"Not if I see you *first!*" was Cynthia's muttered defiance.

"Ma'am?" The elevator operator looked over his shoulder.

"I was talking to myself. Six, please."

Walking down the hall to her room she wondered what Eric meant by "*Everything* is all right now." Had he rid himself of the unwelcome intruder at the rehearsal? Permanently? She shivered at the connotation of that word suggested by his often ruthless nature.

Before her door she stopped and raised her chin resolutely. There was no time to waste on the past; the present demanded action. He would be here at six and she vowed with clenched fist that he would not find her. Another hotel? That would only postpone their meeting, if he could track her so easily. Then where should she go? In her tightly closed hand the gold star pricked with steady suggestion. That fantastic idea which had come to her at the jeweler's window returned, this time as the only solution to her problem.

She must secure the position with Miss Shaw and join her at—was it Newbury Point, wherever that was? No matter, so long as it was not in Boston within reach of Eric Crane. Perhaps she could take a train tonight; she would gladly sit up in a day coach to be out of this city. With lips compressed in determination she returned to the elevator.

On the threshold of the jewelry store her courage almost failed. To get away from Eric seemed all that mattered in her life, but was it worth a lie? She hated liars—but this was a crisis! After all, Miss Shaw did need a secretary and had been unable to find one to suit her. Cynthia would suit her or perish in the attempt, she vowed, pressing the star in her glove as she entered the shop.

Miss Ober looked up with a start when Cynthia, unusually pink as to cheeks but with lovely chin still set in determination, marched into the office.

"Miss Ober, I've had an inspiration," she began, breathless to have the distasteful task completed. "A solution to your difficulty with Miss Shaw—and to my jobless state. Send me to apply for that secretarial position!"

"But—but, my dear, she insists on a married woman!"

Cynthia stripped off her left glove, careful not to dislodge the lucky star, and extended her hand across the desk. The plain gold band on her third finger glistened quite satisfactorily.

"We can *say* that I am married, can't we?" she suggested with spurious calm. "We don't even need to say anything, except that I am *Mrs.* Cynthia Farley—an inexperienced but willing secretary."

Ruth Ober peered from the ring to the resolute face and became paler than usual.

"Why, it wouldn't be the truth! You bought that ring. It would be—be a deception!" she gasped.

Cynthia wondered if the protest was made in fear of possible consequences or if her idea had collided with an immovable New England conscience. Whatever caused it gave Cynthia herself food for thought. There could be endless complications in such a masquerade, unlimited chances for awkward questions. Just for instance, how would she explain being in Boston without a husband?

Nervously she slipped the guilty hand back into its glove. The lucky star scraped her skin—and inspiration flared. Alonzo! Lon in the Orient on business would be priceless as her long-distance husband.

"It would be a *white* lie," she pleaded. "And in such a good cause. Miss Shaw desperately needs a secretary, I just as desperately need the job, and you need to keep one of your best clients happy. Bingo for all of us! We'll simply say that I am Mrs. Alonzo Farley. Alonzo is my older brother, he is in Japan and he isn't married, and I am sure that he won't mind in the least."

The fact that the absent brother would file no protest failed to impress the other. She wrung thin hands in her favorite gesture, one Cynthia had never seen outside of a TV melodrama.

"You would be the perfect answer for Miss Shaw," she conceded unwillingly. "But your suggestion is impossible. You'd never get away with it."

"Why not? I know absolutely no one in this city, nor in New England for that matter, so who could give me away? I can airmail instructions for Lon to address his letters to 'Mrs.' when he writes—if he ever condescends to. I don't expect to be hearing from anyone else."

Cynthia's ever active imagination took off like a jet. Once embarked on deception she discovered that the descent to Avernus was as easy as old Vergil had predicted. It invited with the enticing, though treacherous, smoothness of a greased toboggan slide.

"And it won't be necessary to produce a husband—ever!" She explained excitedly. "After a few weeks, supposing that

I satisfy Miss Shaw, we'll have the absent Alonzo dispatched by—by bandits. That's being done all the time in the Mysterious East. It's a perfect set-up!" she ended enthusiastically. "Come on Ruthie, be a sport—let's do it!"

"Well—I'm tempted, Cynthia, I really am!" The little woman gave an apprehensive shiver as she spoke. "Miss Shaw *is* desperate—and so determined. And I know that she will like you. But—oh dear! I can hardly dare—" Then she firmed trembling lips with resolution.

"I liked you the first time you came in here, but if I am to recommend you, I should know a little more of your background. You have told me that you have no home, come from the West, and live in an hotel at present—a quite nice hotel, I know. You have no business references, naturally, and I'm sure you don't need the other kind. But what about your family?"

"Cynthia Farley, This Is Your Life!" She perched on the arm of a chair and began it soberly. "I had a wonderful home, a distinguished lawyer for a father, an adorable mother, and two older brothers, both oversized and vigorously alive and both determined to bring up their sister in the way *they* thought she should go."

"They sound wonderful!" Miss Ober sighed.

"Right!" Cynthia felt the sting of tears as her thoughts recreated the past. "Then—then we lost Father and Mother—and then we sold the house. That was dictated in the will, and the will also divided the property. It had never occurred to me that Father was so wealthy, I'm afraid I took all our luxuries for granted. And he was perceptive about us, too. Tom was the adventurous type; he was left a tremendous ranch in South America which Father had somehow acquired. He is down there now," she added wistfully.

Ruth Ober was listening enthralled. She twitched impatiently on her chair when the girl paused to mentally bridge the miles which separated her from Brother Tom.

"Alonzo," she continued, "received a very profitable manufacturing company which Father owned, lock, stock and barrel, as he used to say. That's why Lon is in Japan now, on business for the firm."

"And what about you?" the other demanded breathlessly. Then she gasped, "Excuse me, my dear, that was very impertinent of me!"

"Not at all. Isn't this my life story? I wasn't left anything as useful or absorbing as a ranch or a factory. I am the poor little rich girl," she stated without enthusiasm. "I inherit a—a great deal of money—when I am twenty-three, in a couple of years. I suppose Father thought that by then I would have sense enough to take care of it. I wonder."

"But why are you looking for work, with all that money? I thought that you *needed* a job!"

"Oh, I do—until my ship comes in. Until then an uncle in California receives the income and makes a home for me. Only," Cynthia whispered sadly, "it didn't work out. I couldn't stand Aunt—his second wife, and perhaps that is why I got myself engaged—and that didn't work out either. So here I am, marking time in a big, friendless city, and—" she bit her lip to keep from bursting into tears. "If I don't get *something* to do I'll—I'll probably go completely haywire!" she ended with a rush.

"Then—" Miss Ober blinked rapidly and blew her nose. "Then, my dear, I think we'd better try your plan—mad as it seems." She checked a name in her memorandum book, reached for the telephone and dialed a number.

V

CYNTHIA held her breath until Miss Ober obtained a connection with "Mr. Alexander Houston, please, if you are quite sure that he isn't busy." She listened, alternating between buoyant hope and dark foreboding, to a brief conversation punctured by nervous gasps and portentous silences. It ended abruptly, and Ruth replaced the hand set with trembling fingers.

"That was Miss Shaw's legal advisor—and cousin," she quavered. "He is coming right over to meet you and—and—oh dear!"

Cynthia repressed an impulse to laugh away the fears of the jittery little woman, and an equally strong inclination to share in her panic. With feigned nonchalance she remarked:

"Miss Shaw must be really desperate for help if her old lawyer hot-foots it over here, instead of having me present myself at his office for inspection."

"I do wish you wouldn't be so—so flip," Miss Ober moaned. "Mr. Houston is very anxious to have this settled because his cousin is out of town and left the matter up to him, so he— Oh, I might as well tell you! He plans to take you down to Newbury Point, let her see you and decide for herself."

"If he put it like that," Cynthia retorted sharply, "I feel

as though I were a picture she's thinking of buying! Let me assure you that Miss Shaw needn't worry about my pursuing her precious cousin. I dislike him already!"

"You mustn't worry about driving down there with him *alone*," Miss Ober said primly. "I am sure that he is a perfect gentleman."

Cynthia laughed. "Bring on Lawyer Alexander!" she challenged, flexing the muscle in her right arm. "Of course I'll go with him, alone or otherwise; I imagine that I can handle an aging Boston wolf. I might even retain him to divorce me from that wife-beating Alonzo."

Miss Ober was in no mood for levity, her hand shook as she reached for her pen.

"I'll write a note to Miss Shaw about you while we wait," she decided. "I do hope that we are doing the right thing. I have never deceived a client before, but you do appear to be perfect for her—almost, that is. I think that Fate must have sent you just at the right time."

"Not Fate," Cynthia said soberly. "I am sure it was my lucky star. Let's hope it continues to function."

She watched the other finish the letter and then sat silent with her, waiting with beating heart.

The corridor door opened and closed. Footsteps crossed the waiting room and a man appeared in the doorway. Cynthia stared at him while her mind flopped over like an hourglass and her thoughts and conclusions were forced to flow in a new direction, as Miss Ober squeaked:

"Mr. Houston!"

Cynthia shook her head groggily. This man wasn't old! Far from tottering in as she had visioned, he crossed the room with quick strides and studied her with frowning concentration. In a moment the lines smoothed from his forehead and he smiled, and something in her heart leaped to meet something in his eyes. For an instant her lips curved in an answering smile and her heart thumped wildly. Then common sense and caution took charge.

It required a real effort of will to turn her head and look imploringly at Miss Ober, as an inner voice pleaded, "For heaven's sake, say something to break this spell!" Was this the way the other secretaries had begun? No wonder! And *she* had a head start on all of them, for this was the stranger who had carried her from that smoke-filled train—and lost a suitcase for his pains. But that man lived in Philadelphia, why was he practicing law in Boston?

In the midst of her confusion she heard Miss Ober stutter:

"This is Miss—Mrs. Farley, Mr. Houston. I—I hope Miss Shaw will find her satisfactory."

If Alexander Houston remembered Cynthia he gave no sign. Rather he appeared maddeningly cool and detached while he listened to a disjointed outline of her qualifications from Miss Ober. Cynthia wondered if he could be a trifle suspicious. It would be excusable, the little woman could not have acted more guilty if she had been caught red-handed as a shoplifter.

Cynthia attempted a diversion as Miss Ober's voice faltered.

"Mr. Houston, can you tell me exactly what Miss Shaw expects from me in the way of secretarial work?"

"Not *exactly*," he admitted with a smile, sitting down near the desk. "Cousin Eva is unpredictable. A few years ago she amazed everyone in the family by writing a book—and getting it published, too. It dealt with some of the eccentric characters of early days in America, so she titled it *Off-Beat Yankees*. People like Sir Timothy Dexter, who sold warming pans in the West Indies, and Johnny Appleseed, and a strange fellow called 'The Cat Inspector of Little Rest, Rhode Island.' "

"It sounds fascinating!" Cynthia exclaimed.

"It was and it sold well. Cousin Eva did a vast amount of research for it, and she has a style all her own, as you will discover. All this, however, is background. At present she is writing another book, a history of the Shaw Family—and please don't assume that it is a sequel to *Off-Beat Yankees*," he cautioned with a grin.

"All sorts of Shaws will appear in it. My cousin has always had a keen interest in the doings of her friends—to the extent that some people call her snoopy," he added with another smile. "She is equally curious about the affairs of past generations, and thoroughly enjoys digging into family history. Your work, I suppose, will consist of typing her longhand manuscript as she produces it, helping with the research, collating notes—and heaven only knows what else. Are you dismayed?"

"Not in the least," Cynthia asserted. "I am intrigued by the prospect." She might have added, but did not, that she was equally intrigued by the gentleman Miss Ober called "Alexander Houston." That was not the name she had shipped the suitcase to, but she was sure this was the man from the train. Even now she could remember the comforting strength of his arms around her.

"I suppose," he said thoughtfully, "that I ought to ask penetrating questions about you, Mrs. Farley, but as this sort of thing is quite out of my line, I shall leave that to Cousin Eva."

Miss Ober coughed and fluttered.

"Mr. Houston, if you will give this note to Miss Shaw—it contains more information about the applicant."

"Thank you." He slipped the envelope into his pocket. "And many thanks to you, Miss Ober, for finding Mrs. Farley." He smiled at Cynthia and again she responded in spite of herself. "It will be a relief if we can close the deal. Miss Ober knows how much it has been on my mind; while pinch-hitting for my cousin I have really pestered her."

"Not at all!" that lady gasped. "I explained to Mi—Mrs. Farley that you are going to drive her down there—at once." From her tone, the sooner she could wash her hands of the nerve-racking affair the better.

"Only if you wish, I don't want to railroad you into anything," Houston protested, rising. "If it isn't convenient—?"

"I am anxious to have it settled, too." You'll never know how anxious, she added silently. "Let's go!"

As she left the office she yearned to toss Miss Ober a parting wink or two fingers lifted in a V-for-Victory signal, but that would have been risky with Lawyer Houston close behind her. And a little premature, too. The old Roman gladiator's cry of "We who are about to die salute you!" might be more appropriate.

Seated in Houston's shimmering gray convertible they waited for a glowing red traffic light to change. Cynthia stole a glance at his profile. Clear cut, strong—unflinching. "Cousin Alexander's" convictions would be about as resilient as a concrete wall if one ran up against them, she decided. That wasn't going to make her deception any easier.

"I have an idea!" he said so abruptly that she started. "Didn't Miss Ober say that you are staying at a hotel? Why don't you pack a bag for a day or two and bring it along? Then if you get the job, which appears likely, you'd save a trip back here. The hotel could forward your stuff later."

"If you don't mind waiting, I'd like to do just that!" Her enthusiastic agreement surprised him. He would have been more amazed, Cynthia reflected, if he knew the reason and that all her worldly goods would make the trip with her. "I am at the Abbott, quite near."

"I know it. Comfortable place." In response to the command of the lidless green eye ahead he shot the machine up the slope past the State House. Nodding toward the red brick building whose dome and incomparable colonnade glowed in the sunlight he remarked, "Swell, isn't it!"

"If one may call a Bulfinch masterpiece 'swell,' " Cynthia temporized. "Wouldn't *magnificent* or even *breath-taking* be much more appropriate?"

"I am properly squelched. Perhaps I am too used to it to

be suitably impressed. A very weak defense, isn't it? I throw myself on the mercy of the court."

"Are you, and I quote, 'one of those Bostonians whose family has dwelt in the shadow of the golden dome since its creation.' ?"

"Now that you mention it, an early Houston cleared part of the land on which it is built." He pulled into the curb. "Here you are at the Abbott's side entrance, if you don't mind. Easier to park here than in front."

"I'll be as quick as possible." Cynthia hurried into the hotel.

The packing went with satisfactory rapidity, but there was a slight delay when she checked out at the desk and paid her bill. The clerk appeared dismayed and a little hurt at her refusal to leave any forwarding address.

"It isn't curiosity, Miss Farley," he protested. "We simply try to do everything possible for our guests even after they leave. In case there is mail to forward, or a friend inquires for you—"

"You hit the nail on the head," she informed him grimly. "You have been very accommodating, so I don't mind telling you the truth. That man who left the note has been—annoying me, and I propose to lose him completely and finally."

The clerk beamed. "I understand perfectly, Miss Farley. And listen," he dropped his voice to a conspiratorial whisper and leaned across the counter, "before you reach your destination you had better change taxis. That will help to break up any attempt to trace you." He nodded with the assurance of a veteran whodunit reader.

When Cynthia appeared on the sidewalk with a laden bellboy Houston sprang from the car and stowed her bags in the back.

"Next stop, Newbury Point!" he announced as he returned to the wheel.

"May it be my Point of No Return!" Cynthia prayed, as she closed her fingers to feel the reassuring pressure of the gold star in her glove.

"I have an idea it will be," he encouraged. "In the happy sense in which you meant it, Mrs. Farley." With a quick glance her way he added, "It is *Mrs.* Farley, isn't it?"

"Would I be here otherwise? That was one of Miss Shaw's requirements, I believe." She was pleased with the deft evasion.

"Of course. Er—widow—or former wife?"

"Neither." Cynthia resented the hint of amusement in his tone. "Mr. Farley is away on a business trip for some months. We both believe that the occasional separation of a man and his wife keeps married life smoother." She was glad to remember that bit from one of her brothers' vociferous arguments pro and con the prospects of wedded bliss.

"I see. What the psychologists call escape mechanism, isn't it? Absence makes the heart grow fonder, that sort of rot." He could only snatch a quick look at her before he swung up onto the northeast expressway. "Okay, but I hope that when I get a wife she won't feel that way!"

"Then you are not married?"

Houston eyed her again, to her embarrassment. She had meant the question to sound only mildly interested, but the thought of Miss Shaw's succession of swooning secretaries had brought her perilously near the brink of laughter. She stared ahead, expressionless, as he answered:

"Not married. And having settled our respective *status quos*—how's that for modernized Latin?—let me direct your attention to a bird's-eye view of *Old Ironsides* at her permanent berth in the Navy Yard."

"I've been aboard her." Cynthia admired again the tall masts and slender spars of the ancient battle wagon. "I doubt if there is one of your historic sights which I haven't visited."

"From that remark I judge that you are not a Bostonian. Most of us never bother."

"I belong to no such high and mighty caste," she said dryly. "I am Middle West."

"The very flower of it!" Houston smiled, and then as though regretting the gallantry switched the subject. "The Middle West reminds me that I want to entertain you on this otherwise boring ride with a short story. It has been on the tip of my tongue since I met you at the employment office. I don't know that you would call it exactly a story, either. Perhaps it is more of a riddle."

Smilingly Cynthia quoted, " 'Come, we shall have some fun now! thought Alice. I'm glad they've begun asking riddles.' "

Alex Houston chuckled. "If you are going to turn this into the *Alice in Wonderland* tea party, that casts me as the Mad Hatter. Is that the way I impress you?"

"Perhaps you had better get on with the riddle," the girl advised. The gray eyes with laughter in them were unsettling.

"Right! Once upon a time, to coin a phrase—"

"The only proper way for a story to begin," Cynthia cut in.

"Right again, I can see that we are *sympatico*. Once, *et cetera*—a certain young gentleman of our acquaintance was able to be of some small service to a lovely stranger by gallantly rescuing her from a frightful train wreck. It turned out," Houston interpolated with a wry grin, "to be nothing more than a boring delay, but that wasn't our hero's fault. He carried her forth into the rain, and even let her sit on his suitcase while he went to help others in distress."

Cynthia gasped, "I'm terribly upset about that, Mr. Houston. I—I—" He lifted a hand for silence and continued gravely:

"When our hero returned to the station the lovely stranger had vanished. Also *his bag!* Said article was later expressed to him intact by an obliging but mystified friend, one Archie Holme of Philadelphia, who wanted—"

"Archie Holme! A. H.! Oh, good grief!" Cynthia moaned. "But how was I to know?"

"You couldn't possibly," Houston assured her. "But the mystery was in his letter, which explained that the suitcase had been sent to him, according to the tag, by one J. Darcy of Niles, Michigan. *Who,* Archie wanted to know, was J. Darcy—and what the devil was going on? I echo the question."

As the girl remained speechless, he gave her a sidelong look.

"Was your name Darcy—at that time?" he demanded.

"No. I—I didn't want you to feel that you must write me about it, so I used the first name that popped into my mind," Cynthia explained hurriedly.

"Another mystery still remains. Since Arch shared a hotel room with me at the Chicago convention we attended, he recognized the suitcase, complete with initials. And he knew it was mine anyway because of the packet of letters he'd given me—evidence for a law suit in which I represent his company. But here is what *I* want to know. When I said that the bag returned intact, I strayed from the exact truth. When I left it with you it contained a half-dozen neckties, very extra special ones, too, which I bought in Chicago and hadn't yet worn. *They,* Mrs. Farley," he announced with impressive severity, "were not in the case when it reached me!"

"Why, I never touched them!" Cynthia cried aghast. Then it seemed only fair to tell him the whole story, her sudden decision to take the taxi, discovering the abandoned suitcase with her own things, and her effort to identify the owner.

When she reached the point of finding the memorandum fastened to his razor case she exclaimed, "Why, that note did refer to *my* Ruth Ober, didn't it!" She laughed happily. "Just think, if I hadn't seen it—and followed the advice to call Ober—I would never have known about Miss Shaw!"

"And her cousin, Alexander Houston."

Cynthia reverted quickly to the drama of the suitcase.

"When I found the letters with a name which matched the initials I felt very Sherlock Holmesish. There was time in Niles to ship it off while I waited for my train. And I did *not* snitch your precious neckties! I saw them, though—thought they were really super!"

"Ye gods, can it be that after all these years I have found a woman with good taste in ties? Tell me, do you select them for your husband? Or is his taste also impeccable. By the way, what is his name?"

"My—my husband? Oh! Alonzo. Alonzo Farley." Cynthia didn't care for the penetrating look she received, nor the quizzical smile and lifted eyebrow. "He is very nice, and I like his ties."

"Alonzo," Alex Houston rolled the name on his tongue. "A fine old-fashioned name, redolent of integrity and—and common sense. How old is your Alonzo?"

"M-m-m, thirtyish, but doesn't look it." She hoped that Lon wouldn't mind aging rapidly.

"Glad to hear that, but I am still surprised. How come you left the home nest for the uncertain seas of matrimony so young?"

That careless phrase, "the home nest," called up a memory which set a lump in Cynthia's throat. To disguise her emotion she managed a shaky laugh and caught at any excuse to speak lightly.

"I must have left it in search of peace and quiet. A wonderful father and two splendid brothers with one fault in common—they wanted to run my life. Living in our family was like life in the very eye of a hurricane."

Now she was on the solid ground of truth and reveled in it. "To put it mildly, my men-folk were opinionated, and they loved to argue—at the top of their lungs, too! One need only express the simplest opinion; Father and the boys would line up on opposing sides and the battle was on. Our friends affectionately dubbed them, 'The Fighting Farleys,' and—"

"Farleys?" Houston repeated sharply. The car swerved as he turned to stare at her.

Cynthia's heart stopped for a breath, then raced madly. She'd done it! In the first hour of her deception she had ruined everything with a careless word. Desperation nerved her to a supreme effort at recovery.

"Yes, the very same name. Wasn't that a coincidence?"

"Very odd." His tone conveyed such incredulity that she was driven to further improvisation.

"Of course there was a row," she confided with a light laugh. "Father and the boys suspected he must be a relative, and they couldn't approve such a match. Another chance for a house-shaking argument, and how they enjoyed it! Poor Alonzo, they dug into his past for generations, but nowhere could they find the slightest connection between the families, so everything ended happily."

"An unusual story indeed!"

To Cynthia his manner was still unconvinced, but she had exhausted her inventive genius.

"And now," she suggested hopefully, "if you have finished the cross-examination, Mr. Attorney, won't you tell me something about yourself?"

"Nothing very exciting in *my* past," Houston laughed. "You would be bored to death. Born and raised in the shadow of the State House, except when I was away at boarding school—or at Newbury Harbor for the summer, which I may add was *every* summer as long as my parents were alive."

"Both gone now?" Cynthia felt that the double loss was a bond between them and spoke gently.

"Some years ago—but they had full, rich lives. Dad inherited considerable money, so he didn't need to work, and devoted himself to helping less fortunate people. But it wasn't enough, he found. A man has to have some purpose in life for himself, and he made me promise to get one and give it my best. I chose the law, after college and putting in my Army service, and have found it fascinating."

"Do you have other clients besides Miss Shaw?"

Alex Houston grimaced. "Well, I should hope so! Being legal advisor to Cousin Eva is equivalent to acting as a second for the heavyweight boxing champion of the world. She very seldom needs advice and when she does quite often won't take it. She seems to have a sixth sense for doing the right thing. But I have a number of clients who do require my best efforts, and I am often appointed by the courts to act for people who can't afford to hire a lawyer. Helping them is a real satisfaction."

"I know. My father did a great deal of that sort of thing, and loved it."

"So he was a lawyer, too? In Chicago, I take it, since you got on the train there."

"Yes, he was a lawyer," Cynthia admitted, "but I took the train farther west." She shied away from reopening the discussion of her past life and snatched at a new subject. "Tell me about some of these little towns that we are passing so rapidly I hardly notice them. And isn't that the ocean off there?"

VI

NOTHING in all Cynthia's experience with hotels, either on the shores of Lake Michigan or in California, prepared her for the Harbor House at Newbury Point. The impression she had gathered concerning Miss Shaw's social position and affluence had led her to expect something on the order of the newest Conrad Hilton caravansary, shimmering with steel and plastic and bowered in luxuriant formal gardens.

Instead, the Harbor House reared its five stories, clothed in white-painted shingles, above the tops of scrubby spruce trees on the rocky shore. The girl stared round-eyed at the towers which broke the long front wall here and there, making bay windows for several of the rooms, and the long, covered piazza stretching from end to end of the hotel.

"If there is an end!" Cynthia muttered, as Houston drove past the huge porte-cochere of the main entrance and continued along the concrete driveway. To her wondering gaze it seemed a lofty white cliff that stretched for miles. But at last he turned the convertible off the concrete onto a gravel road which led past the northern end of the hotel, pulled over to the side and stopped.

From here Cynthia could view the rear of the Harbor House, a bewildering maze of iron fire escapes clinging like demented spider webs from ground to roof.

"So *this,*" she gasped, "is where Miss Shaw spends her summers!"

"Not in the hotel," Houston said, "although she will have a room there for you. Cousin Eva has an apartment here, in the Annex."

At his nod Cynthia turned. Beside her loomed another five-story building, as tall as the hotel but only the width of an ordinary house, and without towers or piazza, white shingled like the other and of equal ugliness.

"The Harbor House became so popular," Houston explained, "that they were obliged to add the Annex at a later date."

Cynthia burned to suggest, "about 1850," but politely refrained. She could see that everything about the two houses was well cared for, the lawns smoothly clipped and edged, fresh paint glistening on every side—but the architecture!

Perhaps her feelings were too evident in her face, for Houston remarked defensively:

"It may look outdated to you, but for years—generations in fact—it was *the* place to spend the summer as far as our people were concerned. And Cousin Eva is rather set in her ways."

That thought seemed to lead to others, because he halted as he mounted the steps at her side.

"I hope your wings of freedom won't be clipped in this gloomy ark, Mrs. Farley. For the last time, let me warn you that if you accept this position—well, you won't have to read magazine articles on what to do with your leisure time. I am convinced that in a previous incarnation my cousin was the original slave driver."

"I am not afraid of work," Cynthia asserted. "I have been at loose ends so long that I will welcome it." Soberly she looked up at him. "All of twenty-one years old and I have never really worked, never done anything useful in the world. That is nothing to be very proud of, is it? And I haven't even got *this* job yet."

Equally sober, Houston answered, "Don't worry about this job. The ride with you, all too short as far as I'm concerned, convinced me that Cousin Eva is getting a winner."

If Alex Houston's smile was heart-warming, as Cynthia had discovered, the deep admiration now in his eyes was even more upsetting and sent hot blood flaming in her cheeks. He must have seen it and regretted his admission, for he shifted to cheering banter.

"Got your union card ready, Mrs. Secretary?" he smiled. "Then, *en avant!*"

In the entrance hall of the Annex, waiting for the elevator, she alternated between nervousness at the impending interview and amusement at her surroundings. The railing and banisters of the golden oak stairway which wound up around the elevator shaft were deeply and elaborately carved, the carpet on the treads was inch-thick crimson pile. Not a speck of dust was visible, the light and dark oak squares of the parquet floor gleamed with recent waxing.

In response to Houston's jab on the button the elevator whined slowly down to them and stopped with a jarring thud.

"Self-service style, and quite old-fashioned, I'm afraid," he apologized. He slid back the frosted glass paneled door of the shaft and then the wire door of the car for her to enter.

Cynthia found herself both intrigued and amused. The single light in the car was set in the back wall instead of the ceiling. From it dangled a red printed card, *Please Close Both Doors on Leaving Car.* When she turned to face front an identical card blazoned the same message from beside the control buttons.

"They really mean it, don't they!" she laughed.

"Some of the tenants are absent-minded," Houston explained, as he closed the doors and punched the Number Two button. "You can't get the elevator up to you—or down to you—if either door is left open."

His ring at the second floor apartment was answered by an angular maid in a black uniform with white collar and cuffs. At sight of Houston her rather protuberant blue eyes bulged even more and she pressed a hand against her flat chest.

"You, Mr. Alex!" she stammered. "What are you doing here midweek? Has something happened?"

"No, no, everything is all right, Mary! I only—"

"Oh!" the maid squealed, noticing Cynthia, her waxen cheeks pink with excitement. "Oh, dear Lord! I know! You're *married!* Oh, lordy—!"

"I am not!" Houston snapped, his own face flushed. "For Pete's sake, Mary, pull yourself together, and tell Miss Shaw that I've brought Mrs. Farley down to be interviewed."

"Oh." It was not an exclamation, so much as a deflation. "Oh dear—excuse me, ma'am! Come in. I'll tell Miss Shaw you're here."

When she left the room Houston, still shaken, muttered, "Don't mind Mary—she makes a soap opera of anything, if she can."

"Mind? I was flattered," Cynthia corrected, smiling, and took impish delight in his increased embarrassment. As he seemed to have nothing further to say she turned to inspect the living room, her eyes drawn first to the side where the high, old-fashioned windows showed an indigo sea flecked with dashing whitecaps.

After the disillusionment of the Harbor House's exterior she was quite unprepared for Miss Shaw's apartment. The paneled walls were painted a warm gray, the trim old rose. Long hangings of dull gold brocade framed the two windows; between them an oval mirror with a carved walnut frame delicate as old lace hung above an antique tripod table, whose softly glowing top was a single board of swirling burl walnut. Cynthia was grateful for the half-year course on interior decorating she had taken in college, it had prepared her to identify and appreciate many of Miss Shaw's furnishings.

The two straight chairs flanking the table, for instance; those were Hitchcocks with graceful turned legs and charming old faded gold stenciling on back posts and panels. The curiously shaped porcelain bowl on the table, although unknown to her, was clearly the work of a master potter and probably a cherished heirloom. Its clump of lilac spears filled the room with elusive fragrance.

At the end of the room a fireplace of black tile was topped by a carved panel set off with a rope border of pure Colonial ornament. On either side built-in shelves showed the rich browns and tans of old leatherbound books and an array of porcelains, ruby Sandwich glass, dull pewter and glistening silver.

In the midst of her inspection Houston stepped forward with a cheery, "Good afternoon, Cousin Eva!" and she realized that her prospective employer was standing in the doorway of another room.

The suddenness of it jerked her already keyed-up nerves. How long had the erect white-haired and rather grim woman been there unnoticed, weighing any visible attributes—and defects—of the new secretary? *Proposed* secretary, Cynthia amended mournfully, to judge from the expression on Miss Shaw's long and square-jawed face. At last I know, she thought, what is meant by "cold roast Boston"! She gave the lucky star in her glove a convulsive, imploring squeeze while she waited for Houston's introduction.

Miss Shaw did not wait. "How do you do, Mrs. Farley?" She spoke without relaxing her stern expression and with no slackening of her keen inspection. Overriding Cynthia's murmured reply she went on talking. "A stupid greeting, is it not? As though I expected you to furnish a medical report!"

She crossed the room to a long couch, picked up a needlepoint pillow which was set in the exact center and tossed it to one end. When she seated herself in its place she was directly beneath the portrait of a dowager in a shoulderless Empire gown whose every feature was reflected in the living woman's face.

Miss Shaw folded patrician hands, glittering with rings, and arched her imperious eyebrows at Houston.

"Must you stand there like a wooden Indian, Cousin Alexander? Bring a chair over here so that we may all become acquainted."

Houston slanted a humorous glance at Cynthia while he shifted a small wing chair from beside the fireplace to a spot in front of the couch.

"Pray be seated, madam," he invited with comic elegance.

Her move to obey was halted by Miss Shaw's abrupt, "Not there, Mrs. Farley, with your back to the light! I wish to have a good look at you." She indicated the couch and with another sweeping gesture assigned Alex to the chair.

Houstons and Shaws were cut from the same cloth, Cynthia decided. First a cross-examination by Alex, to be followed now by a third-degree complete with the revealing spotlight of the afternoon sun. Devoutly she hoped the ride had not played havoc with her hair or her make-up.

When they were arranged to Miss Shaw's satisfaction Houston handed over the letter.

"This comes from the faithful Ober, full particulars, I assume." He leaned back with folded arms while his cousin adjusted ornate black framed glasses on her formidable nose and opened the unsealed envelope. "From her description, Cousin Eva, Mrs. Farley seemed so exactly what you are after that—"

"You told me that on the telephone."

He ignored the interruption. "—that I immediately shanghaied her down here, for fear someone else would snap her up."

Cynthia bit her lip to cover a smile. Snap her up, indeed! If he knew of her weeks of fruitless seeking and waiting! As soon as Miss Shaw had skimmed through the note and removed her glasses Cynthia ventured:

"I hope Miss Ober made it clear that except for a typing course in college I am truly inexperienced."

"Ober knows her business. That was what I asked for, Mrs. Farley, and that is what I want. Ohio?"

The enigmatic word baffled Cynthia. "My college, you mean? No, I was at Marianna Junior College for two years."

"I meant your accent."

"Oh. I am from Chicago."

"I knew it was Middle West," Miss Shaw said complacently.

Houston growled, "No doubt Mrs. Farley can cultivate a Boston broad "a" if necessary, Cousin Eva."

"Don't be impudent, Alexander! I am indebted to you for all the trouble you were put to, keeping in contact with Miss Ober after I left town, but I will conduct this interview in my own way." She shifted to Cynthia. "Your duties as secretary will be to assist me with the book I am now working on, that is all. I am perfectly capable of managing the household accounts and social correspondence. Did you expect to do that?" she asked with a hint of suspicion.

"Miss Shaw, I honestly had no idea what my duties would be."

"Are you sure you can remain with me until my book is completed? I won't have that husband of yours returning unexpectedly and dragging you away."

"You needn't worry about that," Cynthia asserted, for once on firm ground.

Miss Shaw studied her again, at close quarters, the greenish eyes taking in every detail, from diminutive straw hat to sensible low-heeled shoes.

"She dresses well, Alexander," she stated abruptly.

"I refuse to answer," intoned Houston solemnly, "on the grounds that it might incriminate me." But his look was all admiration.

Miss Shaw chose to ignore him. "You didn't make that suit yourself?"

"Certainly *not!*" Cynthia said with asperity. Once more she had the uncomfortable feeling that she was an *objet d'art* which might or might not be purchased. "Not" was more than suggested by the elevation of the aristocratic nose, the inflexible lips. Cynthia's temper, usually kept well under control, began to simmer. Keep smiling, she warned herself sternly, you didn't expect her to fall on your neck, did you? By chance she caught Houston's signaling eyes; on his folded arms a finger and thumb formed a fleeting circle. That generally meant *success,* she knew, but this time it must be only kindly encouragement.

To her utter astonishment Miss Shaw suddenly reached over and patted her hand.

"I think that you will do nicely, my dear. Your lack of experience is a godsend; I can train you as I wish. You will live in the hotel, at my expense, naturally, so twenty dollars salary per week should be sufficient until you are worth more. Any further details can be discussed at our leisure. Satisfied?"

Cynthia gasped. She had a job—just like *that!,* with a mental snap of her fingers. "Oh yes, Miss Shaw—perfectly satisfied, and thank you. If you want me at once, I brought my things along—just in case."

"A commendable precaution," the elderly lady agreed without relaxing her severity.

"Yes, it indicates a capacity for planning ahead," Houston pointed out blandly.

Cynthia ventured a smile which Miss Shaw crushed by snapping, "Or considerable confidence. By the way, I hope Miss Ober mentioned that I count on you to help me with any entertaining I may do."

"I would love to," Cynthia assured eagerly.

"Splendid! Alexander"—the green eyes impaled him—"as long as Mrs. Farley has a perfectly good husband in"—she glanced at the Ober letter—"in Japan, you need no longer avoid my parties on the excuse of pursuing female secretaries after your money."

Houston went dark red and his eyes glowed angrily. Then the ridged muscles around his mouth relaxed and he contented himself with a forceful, "Rot, Cousin Eva!" He rose to return his chair to its place by the hearth.

Cynthia was impressed. Had he been one of her beloved Fighting Farleys his reaction to the taunting remark would have rattled the pictures on the walls.

"I'll run back to town, now that you ladies are all set," he announced. "Mrs. Farley won't need return taxi service. Shall I drop her bags at the hotel, Eva?"

"Please do, and tell them that I will come over later to make the arrangements. I want to select the room myself and not have Mrs. Farley tucked away in some second-floor-back. Won't you stay for tea with us, Alexander?"

"Another time, thanks." He shook hands with the new secretary. "Best of luck to you, Cynthia, and don't let all this get you down."

"I can't thank you enough, Mr. Houston. I—"

He silenced her with upraised hand as he stepped back. "The pleasure was all mine. And you'd better get used to calling me 'Alex,' most everyone else does. Cousin Eva, *au revoir*—and believe me," he smiled at Cynthia, "I mean exactly that. I'll be seeing you—both!" With a casual wave to them he departed.

"Charming, isn't he!" said Miss Shaw, eying the girl with an unreadable expression. "Alexander can be irresistible—when he chooses. I am relieved that you are not the sophisticated type which seems to appeal to him."

From her own observation of Mr. Alexander Houston Cynthia considered that the only proper reply to that remark would be an inelegant "Oh, yeah?" but this was hardly the time for it. Instead she asked brightly, "Will you tell me more about this book I am to work on? Mr. Houston mentioned that it was a history of your family."

"And you think that sounds unbearably stodgy and dull, no doubt. You are quite right, Mrs. Farley."

"But I don't, Miss Shaw! I didn't mean that—"

"You needn't lie—flatter me, to hold your position!"

Cynthia felt her temper slipping its leash, with sufficient provocation to be sure. Not all the fight in the Fighting Farleys was on the masculine side. She squared her shoulders, as rigid now as the elderly woman, her eyes blazed into the eyes which glared at her.

"Miss Shaw, don't think me impertinent, but I am not accustomed to being called a liar, even by a woman old enough to—" She snapped her teeth shut on that automatic comparison and drew a long shaky breath. "I was not trying to flatter you. *You* said that I thought the Shaw family history dull and stodgy—*I* didn't! Why in the world should I? I know absolutely nothing about it!"

Breathless from her vehemence, she thought, There goes the job! and gathered up purse and gloves.

Again Miss Shaw amazed her, and with the same friendly pat on her hand.

"Good for you, Mrs. Farley!" The green eyes were all warm approval. "You were so patient under my questioning before that I was afraid Miss Ober had sent me another spineless female, so tried some of the treatment with which I keep Cousin Alexander in his place. If I didn't he would become conceited and begin telling me how to conduct my life, as he already does in my legal affairs.

"As to the family history, I hope that you won't find it dull because *I* am fascinated, the deeper I delve. Why, I have come across a Captain Benjamin Shaw whom none of us ever heard of, as far as I know. I can't imagine what he did to be hushed up, but I intend to find out!" she promised vehemently and quite breathlessly.

Cynthia was infected by the other's excitement when she spoke of her work. "Perhaps he was the black sheep of the family," she suggested eagerly.

"That is possible, you know." Miss Shaw considered it with sparks of anticipation in her eyes. "Very possible, when I remember some of the less distinguished branches of the Shaw tree. I did find out that there may be records of him in the Essex Institute—that's in Salem, almost next door—because they have tons of old logbooks and journals of clipper ship captains. That is what Benjamin was, you know. So I closed the town house and came down here weeks ahead of the season to plunge into musty, dusty files, with no success so far." She looked at Cynthia with apprehension. "If that doesn't appeal to you, you can go back to Boston tomorrow, you know."

Cynthia laughed and shook her head.

"Not I! I can't wait to begin. Tell me more!"

"Good! We are going to get along, Mrs. Far—Cynthia. Please ring that bell by the door and Mary will bring in the tea. You will need it strong if you let me ride my hobby!"

Cynthia could hear the distant hum of the bell, presumably in the kitchen of the suite. As she returned to the sofa a large yellow cat appeared in the doorway, where it stood for a moment surveying the room with shining yellow eyes. Its dignity, and the unwinking stare reminded Cynthia forcibly of a similar entrance by its mistress.

Slowly the cat advanced to the couch and sat motionless.

Only the tip of its tail twitched while the golden eyes turned from one face to the other.

Miss Shaw chuckled. "Topaz knows what that bell means at this time of day."

VII

THE FIRST days of Cynthia's job were so crowded with new experiences that later attempts to recall them resulted in only a blur of vague scenes like an overexposed movie film running too fast. It was a difficult time for her, and no doubt, she added honestly, equally upsetting for her employer.

The routine task of copying the accumulated manuscript which Miss Shaw had produced while awaiting a secretary would have kept Cynthia busy enough. Not only must she struggle to regain what little typing skill she had acquired at college, but it was also imperative that she should become quickly familiar with Miss Shaw's ingenious but unprofessional system of indexing her notes.

For the saga of the Shaws, which embraced a multitude of families covering hundreds of years, she recorded the facts about each clan on cards of a certain color. As a result Cynthia, who had to refer often to them in copying the manuscript, labored amid a constantly shifting kaleidoscope of every rainbow hue.

Eva Shaw usually sat at an adjoining table, attired for writing in a well-worn but still resplendent Chinese coat heavily embroidered with golden dragons and leering gods. The Oriental effect was heightened by several spare pencils stuck haphazardly into her swirling white hair. She used dozens of pencils, discarding one the moment its point became too dull for her elegant Spencerian script, as smooth and even as copperplate engraving.

Usually they followed the same pleasant routine. When the French clock on the living room mantel tinkled the hour with truly Parisian gaiety, Mary appeared in her morning uniform of gray and white. She bore a tray with two steaming cups of coffee.

"Ten o'clock, ma'am!" she announced firmly, pushing away a pile of papers to place a cup beside her mistress.

"Be careful, Mary! If you mix my pages I will be lost!"

"I didn't hurt 'em. You drink your coffee and eat your crackers or *you* will be lost."

The maid served Cynthia and paused, nursing the empty tray.

"S'pose I was to make you each a nice sandwich? You've got to keep your strength up."

"Haven't time. And my strength is holding up quite well, thank you." Miss Shaw corrected manuscript while she sipped her coffee. "Where is Michael?"

"Washing the car, of course!" Mary snorted. "Does he ever do anything else, when he isn't driving you?"

"I shall want him at four-thirty. Finished, Cynthia? Run along, Mary, and let us work."

The hours that followed would be interrupted only by a brief luncheon period.

How fortunate, Cynthia thought, to have found just this job, work which she could do acceptably in spite of her inexperience, for a woman she admired more with every passing day. Interesting work, too; the family history of the Shaws, at least as Miss Shaw chose to tell it, was a sprightly chronicle of delightful, if sometimes unrighteous, characters.

Even the room where they labored added its charm. Adjoining the living room it, too, looked out on the ever-changing and fascinating shore and sea, through windows brightened by ivy and African violets. Among the flower pots Topaz lay curled in peaceful slumber. And best of all, Cynthia was completely remote from any connection with her former life. Eric Crane would need to be clairvoyant to trace her here.

Only Alonzo knew her present location, or would as soon as he received the excited airmail letter which she had dispatched to Japan on the evening she was hired. This assumed character of hers should be suspicion-proof when she could carelessly display a missive addressed in his masculine hand to "Mrs. Alonzo Farley." That, she reminded herself cautiously, would depend on whether he approved of her venture. If he shouldn't, thank Heaven he was too many thousands of miles away to do more than protest by mail.

The usual routine was abruptly cast to the winds at noon on her third day. Miss Shaw bundled together her sheets of manuscript and began plucking pencils from her coiffure.

"Cynthia, I am—what is Cousin Alexander's expression—oh—*bushed!*" she admitted. "A wonderful word that, so much more descriptive than worn out or exhausted. Whenever I have to struggle to write, I know I am tired. And you must be equally bushed, my dear; I know I have been working you too hard. So, no more today—and that is an order! Quoting Alexander again."

"You are *not* working me too hard, I love every minute of it!" Cynthia protested. "And it is very agreeable to my ego, after wasted years, to find that someone really needs me."

Miss Shaw tilted her chin to peer at the girl over her glasses.

"Didn't your husband need you?" she inquired sharply.

"Oh, of course!" Cynthia gasped, searching frantically for a believable explanation. "I didn't mean—but you see, he is away now—and—it left me terribly at loose ends."

She arranged the pages she had typed in a folder and clipped the pencil-written sheets to the front so that Miss Shaw could refer to them when she edited the final draft.

"If you are sure you want to stop now, I'll go for a swim before lunch, and be back at two—"

"I said no more for today, and I meant it! I have to call on a deadly dull relative this afternoon and you are not to stay cooped up here alone. Get out in the sun before you grow as dried up and yellow as I am."

Cynthia laughed. "If I look one quarter as well at your age—"

"Leave my age out ot it!" snapped Miss Shaw. "Run along now."

The girl departed, not at all depressed by the curt dismissal; she was becoming familiar with the waspish side of her employer, and beginning to realize that it was sheer camouflage, probably a defense mechanism against those who might take advantage of her.

"As I am doing?" Cynthia asked herself. "But she *does* need me!" came the somewhat comforting afterthought.

The need was demonstrated within a few minutes. Miss Shaw, with the inconsistency which Cynthia had come to expect, having ordered her to take the afternoon off, immediately called her room and begged her help in finding a missing page of manuscript.

Ordinarily Cynthia would not have appeared in that decorous apartment wearing a yellow and tan plaid swim suit partially draped by a white terry beach robe. But because of the desperation in Miss Shaw's appeal she flew to the rescue like a fireman responding to a third alarm. The Annex elevator was somewhere in the upper regions, so Cynthia ran up the stairs, found the wanted page under a pile of Miss Shaw's notes and retired to the hall triumphant. Because she was breathless, this time she punched the button and heard the elevator come complaining down the shaft.

As it reached her floor she saw the shadow of a man's figure on the frosted panel of its door. The car jerked to a stop, the doors slid open and a jovial voice boomed, "Won't you come into my parlor?" A man in a hound's-tooth check sports coat and lemon yellow tie leaned out and stared at Cynthia.

"I beg your pardon, I thought it would be Miss Shaw. Say—you're her secretary, aren't you? I've seen you—Miss Farley. Right?"

"*Mrs.* Farley." Cynthia stepped in.

"Excuse me again." He closed the doors with a flourish. "Going down?" At her nod he pushed a button. He was only slightly taller than Cynthia, stout and beginning to acquire another chin. There were puffy pouches under the eyes which sparkled with friendliness. "I'm a neighbor, Neal Bruce, up in Number Three." He offered a tentative hand.

"So nice to meet you, Mr. Bruce." Cynthia shook hands gravely and was surprised at the strength of his grip. Mr. Bruce must be less flabby than he appeared. "You are the first of the Annexites I've met, although I have seen Mr. and Mrs. Whitehead in the dining room. Miss Shaw told me who they were."

"That's right, they are in Number Five, the top floor. Probably Miss Eva, who knows everything about everybody, warned you to read a book on tropical fish before you meet them, because they are cracked on the subject. Speaking of fish," he eyed her costume with a grin, "going for a swim—or just been?"

"On my way."

"Blast the luck!" Bruce growled. "I have an appointment at the Summer Theater or I'd join you. If invited," he added, winking.

"This being my first venture in the Atlantic I welcome *advice.*" Cynthia stressed the word lest she appear to be angling for him to ditch his appointment. "Any dangers to avoid, I mean?"

"Not a thing, this is a great place for even children to swim. Absolutely no risks. Too early in the season for the floats to be put out, but if you like diving, go over on the rocky point." He consulted his wrist watch, then shook his head. "Sorry I can't go along—this time, anyway."

Cynthia noticed that the car was motionless. How long had they stood here? She reached for the door handle.

With a muttered apology Bruce opened the doors and walked with her to the entrance. Passing the first floor apartment door he nodded toward it.

"Doctor Ferguson, the other—what did you call us—Annexites? That's pretty good! He completes the roll call, because Number Four is empty at the moment and being redecorated—a frightful mess! Ferguson is at one of the big defense plants out in the country from here. Something to do with guarding the workers against radiation poisoning, I think."

"And you, Mr. Bruce? You mentioned the Theater. Are you one of the actors?"

He laughed. "Thanks for the compliment—if you aren't ribbing me. No, unfortunately I am one of those stage-struck dopes who put money into such things just so I can hang around show business. And since I have been summoned there today, I suppose they have run out of cash again. Be seeing you, Mrs. Farley." He went off toward the parking lot behind the hotel.

The long beach curving between rocky points was deserted, but the hotel piazza held several observant guests in rocking chairs. Cynthia felt decidedly conspicuous as she adjusted her cap and waded out into the surf. That, she supposed, was what the people here called the low, slow waves which were surging heavily up across the sand, although they were only distant relatives of the racing combers she was accustomed to on the Pacific coast. The water, too, had an unfamiliar feel, warm enough but with a sort of latent bite that was exhilarating.

She swam expertly out toward the northern point as Mr. Bruce had suggested, for she did enjoy diving. Climbing the steep, weed-covered rocks she searched for a level spot from which to take off, but without success. Perhaps one dived from any cleft or outcrop where there was a foothold. Up here the stone was bare of slippery weeds and up here, also, the sea breeze blew stronger—and colder—against her dripping body. She faced the water and braced her feet.

"Don't jump, Cynthia!"

The urgency in the low-voiced order compelled obedience. Startled, Cynthia looked over her shoulder. Alex Houston stood at the top of the rocks a dozen feet away, staring down at her. Like a Viking on the prow of his marauding galley, was her instant comparison. Except that Vikings were blond and the wind was fluttering shining black hair. And instead of armor he wore a mahogany brown sweater and tan slacks.

Nevertheless, the girl decided, looming against the cloud-splashed blue sky he was the handsomest figure she had ever seen. Following which thought she told herself severely, "Hold everything, gal, the cousins are tired of pursuing secretaries!" And in order to make her own attitude clear said aloud—and with indignation—"What do you mean by yelling 'Don't jump,' I was going to *dive!*"

"Please don't do that, either. Let me explain," Houston began.

"That I am much too far up for safety?" she demanded

sarcastically, the memory of two domineering brothers putting an edge on her voice. "I'm not a beginner." She turned away and again poised to spring.

"Cynthia! *Stop!*"

Really! she thought, this is too much like Alonzo to be borne. Over her shoulder she favored Houston with a frigid glare and arched eyebrows.

" *'Cynthia'?*" she repeated pointedly. "And just *whom* do you think you are ordering about?"

He flushed. "I beg your pardon, Mrs. Farley, but under the circumstances I thought only of your safety. I am sure that you are capable of diving from any height, but you shouldn't do it into unknown waters."

"Oh!" Belatedly she realized her carelessness. "You are right, of course and I beg *your* pardon. I didn't check the bottom. How did you know?"

"I didn't, but I wanted to be sure. I happened to meet Neal Bruce in the hotel parking lot. He mentioned meeting you—and that you were going for your first swim here. When I saw you climbing the rocks, evidently without a look at the bottom, I—" He shrugged and spread his hands in an eloquent gesture. "There are plenty of ledges down there. To be honest, the thought of what could happen to you scared politeness out of me and I guess I was a bit arbitrary without thinking."

"I'm very glad you stopped me," Cynthia admitted. "If you hadn't, a foolish girl might have dented a hidden rock with her head."

"Please don't mention it!" Houston grinned, with a dramatic shiver. "Am I forgiven?"

"And heartily thanked. There was nothing to forgive, anyway. You saved my life and Miss Shaw calls me 'Cynthia,' so why shouldn't you, Cousin Alexander?"

"Oh, come now! Make it Alex and we're all set. If she calls you by your first name you must have made a hit with her. Do you have every afternoon off for dunking?"

"By no means, but Miss Shaw decided she's working me too hard, and turned me loose for the rest of today."

"And I," said Alex solemnly, "am also at liberty by some lucky chance. Shall we combine forces? As a starter, how about lunch in some picturesque shack frequented by lobstermen and other town characters, followed by a brisk drive along the scenic shore line beyond Cape Ann, then dinner in another—"

"How about just lunch?" Cynthia interrupted the inviting catalog, "and see how we get along? I may bore you, so don't commit yourself too far."

"That shoe is more likely to fit *me*—but whatever you

say." He pointed behind him. "My car's up there, can I run you back to the hotel to dress or are you still determined to risk a dive?"

Cynthia looked down at the water and shook her head.

"Frankly, I've lost the urge for the moment. If you will stop at the beach I'll pick up my robe. I hope you don't mind a rather wet passenger."

"Not this particular one," Houston said gallantly and led the way to his car.

The picturesque shack he selected turned out to be a charming tearoom perched at the end of a wharf in Newbury Harbor and aptly, if not too originally, named Land's End. The exterior was lavishly decorated with festooned fishing nets and brightly painted lobster pot buoys, while two enormous crossed oars framed the entrance. Within, however, the proprietor had curbed his passion for marine effects; turquoise walls only suggested the sea, and the plain white tavern curtains at every window were pulled wide to give a view of the harbor.

"Lobster of course?" Alex suggested when a young dark-haired waitress presented the menus. When Cynthia agreed enthusiastically he began to order, suggesting several changes in the advertised side dishes.

Cynthia noticed how intently the girl listened, her brows puckered and lips forming soundless words. As Alex looked up to emphasize a point he must have caught the expression, for he paused and leaned back.

"You are not a Newbury Harborite, are you?" he asked interestedly.

The waitress pondered that. Cynthia could almost see the words being examined, sorted out with intense concentration, and finally identified.

"Newbury Harbor is here, yes?" Her voice was soft, with a throaty accent. "Then, no—I am Hungarian. I don't always understand, sometime. Excuse me."

"You are doing fine," Alex encouraged kindly. "Look, here on the card. Number Two, Broiled Lobster Dinner. One for her, one for me. O.K.?" He smiled at her. "I'll bet you understand that slang already."

"Yes! But you say," she protested with frowning intentness, "Hash potato instead of—"

"Forget all that." He tapped the card. "Just bring each of us a Number Two, no changes."

"O.K." The girl smiled and went away muttering.

"Hope you don't mind taking it as it comes?" Alex asked. "I thought we wouldn't confuse her with complications. She is nervous enough anyway."

"If you had pounded the table and insisted on the changes," Cynthia assured him, "I would have stabbed you with a butter knife. The poor girl can't have been over here very long, no wonder she's nervous. Imagine landing in a strange country and having to earn a living!"

"More or less your own position, isn't it? Alone among strangers and forced to earn a living. But perhaps that isn't a real necessity with you?"

Cynthia didn't care for the subject, and even less for the penetrating look which accompanied its introduction.

"A necessity for the present," she temporized while she groped for a plausible explanation. "You see, Lon needs every cent we were able to scrape up for this Japanese business. If he puts it over, we will have clear sailing. But why bring up dull shop talk," she admonished brightly, "when there is much more interesting sailing to watch in the harbor?" And throughout the four mouth-watering courses of the Land's End Lobster Dinner Number Two she succeeded in holding the conversation firmly away from further discussion of any and all Farleys.

That she achieved her objective without sacrificing any of her charm was attested by Alex Houston's insistence on carrying out the full program he had previously outlined. There was no objection from Cynthia, in spite of secret misgivings as to the wisdom of becoming entangled with Miss Shaw's cousin. She was enjoying herself far too much to call a halt. If the pursued relative chose to turn pursuer, that was his affair—and her gain.

They started for the suggested drive along the shore, but chance postponed the trip. The car was threading through the last of the village's haphazard traffic when a small yellow airplane droned overhead, dropping lower and lower as it flew westward.

With an exclamation of surprise Alex suddenly swung off the main street into a lane and gunned the motor.

"You don't mind a side trip, I hope," he said. "That looked like the new plane of a friend of mine in Beverly. Let's see if it is."

"You expect to catch him in this car?" Cynthia jeered.

"Just that. He was heading for the airfield outside town, it's not far from here," he explained as the car climbed a slope between arching elms.

"An airfield in Newbury Harbor? Nobody has ever mentioned it and I haven't seen any planes around here."

Alex laughed. "That's not surprising. Don't get the idea that this is a La Guardia Terminal. So far it isn't much more than a big level field with a hangar and a couple of part-time mechanics. Quite a few people around here own planes now, or fly occasionally, and they hope to work up into a permanent association that can support a proper field at least."

"That is the way—" Cynthia shut her teeth on the rest of the sentence. Oh dear! Would she never learn to control her impulsive tongue with this man? Almost she had blurted out details of that similar group in California, where she and Eric were practically charter members. The only recovery she could make was a lame, "That is the way to start. I suppose."

"You don't sound very enthusiastic. Don't you care for flying?"

"No."

The flat monosyllable chilled even Cynthia as she uttered it. He would think her impossible! Why couldn't she drive the crowding memories from her mind and live in the present? Suppose Alex was crazy about flying? For all she knew about him he might very well be one of the group he had mentioned. Please, not that! she prayed in her heart; I just couldn't go through it again.

Alex turned off the dirt road onto a bumpy, rutted track, and slowed to a crawl.

"He did land!" he exclaimed, pointing ahead to where the yellow plane sat with spinning propeller at the near end of a long field. He drove through a gap in the low stone wall and out into the open.

Cynthia experienced a sinking sensation as they swayed through the ankle-high grass. This was so like that other field, spreading over the gently curved top of a wide crowned hill. But there were no mountains for a backdrop here, only the blue sea on three sides of Newbury Point, and green fields with scattered houses on the fourth. She studied the plane; except for its color it seemed dreadfully like Eric Crane's.

A small hangar stood at the edge of the field with a storage shed and gas pump. Alex drew up beside the two cars already parked there and stopped. The driver of the larger car stepped out and joined a man in overalls who was walking toward the plane, its motor now silent. In the second car, a battered, dusty coupé, a thin young man leaned from the window to watch.

The door of the plane opened and a man climbed down and stepped out from under the shadow of the wing. Cynthia did not realize that she had been holding her breath until it came out in a sharp gasp of relief. The pilot was no one she had ever seen before; thickset, untanned, with dark curly hair around a glistening bald spot.

He shook hands with the man from the car and smiled at the grimy mechanic.

"You needn't do a thing, son," he instructed. "I've only come from Lynn, and I am leaving in an hour." The mechanic nodded and turned away; the two men climbed into the big car, chatting.

"Scratch my brilliant idea," said Alex regretfully, "it isn't Ned after all. Why, Cynthia, you're pale! Good Lord, have I pulled a boner, bringing you here? Some tragic memory—?"

"What an idea! I am perfectly all right," she protested, so wildly relieved that she bubbled with gaiety. "And you aren't very polite to comment on my lack of makeup." She leaned forward to study her face in the rearview mirror. "*I* think that I look particularly well!"

"Sorry. Maybe it was my imagination."

As the big car started the pilot leaned out and called to the young man in the coupé. "No headlines for you today, Scoop. I came over to sign a lease with Kerriman here, that's all. Too bad."

To Cynthia Alex murmured, "That's young Parker, who runs the local weekly paper, in that broken down car. Everyone calls him 'Scoop.' I guess he thought he had one with a strange plane landing here."

When the two cars drove off he asked, "Mind if I look over the plane for a minute? If you'd rather, we'll pull out for the drive I promised at once."

"Of course not!"

Cynthia tried to make amends for her former lack of interest by going with him while he inspected the little plane. No wonder it appeared familiar; except for the color, and a single control system where Eric's had been dual, it was the model in which she had flown with him.

VIII

THEY were returning to their car when the mechanic came out of the building.

"Hello," Alex said. "We were just looking at the plane. A very neat job."

"Yessir." The young man was frowning, pushing back the hair from his forehead with nervous fingers. He burst out with an anxious stammer, "Say, what do you think I ought to do? There's a couple of kids out there," he pointed toward the sea, "and I think they ought to be brought in! I called the Yacht Club, but nobody answered."

"Probably," Alex suggested, "it's so early in the season that there isn't anyone there and the attendant may be out on the dock. I see the boys now." He directed Cynthia's attention to a bright orange square bobbing far out on the blue water.

"What an odd shape for a sail." Shading her eyes she made out an orange hull below, and the two tiny figures in it.

The mechanic was chewing his lip, his frown intensified.

"It's an inflated life raft, ma'am; they're fitted with a couple of oars and a piece of canvas for an emergency sail. That's the O'Hara boys; their father bought 'em the raft yesterday, but they weren't supposed to take it out until he tested it. It's a Navy surplus, no telling how old it is. I'll bet it's half rotten!"

"I don't believe that the Navy would sell a defective life raft, surplus or not," Alex objected.

"O'Hara didn't get it direct. Some guy at Gloucester sold it to him cheap, so he wanted to make sure it was O.K. before the kids used it. I'll bet they sneaked it out. O'Hara had it stored at the Allens'—that gray house down there. I tried to call them, too, but couldn't raise anyone, and there's no one else this side of the Point that has a boat." He sucked in his breath with a nervous hiss. "Judas, look at the waves pound that raft!"

Inexperienced though she was Cynthia stood appalled at the bursts of white spray which almost hid the craft from view. "How big are those boys?" she asked.

The man kept his eyes on the raft.

"Tommy's twelve or so, I guess, his brother's about nine. The crazy little fools! Gee, sir, I think we ought to do something about them, and quick!"

"So do I," Alex muttered. "How about calling the Harbor, you must know someone there who has a boat?"

"But that's way 'round the other side of the Point; take half an hour to get here. That's why I thought of the Yacht Club. Maybe I should call the Coast Guard?"

"You do that, and fast!" Alex advised. "And we'll drive down to the Club. We might find someone around or a boat that I can take out. Let's go, Cynthia!"

They were in the convertible, backing with spinning wheels to swing around toward the gap in the stone wall, when a frantic yell sent Alex's foot stamping on the brake pedal.

"They've gone over!" the mechanic shouted, beckoning wildly. "They're in the water!"

"Can they hang onto the raft?" Alex slid out of the car and Cynthia followed, her mouth dry with excitement.

"There's nothing to hang onto! It's gone. The darn thing came apart all at once, must have been rotten at every seam! My God, what'll we do?"

Alex laid a hand on his arm.

"Steady, pal. Can those boys swim?"

"Tommy can, pretty good. I don't know about Sam. But they're so far out—and it's mighty rough."

"Call the Coast Guard," Alex ordered, "and be quick!"

Cynthia stood numb, unconsciously counting the times that the two black heads were hidden and revealed by successive waves.

"One boy is in front," she murmured. "That must be the older—Tommy. Oh, Alex, the other one has stopped swimming, he's being swamped with waves—he'll drown!"

"Don't panic, Cynthy." His hand was on her shoulder while he watched. "There, I thought so. Tommy's going back to him."

"How wonderful!" she breathed. "And only twelve years old!"

"That's his brother, gal; he'll stick with him, but how long can he keep him afloat?"

The mechanic charged out of the building. "Are they still there? I got the Guard and they're sending a boat and a helicopter, but they're too far away. It'll take fifteen or twenty minutes to get here!"

"Too long!" Alex growled. "We'll try the Yacht Club, but it's a gamble." He turned toward the car and noticed the yellow plane. "Say!" He whirled on the mechanic. "Can you fly that thing?"

"Me?"

"Yes, you! I can't, but I'll go along and drop a couple of lifebelts to the boys, if you'll take me up."

Cynthia saw the color drain from the young man's cheeks. Her own throat contracted painfully and there was aching emptiness where her heart should have been when he stammered:

"Gee, no sir! I couldn't. I don't fly; I just help around here."

"Damn!" Alex started for his car.

"Alex!" The girl brushed a mist from her eyes and forced dry lips to whisper, "I can fly that plane."

He stared at her a moment before his hand closed on her arm with a grip that made her wince.

"Do you mean that?" he snapped.

"Yes." Now that the die was cast she could speak clearly. "I have flown that type of plane any number of times. I would have qualified as a pilot only—only I never got around to it."

"Can you take me out there and get close enough to drop life preservers right next to them?"

"I—I don't know."

"You can!" His compelling eyes held hers. "I'll bet on you

to come through in any emergency—you've got what it takes, Cynthy. Will you try?"

She drew courage from his eyes and strong hand holding her. "I'll try, Alex," she promised.

"You'll do it!" He turned to bark at the young man. "You, feller! Find a couple of life jackets, Mae Wests, anything. And bring a length of rope." The mechanic dove for the doorway, Alex swung back to Cynthia. "Go ahead—get in and start the motor!"

It was a wonderful tonic for her nervousness to have him take charge with such assurance; how could she hesitate in the face of his confidence? Her heartbeat slowed to normal when she took her seat and settled her feet on the rudder pedals.

"Anything I can do?" he asked, climbing in beside her.

"Not a thing—yet." As coolly as though it was a routine training flight she checked the fuel gauge and the other vital controls.

The mechanic appeared at Alex's door and piled a pair of orange kapok jackets and a few feet of heavy cord onto his lap.

"Hey!" he panted. "Wait a minute! What if the guy that owns this plane comes back? He didn't lock it and I'm responsible—"

"I wish he was here now!" Alex grunted.

"A little more faith in your pilot, please," Cynthia suggested, and drew an approving grin from him.

"I mean," the man persisted, "he may be sore."

"He won't be, and don't worry. If I have to I'll buy him a new plane," Alex promised. "Are the boys still in sight?"

"Yeah. Good luck!" He dropped from the step and slammed the door.

Cynthia flicked the switch, and hoping that the engine was still warm, pressed the starter. The propeller clicked over, whirled faster—the motor roared to life.

"I'll have to taxi to the far end of the field and take off this way, into the wind, so it may be rough riding," she warned.

"Just get me out to those kids!"

As the plane took off at last Cynthia experienced a sensation which she had never known in all her flights with Eric. Was it because another, utterly different man sat beside her that she thrilled to the feeling of freedom? They were together, clear of the earth, soaring into the limitless blue arch of the sky. Eagerly she lifted the plane into a steep circling climb.

The green and brown of Newbury Point wheeled below them, dropping swiftly away to a miniature relief map. The cluster of buildings around the Harbor dwindled to specks with only the sprawling white and black bulk of the hotel still recognizable, and far off the green and white patchwork quilt of fields and highways spreading across the mainland. Then there was only the brilliant blue of the sea below, twinkling with a million diamond-bright whitecaps.

She nosed the plane down, swinging toward the area where the raft had been.

"There they are!" she pointed suddenly.

"I see them." Alex was as composed as though he sat in an armchair on the Harbor House veranda. "Fly as low over them as you can with safety; I leave that to your judgment."

Spurred by his confidence she studied the scene.

"I'd better run past them and come back against the wind as I did when we took off," she muttered. "And I'll drop the wing flaps. All that will slow us up, but I'm afraid we'll still be traveling over fifty miles an hour. Try to make allowance for that when you drop the life preservers."

"I'll do my best, but I never had any bombing practice." He was connecting the two orange jackets with the cord. "Maybe this will help; if either of these falls within reach they can get them both."

The boys disappeared under a wave, reappeared. Cynthia thought that she could see one white face raised toward the plane for an instant before they went under again. Her heart almost failed her at the speed with which the tossing sea and the two tiny dark heads came rushing toward the plane. She throttled down the motor even more, until the plane trembled toward a stall, and in a brief flash of panic she was forced to increase the speed.

Alex unbuckled his safety belt, slid open his window and looked down, the jackets clutched in his hands. The wind whipped his hair wildly as he waited. Then he flung the bundle straight down and watched its fall.

Cynthia was too busy with the controls to look back but her heart jumped with hope when he shouted, "They landed close!" He drew back into his seat, struggled out of his sweater and then bent to unlace his shoes and kick them off.

"Circle over them again," he ordered. "If Tommy doesn't reach those jackets I'll go down and lend him a hand."

"You can't do that! You'd be killed!"

"Looks as if we're only about fifty feet above the water, but I might at that," he admitted calmly. "Just the same, I'm not going to let a couple of boys drown for fear of getting wet."

"Getting wet?" she wailed. "Don't you realize what it might do to you, if you hit the water at the speed we are going?"

"Clamp down on those jittery nerves, gal, you're scaring me." He looked out the window again, then closed it. "Glad to report that I take no high dive today," he said cheerfully, "as I'm not needed down there. The dependable Tommy has both life jackets and is now hauling his brother onto one of them. What a boy!"

"I'd better keep on circling them, to be sure they are all right," Cynthia remarked. "See the Coast Guard anywhere?"

" 'Sister Anne, Sister Anne, do you see anyone coming?' " he quoted with a grin. "That's from 'Bluebeard,' isn't it? No, ma'am, nothing visible as yet in sea or sky. Wait! Correction! There *is* a boat to the south, and from the wake she's leaving it must be the U.S. Cavalry galloping to the rescue."

Alex peered below. "Both kids are in the jackets now, safe and sound, so far. What say we run down to that Guard boat and lead them up here. We might offer them a tow."

Cynthia guessed that his flippancy was meant to relax her, and she acknowledged it with a smile. They sped downwind until they could turn low above the white cruiser.

Alex waved to the figures on the bridge. " 'Thou, too, sail on, O Ship of State!'—Longfellow," he said cheerfully.

At his suggestion Cynthia laid a course back toward the shipwrecked mariners, and the big cruiser swung its bow after her to follow, throwing aside rolling furrows of foam. She continued her watchful circling above the boys until the ship arrived and dropped a boat close to the brilliant jackets. She drew a deep breath of relief when they were hauled safely aboard.

"Haven't you a suitable quotation for that?" she asked Alex disparagingly.

"No, the literary hour is over. Sorry it was so far above the intelligence quotient of the listening audience," he cut back good-humoredly. "The skipper of that ship will take it from here, believe me! I'll bet that the boys will receive a classic dressing down."

He relaxed in his seat with a sigh and closed his eyes.

"What say you take this crate in before you burn up all that poor man's gas," he suggested.

Cynthia laughed lightheartedly. It was heaven to feel so carefree again. "Are you sure you don't mean, before I make a mistake and spill us both in the drink?" She headed back toward the Point. "I must salute your courage, sir, in trusting your life to a girl who suddenly *claimed* that she could fly. How did you know that I wasn't just driven to crazy desperation by the boys' danger?"

"Let's not talk about my courage; you have cast-iron nerves. I sensed it when you so coolly figured how best to approach and drop the jackets. You must have flown a great deal, Cynthy, and yet you acted completely bored with the field and the plane at first."

"Let's not talk about that, either," she protested firmly. "Not now or ever, please. It is a closed chapter." They were over the flying field again. "Here goes for a landing, if I can remember to do everything right!"

She did. The plane ended its run without incident, coming to a stop almost where it had stood before. With the last sputtering of the engine reaction claimed her and she shivered violently. Her hands were wet and trembling when she opened the door and stepped down. Alex was already out and steadied her.

The mechanic met her with outstretched hand, his face pink with excitement.

"Nice going, ma'am! Nice going! I saw the whole thing!"

"So did I!" yelped a breathless voice and the young reporter pushed past him to shake her hand. "You, too, Mr. Houston!" he chattered, and insisted on seizing Alex's hand for a vigorous grip. "What a story! I saw the plane when it took off, and I knew that the owner wasn't here, so I drove back in a hurry. I figured maybe someone was stealing it, but this is even better!"

"You can leave me out of it, Parker," Alex laughed. "I was just ballast. Write your story about Mrs. Farley—and make it good!"

"No, please!" Cynthia begged anxiously. "No publicity!"

Scoop Parker drowned her objection in a torrent of questions. "Mrs. Farley, aren't you Miss Shaw's latest secretary? Sure, you must be. Where have you flown before? Never mind that, though—I want to hear about this flight and then get down and interview the O'Hara boys. Who saw them first?"

"This gentleman!" Cynthia interjected eagerly, hoping to shift Parker's attention from her. "He is the mechanic here—"

"Sure, I know Kenny. I want a picture of him, too." Parker whipped a small camera from his jacket pocket. "Local boy makes the local paper with bells on. Let's go over where you first spotted them, Ken. You can be pointing off to sea." He led the willing subject to a suitable position.

"Alex," Cynthia whispered, "please take me away before he asks any more questions."

"You do dislike publicity, don't you!" He led her unobtrusively to his car. "Have you had an unfortunate experience with it?" he inquired as the machine swayed into the lane.

"N-no." She wondered if it was his legal training which made him ask such disconcerting questions. "Honestly I haven't. I just don't care to pose as a heroine when I didn't do anything heroic. I can fly a plane, so it wasn't spectacular bravery for me to go out there."

"There might be two schools of thought on that," Alex objected dryly. "But as far as publicity goes, I wouldn't worry too much about Scoop Parker. The Newbury *Weekly Messenger* must have all of three hundred subscribers and a lot of them only read the ads."

"Good for them," Cynthia said relieved. "As long as the two boys are safe I'm going to forget the whole affair."

"That is something that I'll never do."

The admiration in his tone lifted her heart to double-time, but she said earnestly, "Don't exaggerate my part. *You* thought of using the plane, and put such trust in me that I had to come through. Now I think you had better take me home."

"And break up this very successful team? Perish the thought! If you recall the program, it included dinner. And I know just the place, in Portsmouth."

"Where is that?"

"Bless your Middle Western ignorance. Never mind, I can find it, and I guarantee you'll like it. Northward ho!"

Their destination proved to be a still flourishing tavern of pre-Revolutionary vintage which more than lived up to his promise. The dining room was a low-ceilinged room where Alex had to stoop slightly to dodge the rough beams. There were many-paned windows and a fireplace so broad that wooden benches were set into it, flanking the ash-heaped hearth.

They sat at a table dark with age and scarred and dented by the pounding of generations of pewter mugs. The yard-wide boards of the floor were worn into hollows by the tramping of countless heavy shoes.

Cynthia drew in a deep breath of the tavern's warm air and tried to sort out the varied odors mingled in it. There was smoke, of course, the faint scent of spices and wine, and something she felt sure must come from the building itself, a haunting aroma of sturdy pine and oak aged for three hundred years but still proof against the onslaughts of time or man.

She smiled at Alex's watchful eyes. "I knew there was New England in my blood, but never felt it more strongly than in this wonderful room."

"The Yankee in us never dies," he agreed. "So you are New England stock after all. You know, I had a feeling that you were, when I carried you off the train that night."

"Otherwise," she laughed, "I suppose you would have dropped me and gone in search of a Bostonian female to rescue."

"At least she wouldn't have absconded with my suitcase."

"You win," Cynthia admitted with a dramatic sigh of

resignation. "As the daughter of a lawyer, I should know better than to try matching wits with one."

"I am interested in your family, Cynthia. Know a number of lawyers in Chicago, but I don't believe I ever met Mr. Farley."

"He—he was before your time, probably," she murmured. "Father died some time ago."

"And is—er, Alonzo from Chicago?"

"Of course." Too late she realized that Alex was referring to her *husband* and not her brother. "That sounds terribly provincial, doesn't it?" she said quickly to cover the mistake. "As though I couldn't possibly marry anyone who wasn't from Chicago."

"Then you could consider it?" His eyes were disturbingly bright. "I mean, if you weren't already married?" he amended, and shrugged. "It would be a blow to my self-esteem if you said 'No,' so I hastily withdraw the question. Your husband's business is manufacturing, isn't it? Also in Chicago?"

"Yes." Cynthia decided that it would be wise to leave Chicago and the Farleys before she committed another error. "Let's not break the spell of this delightful old place by talking of the present," she suggested. "We should discuss Liberty and the tyrannical Stamp Act, and what Old Sam Adams will be up to next. There!" she smiled triumphantly. "You see I do know some history!"

Whatever he meant to answer was lost in the whirlwind approach of three girls who crowded around the table and greeted him with whole-hearted enthusiasm. Alex rose and introduced them in turn to her, but in the babble of conversation she caught only names without being able to pin them on the individuals, except that the tall, gloriously copper-haired athletic-type female was either Babbsy or Bobbsy.

"Mrs. Farley?" This one echoed the introduction curiously. She had linked arms with Alex but studied Cynthia covertly. "A client, Alex?"

"My cousin's latest secretary—and one who seems destined to satisfy even the critical Eva," he smiled, without troubling to withdraw from the clinging embrace. It did not, Cynthia thought, seem to displease him in the least.

"She must be pretty good!" Babbsy—or Bobbsy—took a firmer grip on his arm. "Let's make this a party—we can get a big booth and join forces. Would you mind, Mrs. Farley?"

Alex saved her from having to make polite and very unwilling acceptance.

"We'd better not tonight, Barbara. I am trying to give

Mrs. Farley a line on how to handle Cousin Eva. If she doesn't make the grade, you know, I'll be saddled with the job of finding another secretary."

"Is that so unpleasant?" The redhead gave her question the very lightest flick of sarcasm. "Some other time, then. We haven't seen anything of you for weeks, Alex. Aren't you ever coming to Beverly Farms again?" With another burst of conversation the girls retired to a booth across the room.

"I'm sorry, I didn't catch their names," Cynthia apologized. "They seemed to know you very well."

"Oh yes, particularly Barbara Eliot."

"Eliot? Isn't there an Eliot line among the Shaws? I'm sure there is—on pearl gray filing cards!" At his puzzled frown she explained Miss Shaw's colorful system for separating the notes on the various branches of the family.

Laughing, he denied any family connection with the Eliots of Beverly Farms. "I've known Barbara for years," he added. "We summered at the Harbor House from childhood. Practically brother and sister."

Cynthia was sure that such a relationship would not continue if Barbara Eliot had her way. Evidently secretaries were not the only females who pursued Alex Houston, and no wonder!

"A cocktail before we order?" Alex asked, and when she declined he offered his cigarette case. She shook her head. Alex raised his eyes to heaven, or the beamed ceiling. "Doesn't drink or smoke! Decidedly a paragon among women, and one to know better! By the way, does Alonzo smoke?"

"You seem obsessed by the subject of Alonzo."

The gray eyes scanned her intently. He sighed with exaggerated patience.

"Sorry, thought you would enjoy talking abour your husband. Would you rather order dinner?"

"I *am* hungry." Cynthia put all the coldness she could into the flat statement and succeeded in discouraging him from prying into her past for the rest of the evening. To her relief he showed no resentment and devoted himself to entertaining her through dinner and an hour or two of dancing at a nearby hotel. And such was his skill that long before their private curfew sent them home she decided that Alex Houston was by far the nicest man that she had ever known.

IX

THE MORNING was heavily overcast with a threat of impending rain in the leaden clouds, but Cynthia's high spirits made light of the weather. In fact she was on the crest of the wave when she came down to her breakfast in the Harbor House. Bemused, she hardly noticed an unusual warmth in the greeting of the headwaiter. The friendly smiles of everyone she passed on her way to her table in a bay window she attributed to the canary-yellow dress chosen to enliven a drab day. Reaching the table, however, she descended from her rosy clouds with a jolt. Miss Eva Shaw, who invariably breakfasted in her apartment, sat there stiffly erect and ominous.

"Why, good morning!" Cynthia gasped.

"Good morning. You don't mind my joining you?"

"I am honored—and delighted."

"*I* am delighted," Miss Shaw said without betraying the slightest evidence of that emotion, "to find you unharmed. You might at least have returned at a decent hour to reassure me. I shall never forgive Alexander—but you both must be equally mad!"

Cynthia caught her breath at the unexpected attack and sank into her chair.

"Surely there was no harm in our going out for dinner—or dancing," she protested, and then remembered her role. "Why, Miss Shaw," she assured demurely, "Alonzo wouldn't think of objecting, under the circumstances. And twelve-thirty isn't late."

"You misunderstand. Alexander Houston's conduct is always above reproach. It is his judgment which disappoints me. I know nothing about last night, I am referring to your afternoon's escapade. He was insane to allow you to take such risks!"

Again Cynthia had to adjust to the unexpected.

"Oh, the plane!" she faltered. "Then you have heard about that? Is—is the owner making trouble?"

"Heard about it!" Miss Shaw disregarded the last question in her agitation. "There was some garbled reference to it on the late news last night, and now—" She plucked a newspaper from her lap and slapped it down on the table before the girl. "—Now *everyone* has heard about it!"

Cynthia stared in horror, slowly taking in the awful page with its blaring headline:

GIRL PILOT DARES DEATH
TO RESCUE BROTHERS

Even more dreadful was the large picture below the headline, a startlingly clear photograph of herself snapped at the instant she stepped from the plane, with the legend, "Cynthia Farley and her co-pilot, Alexander Houston, prominent lawyer." To cap her consternation, this was not the Newbury *Messenger* but a leading Boston daily paper.

Her brain literally whirled. She guessed from Miss Shaw's look of alarm that she must have turned white and she fought to regain control, to utter some matter-of-fact comment. The effort was useless when all she could comprehend was that the secret of her location was now broadcast far and wide. If Eric Crane had not yet returned to California—! But he must have! Unable to trace her beyond that Boston hotel he would give up. Even that hope died as she looked more closely at the story; it was credited to a news service, might already be appearing in the San Francisco papers. Eric would know—*everyone* would know where she had taken refuge!

Then common sense helped to rein in her galloping fears. She was borrowing trouble. Why assume that this local story would rate nationwide coverage? It was sheer conceit to feel that her doings were flashed out on every telegraph wire to a panting world.

Somewhat calmed by that thought she schooled her features to a reproving frown.

"Alex will be embarrassed, won't he. Probably furious."

Miss Shaw bridled, indicating that criticism of a relative was her prerogative.

"Why?" she demanded. "It is an excellent picture of him!"

"It is," Cynthia admitted meekly. "I meant that he would be upset because they call him my co-pilot." She sighed. "That reporter must have snapped us while I was still dazed, and then pocketed his camera in a hurry for fear that I would object. And wouldn't I have! But Alex told me he was only from the little local paper."

Since there seemed nothing to gain by further regretting she ate her grapefruit, while with equal relish she read the story. It was a good account; young Scoop Parker possessed the gift for making words come alive. There was even a mention of "Miss Eva Shaw, well-known author." Nevertheless Cynthia would read the riot act to him for disrupting her privacy! Or would she? It would be impossible to make any sensible objection without revealing *why* she preferred to remain anonymous.

Thoughtfully she sipped her coffee, and found Miss Shaw regarding her with surprising tenderness. Had it not been totally out of character one would have said that the piercing eyes were dimmed by tears.

"Don't ever do such a thing again, Cynthia!" the older woman implored. "If anything had happened to you—!"

"But nothing did." Touched by this evidence of human emotion in her formidable employer, Cynthia dared to pick up the hand which was drumming on the table and squeeze it sympathetically. "As I told Alex, I knew how to fly that plane, so it would have been rank cowardice for me *not* to help those boys."

She dropped her eyes to the newspaper.

"I didn't stop to think of the pub—"

She was interrupted by the appearance at her elbow of Neal Bruce, suavely smiling, in Hollywoodish raiment of rainbow-hued sports shirt and old ivory slacks. He seized her hand and pumped it vigorously.

"Congratulations, you daring pilot!" he said excitedly. "I'm proud to know you!"

"Sh!" Cynthia extricated numbed fingers from his grip.

"'Sh,' my eye!" he grinned. "The world should know!" Thrusting a hand into the front of his shirt and teetering back and forth on his toes he declaimed sonorously, "The world will little note nor long remember what I say here, but it will never forget what you did—or words to that effect."

Over his shoulder he acknowledged Miss Shaw's presence.

"A thousand pardons, dear lady, and a good morning to you. I hope you can appreciate that I forgot my manners in the glorious sight of our young heroine."

"Perfectly excusable, under the circumstances, Neal," Miss Shaw admitted primly.

"Why did you tell me yesterday that you were not an actor, Mr. Bruce?" Cynthia challenged. "Surely the theater could use such eloquence."

"In this case I had a good writer—A. Lincoln," he chuckled. "Generally with the producers it's 'Don't call us—we'll call you,' and they haven't called me yet! They let me watch the rehearsals anyway; I am due there at nine-thirty—hence this musical comedy costume."

He leaned closer and lowered his voice.

"By the way, Mrs. Farley, could we persuade you to help us out? We are stuck for one part, short but with a lot of meat in it—a pretty girl—"

The staccato rattle of spoon on plate intervened. Miss Shaw ceased the tattoo and aimed the spoon at him.

"We will have no stealing of stars, Neal!" she advised acidly. "Mrs. Farley has quite enough to do for me."

"Sure. And the Summer Theater couldn't compete with your wages," he laughed, and withdrew with a courtly bow.

Miss Shaw scorned to wait until he was out of hearing. "Neal Bruce is what they used to call 'an eligible bachelor' and has been for twenty years," she confided to Cynthia. "Nice boy, but too much money for his own good. Never worked at anything."

Further revelations were prevented by the arrival of the headwaiter.

"Excuse me, Mrs. Farley." He bowed. "A telephone call for you, at the desk. Important, they said. And may I congratulate you?"

"Thank you, but everyone is making too much of it. Excuse me, Miss Shaw, and do eat your breakfast. It is probably Alex, calling to make sure I survived."

She left the table with a strong impression that her remark had caused Miss Shaw's eyebrows to arch in surprised rebuke. Darn it, she mourned, I keep forgetting all those pursuing secretaries.

She was glad to soothe any displeasure on her return. Her cheeks were pink with excitement.

"It wasn't your cousin," she explained. "It was a television station in Boston, wanting to interview me on the air tonight. And quite excited that I am secretary to Miss Shaw, the author."

"Splendid!" The celebrity immediately assumed command. "You had better go up this morning, I suppose. Rehearsal and so on, you know. Michael will drive you."

"No, thanks. I told them politely to forget it."

"Why, Cynthia! Of course you must go, it's a wonderful opportunity. Who knows, it might lead to a career!"

"On television? Never! I have no talents suited to that. And they aren't hunting talent, they only want to cash in on what the paper calls my heroic deed. Which it wasn't at all."

"I don't know what to make of you," Miss Shaw grumbled. "I wish that someone would invite *me* to appear. I could get some of the publicity you scorn for my book. The publisher reports that its sales are slowing down."

Having finished her breakfast Miss Shaw pushed back her chair. The headwaiter materialized beside her with miraculous speed and assisted her to rise.

"Let go of my arm, young man!" she snapped. "I'm not

senile!" Her annoyance carried over to her parting remark. "Cynthia, don't dawdle, we have loads of work to do."

She swept out of the dining room erect and imperious as a full rigged ship, stopping at several tables to make audible inquiries as to the improved health, the problem children or the business ventures of embarrassed guests. Evidently Mr. Bruce had been right when he said that Miss Eva knew everything about everybody.

Before the day was over Cynthia concluded that her employer's reference to "loads of work" was an understatement, for they labored until five with a brief hour out for luncheon. At times she wondered whether Miss Shaw was punishing her for spending so much time with Alex, suspicious that here, married or not, was another scheming girl in pursuit of her well-to-do cousin.

She was able to discount that disturbing possibility, however, by observing that Miss Shaw worked even harder herself. She seemed bursting with energy, on fire with inspiration, and pencil after pencil was snatched from her hair, dulled and discarded, as she filled page after page of manuscript at racing speed.

The next morning Miss Shaw's dynamic power not only remained undiminished but even seemed redoubled. Cynthia was reminded of the fabled giant Anteus whom no mortal could defeat at wrestling because he arose from each fall with strength increased by contact with his Mother Earth.

Undismayed, Cynthia squared her shoulders and flexed her fingers proudly. Not a sign of cramp, even after yesterday's work load; it was amazing how completely she had regained her former ability. Miss Shaw must be satisfied with her progress, too. Even a few days' acquaintance with that decisive lady made Cynthia positive that if she wasn't suited, Cynthia would hear of it.

They might have completed another eight-hour day had not Fate intervened. In the middle of the afternoon Cynthia paused in her typing to inquire, "What does this mean, Miss Shaw? Describing the Langdon family, there is a question mark in the margin with the letters M.L.U. Someone's initials?"

"Oh, goodness! That means 'Must Look Up'—and I never did!" The author rummaged in a box of lilac-tinted cards. "Langdon? One of the girls married a Shaw in 1745 or thereabouts. Here is the note, Essex Institute, records of the Society, Volume Three. Oh dear, I should have checked it at the time! Cynthia, would you mind getting the book? Michael will drive you to Salem, but hurry before the Institute closes for the day."

"Volume Three, of the Society's records." Cynthia welcomed the respite from steady typing. "I'll be back as soon as I can."

The ride gave her an opportunity to reread the airmail letter which had arrived from Japan that morning.

"The miracle of modern transportation," she murmured, adding the derisive qualification, "its speed increased by Lon's impetuous nature!" For Brother Alonzo must have dashed off his reply the moment he received her report on the present location and marital status of Cynthia Farley.

Alonzo was not pleased. There was no need to read between the lines to gather that impression because with Farley vigor he minced no words. Cynthia repressed a giggle as she read:

> Of all the crazy stunts—and you have pulled some beauts—this is tops! I hoped your California fiasco would knock some sense into you, but you're incurable. If you think I'm going to cancel my trip to come back and haul a fool girl out of another mess you're way off. You've done it again—now you can stew in it! But I'll be home sooner than I expected, thank God! Just see that you've straightened things out by then or you'll be sorry!

It was so typical of Lon, though, and so comforting, to have him scrawl a postscript;

> I'll address this to 'Mrs. Farley' as you ask, only because I don't want to be responsible for any trouble; you make enough yourself. But damned if I'll do it again.

That meant no more letters; the present one might get rather dog-eared from carrying it around to convince people that she actually did have a husband in Japan. She must let Miss Shaw catch a glimpse of the postmark on the envelope at once, the moment she returned from her errand.

This, her first attempt at such a mission, would have ended ingloriously had she not been in the protective custody of Michael, the white-haired chauffeur of Miss Shaw's limousine. It was routine for him. He drove her sedately to Salem, parked before the Institute, descended to open the door for her and, Cynthia felt sure, watched her enter with paternal solicitude.

X

When she returned to the car five minutes later she was empty-handed and crestfallen.

"The book Miss Shaw wanted was there, but they wouldn't let me take it out!" she wailed.

"They wouldn't?" Michael's gray eyebrows drew together and his weather-beaten face darkened. "Huh!" He climbed ponderously from behind the wheel. "They don't know you, see?"

"That's what they said. Miss Shaw should have written a note. I don't blame them—but she will be disappointed in me."

"Like heck she will!"

The burly chauffeur took Cynthia firmly by the elbow and escorted her, rather propelled her, into the museum, politely removing his visored cap as he entered. She had the helpless feeling of a very small tugboat at the mercy of a very large ocean liner as they approached the librarian.

Michael released her to plant his large freckled hands on the desk and lean over the startled woman.

"You know me, don't you? Miss Shaw's chauffeur," he demanded huskily.

The woman leaned back defensively. "Certainly, Michael."

"O.K." He jerked a thumb toward Cynthia. "This is Mrs. Farley, Miss Shaw's sec'atary, see? Now you know *her*."

"Yes, but we have rules about taking out books and—"

Michael brushed rules aside. "Sure. And Miss Shaw sent us over to *get* a book. You want us to go back an' tell her we couldn't have it? She isn't going to like that, Miss. You want Miss Shaw to get mad and come over here *herself?*"

"That won't be necessary!" the woman said hastily. "As long as you are vouching for Mrs. Farley, Michael—It was Volume Three of the Society's records you wanted, wasn't it, Mrs. Farley? I'll get it for you."

Back in the car with the book Cynthia said, "Thank you very much, Michael."

Without turning his head he took one hand from the wheel and gave her a half-salute.

"O.K. Any time you run into a situation like that, ma'am, just mention Miss Shaw having to come in herself to fix things. She don't like to have to, see, and lets everybody know it—and *they* don't enjoy that at all, believe me." He tilted his cap to rub his forehead. "What was that crack she made about me 'vouching'? That's a new one!"

Cynthia triumphantly delivered Volume Three to Miss Shaw in time to put in a solid hour of typing and retired to her room with the satisfactory feeling that she had given a day's work for a day's pay. On impulse she decided to avoid the hotel dining room; the night before she had run an embarrassing gantlet of congratulations on her rescue of the O'Hara boys, and she hoped that her absence tonight might help people to forget it. Slipping out a side door of the lobby she started for Newbury Harbor and supper.

The road between hotel and annex led directly to town, but she chose the longer way of the shore drive. It followed the irregular coastline, alternating outcrops of tumbled red-brown rocks with the sea frothing white against them and small crescent beaches of pale sand where the waves spent themselves in widening curves of foam. At one point the road swung close to the edge of a steep granite slope and widened to form a parking place for sightseers.

She stopped there a moment to watch a distant boat dip below the horizon and leave a faint trail of dark smoke streaking the evening sky. Smaller boats speckled the water near shore, busy at fishing or hauling lobster pots, she supposed, and a few obvious pleasure craft darted about at high speed like waterbugs skittering across a pool.

Presently she walked along the winding way until it entered the village on a street whose shore side was a clutter of wharves and warehouses redolent of the fish they processed and stored.

Cynthia had found no opportunity as yet to explore the possibilities of the town and she was not impressed by the one or two small and unappetizing restaurants she passed. Better play safe by going again to Land's End, where she knew that the food and service were good.

With the evening rush still a half-hour away it was easy to get the window table where she and Alex had lunched together. It seemed a good omen, too, when the Hungarian girl remembered her and offered a hesitant welcome with the menu.

"Good even," she murmured shyly. "Your husband not come tonight?"

"My—?" Cynthia pulled herself together. "He wasn't my husband."

"Excuse, please!" The girl's face crimsoned with embarrassment. "I see your ring, so of course I think—" The apology faded to miserable silence.

Cynthia felt her own cheeks burning. "He is a friend—a relative of the woman for whom I work."

"I am sorry." The waitress bit her lip. "They tell me not to say things to the customers, only I want to learn to speak right. So I watch everybody, and I listen, and I talk too much. Excuse me."

"Do talk to me then, I like it," Cynthia encouraged. "And don't worry so about a perfectly natural mistake. I am Mrs. Farley. What is your name?"

The question dragged the girl out of a brown study. "Anna, I am. Please, what is that 'natural'? 'Mistake' I know."

"A mistake that anyone might make." Cynthia explained it further while Anna listened with painful intentness. "If you want to learn, don't let people discourage you," she advised. "You go right on talking to everyone. And ask me about anything you don't understand, I will help if I can."

There was no doubt of Anna's thirst for knowledge and the meal progressed in alternate periods of eating and instruction. Cynthia was grateful for the girl's company. Land's End tonight was a little disappointing. The clam chowder and sole were fully as tasty as the Lobster Dinner Number Two had been, and the evening tide brought in a succession of interesting fishing boats. The low sun transformed their spreading wakes into ribbons of twinkling fire and cast their long moving shadows far across the glassy water. But Cynthia failed to recapture the pleasure of her first visit. Something was lacking. Alex Houston? She pushed that suggestion back into the deepest chamber of her mind and locked the door.

To return to the hotel by the shorter route she had to cross the main street and stood waiting for a break in the traffic. A policeman stood courageouly in midstream, but he appeared more intent on channeling the cars past than in making way for the pedestrians to cross. He had good cause for his preoccupation, she admitted, watching the unending lines which flowed along the narrow street. For the most part they carried workers home from the many industrial plants which flourished along Route 128, the great highway circling around Boston in a twenty-mile arc. A surprising number of people seemed to live on the other side of Newbury Harbor and be in haste to get there.

The shrilling of the policeman's whistle and a squealing of brakes startled her. His outspread arms had halted everything before and behind him, and now he strode weightily to the sidewalk where Cynthia stood. In his uniform with white traffic belt he looked enormous, and the intensity of his stare sent shivers of apprehension up her back. She stood hesitant as the people about her ducked across.

"You're Mrs. Farley, aren't you." There was more statement than question in the rough voice. To increase her confusion his tanned face slowly turned red. He took off his cap, tucked it under his arm and tugged off one white glove before he extended his large hand. "I'm Fred O'Hara," he said.

It took Cynthia a moment to catch her breath, and another to connect him with a smaller O'Hara known to her only by name.

"Tommy's father?" Smiling, she took his hand. "And Sam's, too. Are the boys all right?"

"They are that, thanks to you, and barring a little soreness where they sit down, if you get me," O'Hara growled. A whistle and a wave allowed the traffic to proceed. He hesitated while his flush deepened. "Look, Mrs. Farley, I can't make a speech—"

"Please don't try," Cynthia interrupted. "I'm so eternally grateful that I could help them that I don't need thanks."

"I wish to God I could tell you how grateful *we* are—me and the wife both—but I just don't know how." Still glowing, the officer replaced his cap and pulled on his glove. "I guess you know what we feel without me making a mess of trying to say it. They're good kids, Mrs. Farley, most times—mighty good kids!"

"One of them is quite a man already. Did anyone tell you that when the little boy began to give up Tommy swam back to help him?"

"I hadn't heard that. Thanks for telling me." O'Hara stood, hands on hips, staring at the glowing western sky. "They're enterprising little devils, that I know. I left the raft with a friend 'way across the point, to keep temptation out of their way until I got the chance to look it over. But the two of 'em rode their bikes over there and found it. My friend was away or he'd have chased 'em off, or tanned their hides for snooping around his boathouse. But I took care of that!"

"Don't be too hard on them," Cynthia urged. "I am sure that they learned a good lesson."

"They'd never have lived to profit by it if you hadn't been on hand, ma'am—but I'm keeping you. You were waiting to cross, weren't you?" He settled his cap firmly and split the evening air with an ear-shattering squeal from his whistle as he stepped from the sidewalk with upraised arms. The traffic ground to a sudden halt with the shriek of tortured tires.

"Thank you." Cynthia was sure that every eye in every car was fixed on her with deep resentment while she walked to the other side in O'Hara's protective shadow. "You are treating me like visiting royalty," she protested.

"A queen you are, if anyone asks an O'Hara," he answered soberly, "and to be treated as such whenever you come to town." When an impatient driver tapped his horn the officer sent a scowling glance among the cars. "Someone wants to speak to me, no doubt," he muttered, "but if I can find him I'll do the talking! Good night to you, Mrs. Queen."

There was a message to "Call Miss Shaw immediately" at the hotel desk when Cynthia picked up her key and she obeyed as soon as she reached her room. The phone was answered so promptly that she wondered if her employer had been waiting impatiently beside it. Another page of manuscript gone astray?

"Cynthia?" Miss Shaw's habitual sharpness seemed intensified. "Where *have* you been? Never mind. You play contract, of course?"

"Bridge?" It seemed to Cynthia that she was forever having to make lightning readjustment of her mental processes. "Why, I am not an expert, but I do play."

"Don't apologize until you have to. You must play with me tonight because I am afraid I put my foot in it. A new couple at the hotel brazenly introduced themselves at dinner. The woman claims that she was absolutely *fascinated* by my book, simply *dying* to meet me." Miss Shaw attempted to conceal her gratification with a caustic aside. "At least she would appear to have *read* it."

"Then of course she enjoyed it," Cynthia reassured.

"Don't interrupt. She seems intelligent, although extremely opinionated. What's that you said?"

"Nothing, Miss Shaw. Excuse me, I stifled a sneeze," Cynthia explained meekly, although it had not been a sneeze.

"If you come down with a cold from your swimming and late hours—However, as I was saying, although we disagreed on the psychology of several of my eccentric Yankees, her interest was flattering to an author, of course. I am afraid I let them both soft-soap me, as Alexander would say, and invited them to call tonight. But I am sure I can't stand that woman for an entire evening without some distraction, so you must make a fourth at bridge. Unless you have other plans?"

"No plans. I will be there—at about eight?"

When she hung up Cynthia wondered if it were her imagination or had there been an acid emphais on Miss Shaw's last question. Possibly the outing with Cousin Alexander still rankled. Better be prompt tonight, to avoid any criticism. And dress with extra care! Miss Shaw always took inventory of whatever new costume Cynthia appeared in, and announced her reaction, favorable or otherwise, with complete frankness.

Mary was shooing Topaz off the couch, leaning over a half set up card table to do it, when Cynthia arrived. She helped the maid arrange the cover, remarking "Evidently Miss Shaw isn't going to waste any time in conversation."

Mary tittered. "This is swell," she confided. "She needs a little fun; been working nights on that book instead of enjoying herself like she usually does down here. There's none of her friends here yet, that's the trouble. Wish we'd stayed in town where she's out most nights, and I can get out, too."

"Can't you go out here?"

"And leave her alone? I guess not!" Mary placed cards and score pad on the table. "Don't you read the papers? Look at the awful things happening, thugs breaking into houses, robbing folks right in their own homes, shooting them!"

"But it's different in a hotel, Mary, with so many people around all the time."

"How many in this annex? Mr. Bruce and Dr. Ferguson are out most every night. One's a bachelor and the other might as well be, his wife's gone to Arizona for her health, she isn't long for this world." The maid's pale face drew into mournful lines at the thought. "Number Four is empty now, and what good would them Whiteheads be, way up on the top floor? I wouldn't leave Miss Shaw alone here at night for a king's ransom."

The lady in question put in an appearance before the maid could enlarge further on her mortal danger. Mary had to content herself with a frowning nod to Cynthia and a significant gesture toward her own thin neck as she gathered up Topaz and retired. It was enough to draw attention to the rope of gorgeous pearls looped twice around Miss Shaw's throat, the longer strand reaching to the top of her orchid silk evening dress.

Before Cynthia could comment on them the elevator announced the arrival of the guests by shuddering to a stop in the corridor.

Without waiting for the bell Miss Shaw, like one taking an unpleasant plunge into icy water, stalked to the door and opened it.

A stout, red-faced and gray-haired woman in a low-cut dress of olive green satin strode in. Behind her a man was carefully closing the shaft door.

"Evening, Miss Shaw!" she boomed. "So nice of you to take in perfect strangers."

"Not at all." Miss Shaw barely nodded. "Miss Crane, this is my secretary—and friend—Mrs. Farley." As the man entered she added, "And, Cynthia, this is Mr. Eric Crane."

XI

CYNTHIA clenched her teeth to suppress a hysterical laugh as she stared at the slender figure with the short, crisp blond hair, the jutting nose and the thin lips twisted in a sardonic grin. Only yesterday she had convinced herself that Eric Crane, balked by her disappearance from the Boston hotel, must have acknowledged defeat and returned to California. Her spirits had soared accordingly. Tonight he appeared with the suddenness of a conjurer's trick to plunge her back into the depths. If she had stepped from a high flying plane without a parachute the earthward tumble could have been no more sickening.

Her sensation now was very similar, the breath driven from her body, the gray walls of the room seeming to wheel slowly around her. She could not speak, nor even form words in her mind.

Fortunately Miss Crane saved the situation, although not by intent. With an exclamation of delight she plowed between Miss Shaw and Cynthia and stamped to where the shelves beside the fireplace displayed their porcelain and silver treasures.

"My *dear!*" she trumpeted, spreading her arms like a plump hen attempting to fly. "Your heirlooms? Delightful! Gad, a Chester saltcellar! May I?" She assumed consent and upended the silver piece to inspect its assay marks. "Without King George's head—prior to 1784, then! And this cup dish!"

Miss Shaw joined her at the collection, leaving Cynthia still wordlessly facing Eric Crane.

"The lost is found," he murmured. "But—*Mrs.* Farley?" His eyes went to the ring on her left hand; it brought a suspicious frown. "This *is* a surprise, if I can believe it."

"Please, Eric!" she whispered, hoping that the others were sufficiently immersed in antiques to be deaf to her plea. "Don't say anything now, I'll explain everything later."

"Tell me one thing and I will wait for the rest. Married?"

"N-no, but—"

"That's enough." His smile returned, more disturbingly confident than before. As though in further evidence of that confidence he dropped the subject. Raising his voice he asserted grandly, "Really a charming bit of America here, Mrs. Farley! Such beauty. I haven't seen anything to compare since I left California." The look which accompanied his praise made it purely personal.

Miss Shaw heard him and turned with a sharp, "You are from California, Mr. Crane? I understood your sister to say England."

"Birthplace, King's Lynn in Norfolk. I am in this country for a visit. I rushed from California to Boston to—er—" His smooth explanation faltered but he recovered. "To meet Margaret's boat, you know. Jolly to see her again, it's been years."

"What rot!" Sister Margaret snorted. "It isn't much more than six months since you left Midlands Aircraft, Limited, Eric. Why you threw up that splendid position I'll never understand." She turned to Miss Shaw. "He was a test pilot with them, you know."

"I didn't know. Do you fly here, Mr. Crane?"

"Off and on," he said. "Been too busy to fly much in California because I was visiting airplane plants and such. I mean to do a bit of that here, too. Rather a good-will tour, you know. Hands across the sea, and all that."

"Are there airplane factories in this part of the country?" Miss Shaw asked.

"Well, missile plants and similar defense work, all tied in with the plane industry. I try to take them in, too." He hesitated, and with every evidence of modesty added, "Sounds brassy, I know, but as a matter of fact I'm quite well-known as a pilot." He shrugged and smiled.

"Was that why the man in Boston loaned you his car?" his sister demanded crossly. "Heard of your daring exploits, no doubt?"

"Oh come now, Sis. He is a friend of a fellow I did work for—knew in California. Very decent of him to offer the car."

"The only decent thing about him then!" Miss Crane lit a cigarette with impatient puffs. "Disgustingly common sort! Still can't understand why you chose to drag me to this place. Not at all what I was led to expect."

"Read about it in the papers," Eric said brightly, and managed a covert wink at Cynthia. "Sounded interesting, in a way, varied attractions. Don't you agree, Mrs. Farley?"

"I have been very happy here," she murmured, and was glad to see that the statement gave him pause.

"Can't imagine why." Miss Crane waved contemptuously toward the barren shore and deserted ocean beyond the windows. "Dead! Dead as Marley. You Americans should travel, see the Cornish coast—"

"I have!" was Miss Shaw's tart rejoinder. "Spent a summer there, half frozen. Also Brittany. And several winters in Italy and on the Riviera. And I still prefer our own North Shore. Peculiar, isn't it? But *I* am peculiar. Shall we play bridge?" She went to the card table and spread one deck of cards. "Draw for partners."

"Hold on!" Eric objected. "It would hardly be fair if Margaret and I play together, since we know each other's game so well. Suppose Mrs. Farley and I take on you two ladies?"

Cynthia barely stifled an indignant protest, but apparently Miss Crane shared her sentiment without her reason, for she scowled at her brother.

"Don't be rude, Eric!" she exclaimed. "Our hostess wishes us to pair off in the accepted manner, high and low." She flipped over the ten of hearts.

Miss Shaw turned up the king of that suit. Cynthia's was the five of clubs. She watched Eric hesitate, then select a card with a dramatic flourish so characteristic of him that she winced. It was the six of hearts.

He laughed. "Lucky at cards—!" He left the adage unfinished except for another of those irritating self-satisfied smirks in Cynthia's direction. "Now for a battle, The Misses Shaw and Crane *versus* Mrs. Farley and Mr. Crane. To the death!"

Even if she had been completely at ease it is doubtful that Cynthia would have enjoyed that game. She had played with Eric occasionally before and knew him to be expert, but they had never opposed such warhorses of the card table as the two older women proved themselves to be.

Miss Crane smoked incessantly and Miss Shaw nibbled mints without permitting either occupation to interfere with their game. Neither of them wasted a word in conversation and both played at lightning speed, taking full and instant advantage of every mistake made by Cynthia in her confused state. Eric battled them stubbornly but in vain as they swept to a crushing victory in the first rubber.

"Change partners," Miss Shaw immediately announced.

"Never!" Eric declaimed with upraised fist. "Mrs. Farley and I insist on a chance for revenge."

"You are unusually discourteous tonight," Miss Crane rebuked. "The young woman might prefer a more skillful partner."

Miss Shaw intervened with surprising gentleness. "Suppose we take a break, as the young people call it, and restore ourselves with a cool drink."

"Splendid!" Eric agreed enthusiastically.

"Ginger ale," explained Miss Shaw, preserving a mask of innocence at his unconcealed disappointment. "Cynthia, do you mind serving it. I sent Mary out for the evening, she mopes in her room too much. I am sure that she left everything prepared, however."

Gratefully Cynthia retired to the kitchen where she was greeted by a muted yowl from Topaz who sat on the fire escape and peered in through the window with mournful yellow eyes. Ordinarily she would have taken pity on her, but tonight Miss Shaw might have decreed the banishment, so she only tapped on the glass, waved sympathetically to the cat and went about her duties.

As promised, Mary had taken care of every detail. Tall glasses and a large hors d'oeuvre plate of crackers and assorted cheeses under a crystal dome waited on Miss Shaw's favorite Sheffield tray. In the front of the refrigerator twin bottles of ginger ale stood guard beside a tray of ice cubes. She was lifting out the tray when a hand reached over her shoulder to seize it.

"Now then," said Eric Crane, with impatient coldness, "I'll do the bartending while you talk. And talk fast. What's this wedding ring and *Mrs.* Farley routine?"

Cynthia hesitated. Every instinct rebelled against taking this man into her confidence; after that soul-searing interruption of their wedding rehearsal she put no trust in him. Even the expression on his thin face and in his cold eyes repelled her. And yet that very lack of trust would force her to explain why she was sailing under false colors, lest he expose her anyway. So she must suffer the humiliation of begging him not to, if only because she knew that Eva Shaw regarded her as a friend. The deepest wound that he could inflict would be the shattering of the older woman's faith in Cynthia Farley.

Briefly she sketched her search for work in Boston, Miss Shaw's equally desperate need of a married secretary, and Cynthia's inspiration which seemed to solve both problems.

"Eric," she urged, "don't tell her! Don't tell anyone. I'm not doing any harm and I *am* helping her. I'm sure that I am more than a secretary to her now, that she truly likes me. Perhaps I am the first person, except for her cousin Alex Houston, whom she relies on completely—the first in years, I think. It would be cruel to destroy that."

Crane dropped ice cubes into the glasses and slowly filled them with ginger ale.

"Maybe I won't tell her, if you co-operate," he said thoughtfully. "It might be just as well to keep up the pretense. That wedding ring should ward off any competition."

"Competition?" Cynthia had been too preoccupied with Miss Shaw's possible disappointment to remember her own insecurity.

"That is what I said. It was a nasty shock when I saw your picture in the paper with some handsome collegiate type. Who is this Houston, anyway, and where does he fit in with *Mrs.* Farley?"

"Besides being Miss Shaw's cousin he is her lawyer," said Cynthia. "He arranged for my position here."

"Does he know that you are not married?"

"Of course not! He wouldn't allow anyone to deceive her."

"Very decent of him, I'm sure. But he doesn't object to running around with another man's wife?"

"You are being as hateful as—as I dreaded!" Cynthia was sure that her cheeks were pink and spoke sharply. "He is *not* running around with me, as you so elegantly put it. Our being together in that plane was accidental."

"Mr. Houston looked as though he was thoroughly enjoying the accident. You'll have to put a stop to that sort of thing, Cynthy, and at once. That is what I meant by competition, and I want none of it around my fiancée."

"Your—!" She could not bear to utter the word. "After what happened, you have the effrontery to call me that!"

Crane's face was white; he spoke harshly. "Still harping on past history? Forget it! I have. It was an outrageous attempt at blackmail, and I put a stop to it in short order."

"I can't believe you. That afternoon at the rehearsal I knew from your expression that it was no 'outrageous attempt'—it was real. That girl had a claim on you, and you couldn't deny it. Can you deny it now?"

"Forget the whole thing, I tell you!" Eric kept his eyes on the tray, rearranging the glasses. "I would have explained everything then, if you had given me time," he said angrily. "But you went off half-cocked and disappeared with your surly brother! If Debbie Winfield hadn't felt sorry for me and let out that you had headed for Boston I might never have found you. Now that I have, thanks to the heroic exploit of Mrs. Farley and co-pilot Houston," he sneered, "you won't get away again. I am here, and the past is done with, my dear, so let's forget it and start fresh."

"You seriously expect me to—to be even *friendly?"* she gasped.

"We are making a fresh start, remember?" he said easily. "From the beginning, if you insist." He bowed. "Charmed to meet you, Mrs. Farley, I've heard a lot about you." Forcing a smile he picked up the tray of drinks. "Shall we join the ladies?"

Too angry to reply Cynthia led the way back to the living room.

Miss Crane ground out a cigarette impatiently.

"What were you doing so long, Eric?" she demanded acidly. *"Making* the ice?"

"Breaking the ice," he murmured, as he set the tray down. "Do have some ginger ale to cool you off, Sister!"

When they resumed the game, although they changed partners, it turned into an endless nightmare for Cynthia. The presence of Eric, and his attitude, sapped all her skill and destroyed her concentration. His habitual tricks of speech and mannerisms, formerly noticed subconsciously if at all, now stung her with memories of their romance.

Romance! she mentally scoffed, but the ache persisted. Added to that was the constant gnawing fear that he would change his mind and tell Miss Shaw the truth about her trusted secretary. He would not hesitate if he decided that exposure might serve his purpose better than silence. Cynthia was certain of that. She had long known, but closed her eyes to, his utter lack of consideration for anyone but Eric Crane.

There was danger, too, that he might let slip the secret unintentionally, for he seemed obsessed with his possession of it. He missed no opportunity to make sly remarks which held no meaning for the others but flicked like a whiplash on her nerves.

Once he came perilously close to disaster for Cynthia. He was shuffling the cards, staring at her admiringly.

"Exceptional taste, all you American women have," he commented. "That dress, now. I wouldn't know whether it's silk or satin—or sackcloth—but the delicate golden sheen matches your skin and puts an amber glow in your brown eyes." Entranced by his own eloquence he blurted, "I always said you—" The panic in her look brought him up so short that he fumbled the cards. When he retrieved them he ended awkwardly, "—Always said you Americans know how to dress!"

"Stop mangling those cards," his sister ordered, "and pick up your hand."

Cynthia was still so shaken by the narrow escape that she found it difficult to arrange her own cards, dropped one and stammered an apology.

Miss Shaw studied her. "Shall we make this the last rubber?" she suggested. "You look tired out, Cynthia." To the Cranes she explained. "We worked like fiends today on my new book; I became so engrossed that I forgot the clock."

Crane clucked in sympathy. "Mrs. Farley does look as

though she's had it. Why not call it off right now? I'll take her back to the hotel for her beauty sleep, and then return for you, Sister. I know you are dying for another look at Miss Shaw's superb antiques."

"No," Miss Crane objected, "if the game is over I will call it an evening." She punched her cigarette into the littered ash tray and rose majestically. "A delightful time, Miss Shaw. Nice of you to have us, and a pleasure for me to find someone who can play so well. We must do it again. Ready, Eric?"

"If Mrs. Farley is." He made an exaggerated bow to his hostess. "I echo my sister's sentiments as to your skill, Miss Shaw. Glad that we weren't playing for money. Or were we?"

"I do not gamble, Mr. Crane."

"A pity. You would do well at it. Coming, Cyn—Mrs. Farley?"

"Please don't wait for me," Cynthia said, picking up the silver tray. "I'll clear away, and then Miss Shaw will go over what she plans for tomorrow's work."

"You do keep her at it!" Crane reproved Miss Shaw jovially as she escorted them to the door. "Glad I'm not on your payroll, I couldn't stand the pace. Good night, and thank you again."

"Good night." Miss Shaw closed the door, turned and gave Cynthia a long steady stare. Nervously the girl piled coasters, glasses and plates on the tray. In the silence the elevator's labored descent sounded like the groanings of some subterranean monster.

"Cynthia, what happened in the kitchen?" Miss Shaw demanded.

"Happened? Why—nothing, Miss Shaw."

"That Crane fellow didn't bother you? You know what I mean."

"He helped with the drinks, that's all. And we talked. Were we really gone so long? His sister acted annoyed."

"She evidently has the maternal complex doubled in spades," Miss Shaw said contemptuously. "If she was annoyed, *I* was worried. You didn't seem like yourself all evening, more noticeably after you came back from the kitchen. And you avoided walking home with Mr. Crane, alone or chaperoned, with a transparent subterfuge. When have I ever planned what we would work on the next day? Ridiculous! I never have the slightest idea. And staying to 'clear away'! You know perfectly well that Mary will do that. Now put down that tray and go to bed."

"Very well, Miss Shaw." Cynthia was glad to retreat to the door.

"Never saw anyone play as badly as you did!" was the lady's parting shot. "You must have had *something* on your mind!"

Cynthia burned to add a fervent, "And *how!*" but only murmured, "Good night, Miss Shaw," as she fled to the corridor and, disdaining the elevator, ran down the stairs.

XII

CYNTHIA expected that the arrival of Eric Crane at the Harbor House would immeasurably complicate her life, but to her relief she saw little of him for several days. They met only at breakfast or dinnertime and even then with the briefest of greetings because his sister invariably accompanied him. In fact Miss Crane was so omnipresent that Cynthia wondered if she had dedicated herself to protecting her young brother from the designing married woman, Mrs. Farley. If that were the case, Cynthia thought, Eric must be highly amused at the spectacle.

The one redeeming feature of his presence was that it shifted the spotlight of public interest away from her. Whether Miss Crane had broadcast her brother's fame as a pilot, or the local paper's sketchy outline of his career excited the guests, the Harbor House buzzed with talk of Eric Crane.

The general curiosity was proved when Cynthia chanced to meet another of the Annexites, as she had dubbed Miss Shaw's neighbors. She came down to breakfast earlier than usual and found the dining room almost empty. Almost—for at her table sat a small, gray-haired gentleman in rimless glasses eating toast and honey while he read the morning paper.

At her approach he looked up and rose hastily.

"Good morning, Mrs. Farley. Don't know me, eh? Dr. Ferguson."

"Oh, in Number One!" she said with a smile. "I have seen you going in and out, and assumed you were the doctor."

"I am indeed. My apologies for sharing your table. I breakfast earlier than this as a rule, so we haven't overlapped. I shall retire and leave you to—"

"But you haven't finished!" Cynthia protested. "Please stay, or I shall worry about your undernourished state all day."

"Can't have that," he chuckled, sitting down at once and buttering another piece of toast.

Cynthia gave her order to the hovering waitress and then

asked, "You are with some defense plant, aren't you? I think Mr. Bruce mentioned that."

"Ah, then Neal Bruce has stolen a march on me, met you before I did." Dr. Ferguson twinkled an arch glance through his glasses. "But he would! Neal is notorious for finding lovely women wherever he chances to be. Almost a life work with him."

Cynthia bypassed both the compliment and the possible criticism of Mr. Bruce's activity. "There is so much classified and top-secret work being carried on around here now that unless you are an M.D. doctor I wouldn't dare ask what you do."

He chuckled again, almost silently "M.D. is the proper title and there is nothing secret about *my* job, I assure you. I only try to prevent careless operators from injuring themselves—exposure to radiation, that sort of thing—and doctor them when they do. And speaking of the plant, meeting you today is a happy coincidence, because you apparently know Mr. Crane, and I am curious about that gentleman. What does he do?"

Cynthia was at a loss. "I—I don't know," she admitted. It was humiliating to think that, close as she and Eric had been, she never had shown common sense enough to inquire how he earned a living. With the doctor waiting expectantly, she took refuge in a half-truth.

"I met him at Miss Shaw's a few days ago," she said. "His sister told us that he had been a test pilot for some English firm."

"So rumor has it in the Harbor House. But he seems to have abandoned aircraft. I wondered about him, because yesterday he dropped in at our plant, Mass-Atomic Lab."

"Mr. Crane did mention that he is visiting defense plants around here," Cynthia remembered. Perhaps that was why she never ran into him during the day. "A good-will tour, he called it. I imagine that he discusses new developments in British plane or missile design, compares notes with our manufacturers. Wouldn't it be something more or less like that?"

Dr. Ferguson, who was listening with a dubious frown, looked up so suddenly that Cynthia followed his glance. Eric Crane stood at the next table, his head cocked in a listening attitude, his eyes on them.

He nodded to Cynthia. "It's flattering to be so much in your thoughts, fair lady. I believe you were discussing me?"

"Yes—yes, we were," Ferguson stammered. "Odd that you should come by—"

"Speak of the Devil, and so on?" Crane suggested with a sarcastic grin.

"No, no! I merely inquired about your visit to our plant and wondered—"

"And Mrs. Farley kindly explained," Eric interrupted sourly. Scowling he walked slowly toward them, hands in his pockets. "I hope that you are completely satisfied, Mr.—?"

"Ferguson, Dr. Ferguson," the gentleman introduced himself, pink with embarrassment. "A neighbor of Mrs. Farley's employer." Crane's ominous advance made him stammer. "I wondered about you—I mean, I was curious—because you seemed to spend more time with our mechanics and foremen than with the engineers, and so on, where one would expect to find you."

"But one can never tell where one will find a person, can one?" Crane mocked, barbing the remark with a sidewise grin at Cynthia. "If it will ease your mind, Doc," he sneered, "I like to mix with the workers as much as possible, meet all sorts. Studying human nature is my hobby." His voice shook with suppressed anger as he added, "Yours is apparently sticking your long nose into other people's business. Kindly keep it out of mine!"

Any reply which the startled doctor might have summoned courage to make was prevented by the advent of Miss Crane. With a curt nod to Cynthia she grasped her brother's elbow and conducted him to their table at the end of the dining room.

Dr. Ferguson was too shaken by Crane's evident hostility to attempt further conversation and he left the table with a mumbled apology.

Cynthia had been even more shocked, although Eric's treatment of her at Miss Shaw's should have prepared her for some such exhibition. She had known him to be temperamentally impatient and tense, but now he seemed to have lost control of his nerves and be childishly quick to take offense. His profession of interest in the common man, too, was out of character. In California his cavalier attitude toward clubhouse servants and filling station attendants had often embarrassed her.

She could be grateful that Eric had practically ignored her during his tilt with the doctor, and she determined to expose herself as little as possible to any contact with him in the future. His absences from the hotel should make this easier, and perhaps, absorbed in his business of covering the factories thereabouts, he would even forget the purpose for which he had trailed her from the West.

Cynthia had anticipated a full day's work on the growing history of the Shaw family, which continued to enthrall her, but at three o'clock Miss Shaw called a halt.

"No more this afternoon," she announced. "Cousin Alexander is arriving at four."

"How nice," Cynthia remarked with perfect sincerity.

Her employer made a sound which from anyone less genteel would have been a snort. "He is coming to explain some complicated legal maneuver he has undertaken for me. Why don't you go for a swim?"

"Perhaps I will." Cynthia ignored the hint of rebuke, cheerfully covered her typewriter and departed to carry out the suggestion. Presently, in swim suit, robe and sandals she emerged from the hotel into a perfect sunlit June afternoon.

The Harbor House beach seemed destined to remain her private property until the closing of the schools released some young people for the summer. But it did not suit her present craving for invisibility, as it lay directly under the eyes of a dozen elderly ladies and gentlemen taking their ease in comfortable chairs on the veranda.

She walked along the shore road past two sandy coves inhabited only by darting sandpipers before she felt far enough away to be comfortable. There she climbed down the tumbled rocks to the beach, dropped robe and shoes on a convenient boulder and waded in. A little way offshore a serrated ledge of weed-grown rock beckoned. She swam to it and climbed its slippery side, startling a roosting gull to a thrashing take-off. As she turned to dive for the return swim a brown arm shot from the water at her feet, followed by a dripping head in a rubber mask. Through its amber window enormous eyes glared up at her, while green flippers thrashed the water.

The suddenness of the apparition took her breath, but only for the instant until she realized that it was no monster of the deep but a skin-diver coming up for air. It would have been a very immature monster anyway, she thought, from the lanky arms and legs which emerged and the narrow chest with every rib showing as it pumped breath into laboring lungs.

The diver scrambled up the rock beside her, the huge flippers slapping loudly. He pushed the mask up from a grinning mouth to reveal the freckled face and laughing eyes of a boy.

"Hi! Scared you, huh?" he demanded eagerly.

Cynthia repressed an indignant denial and delighted him with a shuddering, "You frightened me out of a year's growth! Don't you ever spring out of the ocean like that at a defenseless girl again!"

"Didn't mean to—never saw you till I came out," the boy admitted. "You didn't really look *very* scared."

"What were you doing down there, catching lobsters?"

"Naw! There's none in this shallow water. I was just exploring. There's always something interesting to see underwater."

"It must be exciting." Cynthia judged he was no more than ten or twelve years old. "Isn't it dangerous, though, to dive all by yourself?"

"Yeah. The book says never to do it, that's Rule Number One. But I'm all right. I only do it here, in front of my house." He pointed to a white cottage across the road. "Grandpa sits over there with a stopwatch, see him?"

Cynthia had thought the cove completely deserted but now she noticed a white-haired man in shorts and T shirt lolling in the shade of an overhanging ledge and calmly puffing a pipe. Seeing himself observed the man waved his pipe politely.

"Gramp times me ever time I dive," the boy explained. "If I didn't show up when he thought I should he'd be down here like a shot."

"Your *grandfather?* But what could *he* do?"

"Haul me out, of course, and re-sus-itate me. That's right, isn't it?" When Cynthia nodded he went on, "Don't worry, Grandpa O'Hara knows all the tricks, he was a lifeguard at Revere for years and years."

Cynthia started at the familiar name. "Are you Tommy O'Hara by any chance?"

"Sure. How'd you know?" He eyed her with sudden sharpness. "Golly! You're from the hotel, aren't you. And Dad said that Mrs. Farley was a beauty—! Hey, are you really her?"

Cynthia nodded. "But don't you dare begin thanking me, your father covered that beautifully and completely."

"Well, gee! But I'm—I'm very grateful—"

"Skip it!" Cynthia's terse command in his own language brought back his grin and put him at ease. "Where is your brother? Is he all right, too?"

"Sure, he's O.K. Off playing with some little kids, I guess. Say, you want to try a dive with my mask and flippers?"

"I'd love to, if you will tell me what to do."

"It's a cinch," Tommy assured her, pressing the equipment on her. "Don't dive, though, just slip into the water. Take a deep breath when you go under and stay as long as you can. It would be more fun, of course, if we had a snorkel tube, but I haven't saved up enough for that yet." He yelled to the watching man, "Hey, Gramp, *she's* going to try it! First time for her." Gramp acknowledged with another wave, but added nothing to Cynthia's confidence by knocking the ashes from his pipe and descending to water level as though he expected to be called on for immediate rescue work.

With Tommy's assistance she fitted the grotesque fins on her feet, adjusted the mask to cover her eyes and nose, dropped off the reef and discovered a new and exciting world.

Often in swimming she had opened her eyes below the surface, seeing everything through a shifting, blurring veil of water. With the protective glass every rock and wavering frond of weed showed clear as though in the open air, enlarged by refraction and their colors altered to enchanting hues by the amber tint of the mask. The flippers, so awkward on land, gave her an ease of motion like flying in a dream, the slightest kick shooting her forward with the lightning dart of a fish. She pried an oversized purple and yellow snail from its perch on a shelving ledge and was searching for more treasures when she realized that the blood was pounding in her ears and her chest ached. She surfaced with a rush and gasped for breath.

"Better not stay so long at first," the boy advised with a superior smile. "You'll get used to it, though. Did you like it?"

"Wonderful! May I try it again?"

"Sure, go ahead. Then you'd better rest while I dive a couple of times."

They spent almost an hour at the sport, and as Tommy had predicted, with every dive Cynthia became more proficient, both at holding her breath and maneuvering under water. Grandpa O'Hara acknowledged her competence at last by returning to his comfortable seat on the rocks and relighting his pipe, but for Cynthia the excitement continued.

The first time a fish swam past her face at close quarters it gave her a disturbing jolt, thereafter it became a routine and pleasing gesture of friendly confidence. She found a rusted bolt so firmly buried in the sand that two dives were needed to exhume it and bear it ashore with a triumph out of all proportion to it worthlessness.

"It may be part of a wreck," she told the boy. "A treasure ship or the wreck of the *Hesperus* in Longfellow's poem! That was on the reef of Norman's Woe—a wonderful name. Do you suppose that this is the reef?"

"Nope, that's miles from here. Besides, that isn't a ship bolt. Probably somebody just chucked it in from the road, to get rid of it," he explained unenthusiastically.

"You have no romance in you, Thomas!" she sighed.

They had worked inshore during their explorations and Cynthia emerged from a dive to find Alex Houston sitting on the rocks and watching her with amused interest.

"Behold the mermaid," he called, "or Venus rising from the waves."

Conscious of her disheveled appearance and unladylike gasps for breath, she removed the mask so that she could frown effectively.

"You are becoming a slave to habit," she reproved. "Every time I go for a swim I find you standing guard. It's not complimentary, you know, I'm not helpless. And today it was especially unnecessary. Mr. Houston, meet my instructor, Tommy O'Hara."

"Hi!" It was the boy's habitual greeting. "Say, are you the Mr. Houston that rescued me and my brother?"

"Not guilty, Tom. I just went along for the ride."

"Yes, Tommy," Cynthia agreed slyly, "Mr. Houston went for the ride, but did you know that he prepared to dive from the plane to help you if you couldn't reach those life preservers?"

"Honest?"

"Strictly a grandstand play," Alex interposed hastily. "Meant to impress the lady pilot. You know how it is, pal."

"Yeah, sure." Tommy eyed Cynthia with admiration. "I don't blame you, Mr. Houston." Then he studied Alex with sober intentness. "But I don't believe that you were grandstanding."

"Neither do I," Cynthia said quietly, and her look held the man speechless.

In the taut silence Tommy gathered up mask and flippers.

"I better go home now, I guess," he muttered. "Gramp will be getting tired of watching me." He drew a deep breath of determination. "But I'm going to say 'Thanks' to both of you, whether you like it or not."

"Thank *you*, Tommy," Cynthia said with a smile, "for letting me use your diving gear. You certainly converted me to the sport."

"Try it again?" the boy asked eagerly. "Any time you say, Mrs. Farley. And you, too, Mr. Houston, if you want to."

"I might at that," Alex admitted. "Some day I'll come prepared for undersea work and you can show me the ropes. So long, Tom."

"So long." He ran across the beach and joined his grandfather.

"I had quite a job locating you," Alex said while Cynthia put on her robe and shoes. "Don't you like the Harbor House beach?"

She preferred not to mention her reason for avoiding the hotel. "I was told that you were coming to see Miss Shaw on a business matter. What are *you* doing here?" she changed the subject.

"So you disappeared?" he ignored her question. "Unkind of you, to say the least. After a business session with your employer I crave relaxation. Cousin Eva inherited all of the Shaw's Yankee shrewdness but shares Hamlet's aversion to 'the law's delays.' She wants what she wants when she wants it. Perhaps in your short time with her you have noticed it?"

"I would say that she is a little inclined that way," Cynthia laughed as they climbed the rocks.

"The understatement of the week!" He lent her a hand over the steeper places. "Now as to the relaxation I spoke of. I have to come down this way again tomorrow. A client with a plant on Route 128 is having trouble with the employees gambling and wants to call in the Treasury Department sleuths—but never mind that. It happens that the first dance of the season at the Harper House also comes tomorrow, and I thought that I would stay for that. With the hope," he added hesitantly as they walked toward the hotel, "that I could get you to go with me. Everyone will be there."

Cynthia had thrilled at the prospect until the word 'everyone' conjured a vision of herself pursued all evening by Eric Crane. For of course he would attend, if only to bask in the general admiration for "that glamorous test pilot," and his present ugly mood was bound to turn her pleasure into a nightmare.

"Thank you for the invitation," she said, "but I don't believe I will take in the dance."

"Oh, come on!" he urged. "You won't be stuck with me all night, I promise. A number of my friends from the North Shore will be here—alumni of the Harbor House, like me. This first dance is the same as a college reunion for us, you know—reminiscences of our youthful romances, who pushed whom off the float, and whether Joe Alcott intentionally fouled three other boats the summer he won so many races. It's a lot of fun, Cynthy."

"It must be," she sighed, thinking how much it would be like her own dances of more youthful days. "But, having no memories of Newbury Harbor to share, I would be out of place."

"You could never be that! Besides, a lot of the wives haven't the Harbor background either, so you won't be alone. You might like some of them."

"I am sure that I would, but—thank you, I guess I will skip the dance this time."

Alex shrugged. "The absent Alonzo might object to your going to it with me?"

Cynthia almost burst out with an indignant, "Not at all!" but smothered the exclamation in time. Much as she wanted to accept, it was out of the question. Better to use her nonexistent husband as the excuse than risk having Alex's insistence prod her into revealing the true cause of her reluctance. Unhappy, she walked on without speaking.

"O.K." He accepted the silence as final refusal. "Sorry to bother you—"

"You don't!" she denied softly, aching to tell him that nothing could give her more pleasure than his company. "Truly, I'd love to go with you—but I don't think that I should." Rather than prolong the unsettling interview she hurried to her room.

Her mind whirled with conflicting thoughts while she showered and dressed for dinner. The more she thought of an evening with Alex the less reason there seemed for letting fear of Eric Crane deprive her of it. Escorted by Alex Houston need she worry about complications? Hardly! If she showed the least trace of annoyance at anything Eric might say or do, wouldn't Alex take prompt charge with force and authority? On second thought, though, that probability gave her little encouragement. In Eric's present high-strung state such interference could be disastrous. Better to forget the whole affair and swallow her disappointment.

With this firmly resolved she joined Miss Shaw in the dining room, to be thrown back into confusion by that lady's first remark.

"Tomorrow night is the first hotel dance," Miss Eva announced brightly. "A fixutre at the Harbor House ever since I came here as a girl. I shall attend, I think, for the nostalgic pleasure of the occasion. You had better come with me, Cynthia, so that I will have someone to talk to."

In the struggle between anticipation and dread Cynthia felt anticipation winning hands down. This was an order from her employer and she now had no choice in the matter.

"Are you sure that you want me, Miss Shaw?" she asked doubtfully.

"I shouldn't ask if I didn't! You may dance of course, if invited—and no doubt you will be. At other times you will sit with me. Alone I would be an unsightly wallflower. It starts at eight-thirty, I believe, meet me at eight-fifteen. I want to be there early to see the different people make their entrance. It is formal, of course."

"Very well, Miss Shaw." To herself she added the paraphrase, "Cynthia proposes, but Miss Shaw disposes."

XIII

THE HOTEL ballroom at the northern end of the lobby had been opened for the gala occasion of the season's first dance and its white paneled walls, long rose-colored curtains and wide floor glistened from hours of preparation. On a platform banked with pots of red tulips and golden daffodils an orchestra of college boys was whipping through one of the season's hit tunes with professional competence. Cynthia's toes tapped in sympathy while she waited near the doorway for Miss Shaw.

"Punctual as always," the lady praised on her arrival. She tilted her head to scan the girl's tanned shoulders, clover-blue full-skirted dress and white pumps. "Quite appropriate, my dear. You have an instinct for that, haven't you?" Her long finger indicated the miniature golden star which hung on a slender chain at Cynthia's throat. "The perfect finishing touch. An heirloom?"

"Far from it," Cynthia admitted with a smile. "Only a good luck charm I picked up the other day in Boston, although I may hand it down to my children as an heirloom. I am sure that it brought me to work for you, so it has proved its benign power already."

Her employer sniffed. "From anyone else I would consider that fawning flattery, but you are so thoroughly honest that I believe you really mean it."

"Of course I do!" Cynthia was uncomfortably conscious of how little she deserved such praise from Miss Shaw of all people and went on hurriedly, "I hope my lucky star is still on the job."

"Tonight, you mean?" There was sudden sharpness in the question. "Whom do you intend to bewitch at this dance?"

Cynthia suspected that concern for Cousin Alexander prompted the abrupt query and was all the more annoyed because he had popped into her mind when she spoke. But actually he had been an afterthought, and she could answer honestly.

"I did not refer to this evening in particular," she explained. "I was thinking of the future."

She followed her employer to a row of armchairs arranged so that they faced the dance floor while still commanding the view through the tall French windows opened on the sea.

For a moment Cynthia ignored the scattered groups of people to absorb the beauty of the evening. The last crimson of the sunset was fading from the sky, allowing a soft luminous haze to veil the black water. A cruiser rounded the point and passed the hotel, its white sides reflecting the ruddy afterglow. Car after car drew up to the main entrance, debarked the guests and hummed away to the parking lot.

The dancing had begun and the hall was thronged now, as it would be during the summer season, Cynthia supposed. A group near the door, with a sprinkling of uniforms among the men, attracted her attention by their evident preoccupation with a girl in their midst. Between broad shoulders in white dinner jackets she caught a glimpse of Neal Bruce laughingly fending off the others from this person in a daring dress of tangerine hue.

As she watched, the girl's blond head nodded and her feet shuffled as the orchestra swung into a frantic rumba. She said something to Bruce who shook his head with a wry face. The next instant she was in the arms of an Air Force captain and gone among the dancers. Bruce shrugged off the jokes of the other men and walked over to bow to Miss Shaw. He was resplendent in a champagne-colored dinner jacket and cocoa brown trousers.

"It wouldn't be a Harbor House *première* without you on hand," he said gallantly. "And you, Mrs. Farley, add the final glamorous climax to the scene!"

"Stop talking like a stage director, Neal." Miss Shaw was adept at taking the wind out of pretentious sails. "Your glamorous friend seems to have deserted you at the drop of an airman's hat."

"This dance is what they call a 'cha-cha-cha,' " he growled. "Too much for me—but look at *her* go!"

Miss Eva studied the lively blond thoughtfully.

"The girls grow up so fast, and change," she sighed. "I don't place her at all."

"No reason why you should, she's never been here before. Claire Herbert, playing the part I wanted Mrs. Farley to try in our show," Bruce explained. "Real luck for us to get her, too. She came down here without knowing there was a Summer Theater in Newbury Harbor, but I mentioned it when I took her to supper at Land's End and—"

"Then *you* knew her before?" Miss Shaw asked pointedly.

"Well, no—but you know how it is. If you see a stranger wandering around looking lost, you try too make them feel at home." He switched back to the less embarrassing subject. "As I say, I spoke of the theater, and it turns out that she's an actress. And tickled to death to help us out."

"Is she staying here?" Cynthia asked. "I haven't seen her."

"I doubt it," Miss Shaw murmured. "A Summer Theater salary would hardly enable one to enjoy the Harbor House."

"As a matter of fact she *is* staying here—as of this evening," Bruce announced with some hesitation. "A new neighbor for you in the Annex, Miss Shaw." When that lady's eyebrows arched in obvious shock he added hastily, "Don't think she's moving in with me! Claire will be staying in Number Five, while the Whiteheads are away."

Miss Shaw frowned. "Darn this writing of mine! I miss half of what goes on in my own building! *Why* did the Whiteheads go away when they were settled for the summer? And what becomes of their precious aquarium?" she demanded with a derisive laugh. To Cynthia she explained, "A charming couple except for their preoccupation with tropical fish."

"So I've been told," said Cynthia. "Mr. Bruce, you commented on that the day we met in the elevator. Remember?"

"Did I?" he laughed. "Probably; the Whitehead collection of swordtails, red tetras and such is notorious. They truck a load of them down here from Springfield every summer and install them in a big tank up in Number Five, with electric controls for water temperature and the Lord knows what other luxuries."

Shaking his head in humorous disapproval of such folly he turned to Miss Shaw.

"To answer your questions, the Whiteheads have gone to St. Louis because a granddaughter is getting married. They were at their wit's end about the fish, naturally; someone has to check them regularly, to feed them and to see that they're happy, I suppose. And the hotel declined the responsibility."

"Odd that they never mentioned this wedding to me," Miss Shaw complained. "And why move down here if they were going right off?"

"It was totally unexpected," Neal soothed. "Really threw them into a tizzy, believe me. As for asking you to assist with the aquarium, they wouldn't do that when they know how busy you are with your new book. No, ma'am, they brought their headache straight to me."

He patted his ample chest complacently and beamed.

"Efficiency Expert Bruce put his mind to it and settled their problem at once. Here was Miss Claire Herbert suffering in a Newbury boarding house, and there was an empty apartment with a priceless collection of tropical fish needing a baby-sitter. The obvious solution was for Claire —Miss Herbert—to move in with the fish. And there she is."

Cynthia thought that she had never seen a more self-satisfied expression than that on Bruce's round face, and wondered why it faded so quickly until she noticed the prolonged and critical stare he was enduring from Miss Eva Shaw.

"I wasn't born yesterday," that lady reminded sharply. "The fish will not be the only beneficiaries!"

"Now, Miss Eva!" he protested flushing. "Let's not harbor unkind thoughts. She is a perfectly nice girl and I will introduce her at the first opportunity so that you can form your own opinion. I'm sure that you will like her." He saw a chance to retire from the uncomfortable position. "That confounded cha-cha-cha seems to be ending. I'd better find my partner or I'll lose her again. A dance with you later, Mrs. Farley?" He nodded, turned, and threaded his way through the dancers in search of the blonde.

Miss Shaw watched his retreat with pursed lips as her fingers drummed on the chair arm.

"I hope that my thoughts are as unfounded as they are unkind," she remarked. "Rumor has labeled Neal Bruce a typical playboy, but he never intruded his affairs among the family before. I say family, Cynthia, because he is a distant relative. And a dreadful waste of good material," she sighed. "He could have been successful in business, I'm sure."

"Perhaps his interest in the theater will lead to something," the girl suggested.

"A chance to pick up pretty actresses!" Miss Eva squashed that idea with finality.

A young man in a slightly worn and wrinkled white jacket halted in passing to bow. "Good evening, Miss Shaw." His thin, high cheek-boned face which gave him somewhat the look of a boyish Lincoln seemed familiar to Cynthia, and when he removed thick-rimmed glasses she recognized Scoop Parker, the reporter of the local paper.

"How do you do, Franklin," Miss Shaw responded graciously. "I believe that you have met Mrs. Farley?"

His grin at Cynthia was cautious. "I sure have. Hope you didn't mind my publicity, ma'am, it was too good a chance to pass up."

"It was very well done, Mr. Parker, although I would have preferred to remain anonymous." She did not tell him why.

The young man shook his head. "Couldn't sell that kind of story without names, honestly. I guess it would have been more polite to get your permission first, but you pulled out too fast, if you remember, and I wanted to call in the story while it was hot. Any time that I can hit the news services with an exclusive it's real money in my pocket, you see. On just our local weekly I'd starve, so I have to keep on the prowl for the big stuff."

"Are you after something big tonight, Franklin?" Miss Shaw's tone suggested that she had pricked up her ears.

"I wish you'd call me 'Scoop' like everyone else," he complained. "Franklin makes me feel ten years old. No, ma'am," he answered her query. "Nothing big; I always drop in at these dances. During the evening I hope to interview Mr. Crane; get a little more dope on him to pad this week's issue. I was talking to Dr. Ferguson, just now, and he said that there might be a story in what Crane's doing here."

Cynthia wondered if resentment prompted that hint; Eric had behaved badly enough to the doctor. It would be unkind to expose this pleasant young fellow to similar treatment.

"I wouldn't ask Mr. Crane about his work," she advised quietly. "I understand that he doesn't care to discuss it."

"Is that so?" Parker adjusted his glasses to stare owlishly at her. "Dr. Ferguson said that, too, and it made me curious." After a second's hesitation he shrugged. "Well, maybe I'd better drop it, eh?" With a nod and a smile he moved away.

"If he means that," Miss Shaw murmured, watching his departure, "I don't know Franklin Parker! Well!" she exclaimed with an abrupt shift of topic, "here is Cousin Alexander at last!"

It was a meeting Cynthia had dreaded, so she was not surprised by Houston's display of chilly resentment. Long familiarity with that glare from indignant brothers had taught her the wisdom of meeting it halfway.

"You look prepared to tear me limb from limb," she accused with a smile.

"Not at all," Alex denied grimly. "No reason at all for you to accept my invitation if you preferred someone else."

Cynthia yearned to deny the accusation but it seemed wiser to say only, "I came with Miss Shaw."

"At my orders," the lady added, glaring at him. "What has been going on? Did you invite *Mrs.* Farley to this affair?" No one could miss her emphasis on the title.

"I certainly did," with a relieved smile. "And since she is present, for whatever reason, I would like this dance?"

"Thank you, Alex." Cynthia rose at once, hoping to forestall any objection from her employer in case that already irritated lady meant to offer one.

Houston leaned down to pat his cousin's hand.

"Thanks for bringing your secretary to the party," he smiled. "We won't leave you in solitude too long, and then we'll both come and keep you company."

Miss Shaw snatched away her hand and folded her arms as she continued to glare at him.

"Don't treat me like a grandmother!" she scolded. "I have plenty of company. Why, here comes Mr. Crane!"

Cynthia smothered a gasp of apprehension which was well founded, for Eric Crane ignored Miss Shaw, even turning his back on her as he faced the girl.

"Found you!" he announced, briskly triumphant. "Always having to hunt for Cynthia, it seems." He grasped her elbow. "This music is good; shall we dance?"

Before she could protest Alex stepped forward and deftly removed the possessive hand.

"Sorry to disappoint you," he said [illegible] Farley is dancing with *me*."

"Yes, Mr. Crane." Cynthia's look begged him for restraint. "Mr. Houston has already asked me."

"So *this* is the Houston I've been hearing about?" The effect of Eric's supercilious stare was weakened by his having to look up several inches to meet the other's eyes.

"So it is," Alex assured him calmly.

Cynthia murmured, "Mr. Crane—Mr. Houston," but the introduction failed to ease the tension which showed increasingly in Eric's pale face. He snapped his fingers impatiently.

"If you will pardon me, Houston," he growled, "I will borrow your partner for this dance, as we have a lot to talk about. Perhaps Mrs. Farley can persuade you," he suggested sarcastically, "by pleading a prior engagement."

It seemed to the girl that the words which had shaken her caused a flicker of doubt in Alex's eyes, but he shrugged and smiled impartially on them both.

"Mrs. Farley doesn't have to *plead* with me," he stated gravely. "If she wishes to dance with you she has only to say so and I will retire. But she hasn't." He waited an instant, watching her, before he continued. He kept his voice to a conversational pitch but the words suddenly cracked sharply. "Until she does, Crane, why don't you take yourself off and stop bothering her?" Without waiting for more he brushed past Crane and swept Cynthia away among the dancers circling the floor.

Her thrill of relief vanished when she looked back.

"Alex, he's—he's coming after us!"

"Good!" He smiled down at her. "We'll work over toward the French windows. If I can lure him out on the porch it will be a great pleasure to knock him off it."

"No, please—no trouble!"

Alex laughed and whirled her to the center of the floor. "Relax! I was joking. Even for *you,"* he admitted, "I would hesitate to brawl in the staid old Harbor House."

Cynthia chose to ignore the compliment and stole another look at Eric.

"He isn't coming after all!" she exclaimed with relief. "He's going—no, he's following another couple, trying to cut in. Why, it's Neal Bruce and his new blond friend!"

"Crane gives the impression," Alex observed with a grin, "of being either drunk or off his rocker tonight, so let's forget him. Present company is more interesting. You are a woman of mystery, Mrs. Cynthia Farley, and mysteries have always intrigued me. Tell me, would you object strenuously to having a detective on your trail?"

"A *detective?"* It was a panicky whisper and she tipped her head back to stare up at him wide-eyed.

"Did I scare you, Cynthy—I meant myself as the gentlemanly plain-clothes operative. A clumsy joke which fell flat," he apologized. "However, I am making discoveries already; your brown eyes turn to bronze flame when you are startled. Please forget my silly remark about detecting. Anyone would object—"

"I don't think that I would object to anything you do." The admission was out before she knew it, and her partner reacted by holding her more tightly while executing a lighthearted series of improvised steps which left her breathless.

Unfortunately it also brought her around to face a corner of the hall where Crane and the blond girl had stopped dancing to talk with conspicuous vehemence. Then, between intervening couples, she caught a glimpse of the two leaving by the French windows.

"There go Eric and his partner out on the porch," she announced. "He seems to have cut out Mr. Bruce permanently."

"My dear Cynthia!" Alex sighed. "If you have any idea that I want a blow-by-blow report of that gentleman's activities, forget it. Must you concentrate on him all evening? Even if he is an old friend—"

"Not a friend!"

"Acquaintance, then. Although there seemed to be a hidden meaning in his crack about a 'previous engagement' which drove the color from your face. Or did I imagine it?"

Cynthia shook her head, unable to meet his eyes. She could not lie to Alex.

"You're right," she admitted. "I—I was engaged to him, but only for a short time. I was pushed into it—*no!*" she interrupted herself harshly, "that isn't fair to my aunt! It was my own doing, because I was young and foolish—and as much of a snob as Aunt Julia. Eric Crane has titled relatives in England. Look, there is his sister now, talking to Miss Shaw."

"Looks like a dowager, doesn't she? When did all this youthful romancing take place?" Alex asked, showing only lukewarm interest.

"A few months ago. In California." Cynthia was too enmeshed in memories to realize what she answered. His next remark, still carelessly made, snapped her rudely awake.

"This was before your marriage, of course."

She missed a step and it was a moment before she could rally her wits to stammer, "Why—yes. Yes, of course!" She managed an almost presentable laugh. "What a strange thing to say."

"The whole affair strikes me as more than strange. A few months ago you were engaged to Crane, now you are married to—Alonzo, is it?—and Alonzo deserts his bride of a few weeks to rush off to the Orient."

"It was a crisis in his business." While she tried desperately to imagine a plausible "crisis" she chattered, "Besides, I told you that we both believe a husband and wife benefit from an occasional vacation from each other. What the colleges call a sabbatical year, isn't it?"

"That's not what I'd call it! You say there was a business crisis, too?"

Still unable to come up with a convincing explanation she took refuge in a haughty, "I'd prefer not to discuss it—any of it—if you don't mind." This dance with Alex, so ardently desired, was turning into an ordeal and all because of her deception. "Could we go out for a breath of air?"

"The motion for adjournment is entirely in order," Alex agreed, leading her to the porch. "Trying to figure out your missing husband has me stumped. I look at you and wonder what conceivable catastrophe in business could drag him from your side—"

"Please!" she protested, "no more about me. Let's just admire this incomparable view."

Cynthia leaned against the railing and tried to concentrate on the sparkling waves, the stars blinking between ruffled clouds and the velvet breeze bringing ashore the salty tang of the sea. Tried to concentrate, and failed, for she was acutely conscious of Alex Houston's white dinner coat close to her shoulder, his eyes fixed steadily on her face. In admiration—or in skepticism? She was beginning to fear those probing eyes and avoid them; eyes she would have met eagerly if she had nothing to conceal.

When the silence became more disturbing than his questions she was driven to hopeless unoriginality.

"A lovely moon, isn't it?" she murmured. "Beautiful!"

"Yes," he said softly, "you're beautiful!"

Fervently Cynthia regretted introducing what she had considered a safe subject, but one which threatened like a ticking bomb. Attempting a lighter touch she pointed to the sky.

"Whenever I see the moon like that, I hear a line of poetry which always gives me a thrill. 'The moon was a ghostly galleon tossed upon cloudy seas.' Isn't that delightfully shivery? By Coleridge, I think."

Her studied calm was shattered by an impatient snort behind them and Miss Shaw's tart, "*Coleridge* indeed! That's 'The Highwayman,' by Alfred Noyes, and don't you forget it again!" She turned a frosty glare on her cousin. "I'm mortified that *you* didn't correct her, Alexander. That was always a favorite of yours."

"You beat me to it, Cousin Eva," he defended. "I would even have added to the quotation for Mrs. Farley's benefit." Soberly he looked down at Cynthia. "Like this:

> 'Watch for me by moonlight,
> I'll come to thee by moonlight,
> though hell should bar the way.'

Somehow that seems appropriate, Cousin Eva," he added smiling.

"That's enough poetry," Miss Shaw decreed sharply. "I came out here for fresh air, after bearing with Miss Crane until I wanted to scream. Fortunately at last she missed her brother, on whom she has been keeping an eagle eye, and galloped away to scour the cocktail lounge. Anyway, I'm tired of sitting. Walk with me, Cynthia."

Slowly they paced down the seemingly endless veranda past the couples and groups talking and drinking around the tables which had been set out for the evening. Once Alex paused to greet a friend and from the same table Dr. Ferguson popped up with a hopeful, "Could I lure you inside for that waltz they're playing now, Mrs. Farley?"

"Why, thank you—"

"Not now!" Miss Shaw broke in. "Later perhaps, Doctor, after she has taken me for my constitutional." As they walked on, her elbow prodded Cynthia's side. "Be careful with Dr. Ferguson," she whispered. "A middle-aged romantic, and his wife is away." She frowned at the girl's light laugh.

Alex paused to light a cigarette so that Cynthia and Miss Shaw reached the farthest end of the porch alone. They were turning to stroll back when a voice from the shadowed driveway below brought the girl to an involuntary halt.

It was Eric Crane, she knew, speaking in a low tone but with characteristic angry harshness. "Do we have to hash over all that again? I told you I could work things out if you gave me the chance, but you keep barging in! What the devil are you doing in Newbury, anyway?"

"Looking after Number One," a woman answered, and gave a mocking laugh. "You taught me how, Eric! I read the papers, too, you know, and it looked like I'd better get down here."

"No need for that," he growled. "You'd better go away for a while."

"And let you run out on me *again?* I'm not that dumb, you double-crosser!"

By this time Cynthia had recovered from her surprise and attempted to lead Miss Shaw away.

"We seem to be eavesdropping," she whispered. To her embarrassment her employer held her ground with a nod and a delighted smile.

"You're the double-crosser!" Eric was saying. "You promised to play ball, Claire! But you didn't!"

Cynthia was startled again. Claire? It must be Claire Herbert, Bruce's blond friend. She remembered Eric's pursuit of the couple on the dance floor, apparently he knew her. Then she forgot such trivial details at his next words, shaken by rage.

"You fool! Why did you have to come to California and spill the beans? In a short time that stupid girl would have come into her money and you and I would be spending it!"

"Yeah, if I could find you!" Anger as hot as his burned in the other's tone. "I fell for your line once, Eric Crane, but you can't get away with it again! You belong to me!"

Cynthia heard no more. Alex was beside her, leading her rapidly along the porch out of earshot, his other arm propelling his cousin with equal force. Dimly she realized that he was muttering reproaches to the inquisitive Miss Eva, to be met with a satisfied laugh. It was a jumble of sounds seeping through her stunned dizziness, through the sick turmoil which made her steps falter, her head spin.

The two cousins had overheard a quarrel which had no connection with them, no interest except to Miss Shaw's impertinent curiosity. Only Cynthia knew that *she* was the cause. Eric's reference to the California incident would have been enough, but complete realization burst on her like a destroying bolt of lightning at the furious woman's voice, harsh and breathless, and the words which were like a torturing playback of that nightmare rehearsal in the little church.

"You belong to me!" Claire Herbert was the intruder who had broken up her marriage to Eric—and now Claire was here in Newbury Harbor.

XIV

IT WAS fortunate that Cynthia had no opportunity to give way to the whirling confusion in her mind or she might have attracted instant sympathy—and questions—from Alex. In the nick of time Neal Bruce appeared and with only token apology detached her from the cousins to rush her unresisting to the dance floor, this time a lively fox-trot.

His interpretation of the steps became so exuberant that she wondered if he meant the world to see that the loss of his partner Claire meant nothing to him. But that was strictly his affair. She had her own thoughts, and skill enough to follow even his erratic leading while she brooded on past history and present complications.

Her first hot flame of hatred for Claire Herbert gradually cooled as honesty took charge. Actually she knew nothing against the girl, nothing about her claim on Eric except that it seemed to be genuine. Cynthia could never forget his expression when she begged for an explanation, a denial in the church. Instead of bitterness she ought to feel eternal gratitude to Claire for forcing him to show his true colors before it was too late and bringing to an end what had been foolish infatuation on her part.

In this calmer mood it did not upset her when she noticed Bruce's eyes fixed on someone behind her and color flooding his round cheeks. Following his look she saw Claire Herbert standing alone near the orchestra, and was not surprised to have Bruce begin a stammered apology.

"You will think I am—that I haven't any manners, Mrs. Farley—but would you mind if—unpardonably rude to leave you, but there is Claire—Miss Herbert—she doesn't look at all well and—"

"Certainly, go to her at once." Cynthia read in the girl's pallor and haunted eyes what torture the recent encounter with Eric must have been. "She does look ill, doesn't she? It's all right to leave me, truly. I'll find Miss Shaw, who must be wondering what has become of me."

That lady did welcome Cynthia warmly, but with a nervousness which sat strangely on her usually composed self. She commented twice on the hectic pace of the orchestra, repeated a banal remark about the beauty of the evening, and drummed her fingers on the chair arm faster than the music.

"Are you getting tired, Miss Shaw?" Cynthia asked anxiously.

"Certainly not!" The snappish answer seemed to restore some of her assurance. "Cynthia, I am in a state! I want you to do something for me, and I don't know how to ask. I suppose I've given orders so long that when it can't possibly be an order I'm lost."

"You know I will do anything for you, Miss Shaw."

"That is the trouble! Cynthia, you are so—so sweet to me that I ought not to impose on you. I do it all the time, I know, but I can't help it. Why don't you call me a bossy old woman?"

"Because you are not. What do you want me to do that is so out of the usual?"

"Well—my Mary has to leave. She received a telegram tonight and appeared here almost in hysterics. Her sister is having another baby, and there are complications. Mary must go to her at once."

"I'm sorry for Mary—and her sister."

"Rubbish!" Miss Shaw was back in stride. "The woman's had six children already, why should a seventh bother her? But you know Mary—she worries a smoking chimney into another great Boston fire. And the silly girl insists that she can't leave me alone here!"

Cynthia nodded. "She thinks it isn't wise—"

"Rubbish again! Mary doesn't think. But she will be on pins and needles unless I let her go, and have me in nervous prostration before the week is up." Miss Shaw took a deep breath and rushed at the critical question. "Will you move over to the Annex with me?"

"Why, of course!" Cynthia's laugh was relief. "What a to-do over a simple request. I will bring my things over tonight."

"You'll do nothing of the kind! Call a bellboy and don't you dare tip him, I will take care of that. Tomorrow will do nicely. Mary can't get a train until morning. And don't think for a minute that you are to act as a maid, I won't hear of it." With a satisfied sigh Miss Shaw sank back in her chair, only to start upright again as though a pin had prodded her.

"Cynthia, that's settled—go away and dance! Here comes Miss Crane, and you needn't put up with her as I have to. She is a crashing bore at best, and tonight she has had too much punch. I made a great mistake when I became involved with the Cranes."

Mentally Cynthia repeated the sentiment, took advantage of the screen provided by passing couples, and slipped away unseen to the veranda. Choosing a dark corner she sank down on a swinging couch before she noticed that the adjoining easy chair was occupied by a lounging man. Even that dim light was enough to reveal the drawn face of Eric Crane.

"Well, well!" He set a tall glass aside and pulled himself more erect. "What lucky wind blew you here? Sit down!" he snapped when she started to rise. "We have a lot to talk about, my dear."

"We have nothing to talk about!" She stood up defiantly.

"But we have! We are to start over again, remember? We become better acquainted, then dear friends—"

"It's too late for that, Eric. Become better acquainted?" Her laugh was bitter. "You forget how well I know you. You were never very easy to get along with, and now you are impossible. You act like a spoiled child, not only with me—with everyone. Why, you even threw a tantrum when that nice Dr. Ferguson asked about your work—and embarrassed him dreadfully!"

"That old goat! He had no business prying into my visits to plants around here!"

"*Prying,* because he asked a polite question?" She remembered Alex's remark about a client's troubles in one of the plants and scoffed, "Anyone would think that you are a G man on a supersecret mission after gamblers!"

"I can't stand nosy old men, that's all—" Eric began harshly, and then stopped. His pale face wrinkled in thought for an instant before he went on more quietly, "A G man, you said, Cynthy? What put that into your pretty head?"

"I was being as sarcastic as possible, that's all!" she answered shortly.

"I hope so." He flashed his twisted smile as he sat on the couch and drew her down beside him. "I hope no one has been talking, for you've hit my secret, darling. But keep it to yourself."

She jerked her arm free from his grasp and stared at him. "What are you talking about?" she demanded.

"My business here," still with that faint smile. "I do spend a lot of time with the workmen in these plants, just as your brilliant doctor noticed, and I'll tell you why. There is a lot of gambling among fellows of that class, betting on races, and the numbers game—anything, in fact. Bookies have men there to take bets, get the results by phone, and pay off. It goes on all the time, winked at until it gets out of hand, causes too much wasted time, and the management has to step in. Then they call on the government to clean up the place. And that is where I come in."

Cynthia eyed him dubiously. "*You* are working for the government?"

"That's what it amounts to." He waved carelessly. "They asked me to circulate among the plants and find out who the bookies and agents are, so they can pick them up. You can see how my reputation as a pilot helps," he explained modestly. "The men are flattered when I talk to them and like to brag about their winnings, tell me anything to impress me, even who handles their bets. It works out very well. You mustn't breathe a word to anyone, Cynthy. This is between you and me, because I trust you."

He spoke so smoothly, and his explanation was so unexpected, that she momentarily forgot her anger in puzzled consideration. Alex had mentioned that a client was having trouble with gambling and had called on the Treasury Department for help.

Eric's habitual arrogance must have convinced him that her silence meant all was well once more, for he pressed her hand.

"Having disposed of dull business," he said softly, "suppose we make a start on the really important thing, putting me back in the Number One place in your heart."

Incredulous, she stared at him, wondering wildly if perhaps he *was* intoxicated, as Alex had lightly suggested. What else would account for his callous disregard of their shattered romance and what had caused it? Even though he was unaware that she had overheard his talk with Claire Herbert he should realize that the dreadful end of their wedding rehearsal had wounded her beyond healing.

With all the icy finality she could put into the words she said, "I shouldn't have to tell you, Eric, you are wasting your time."

"Not at all. You underestimate me, my dear. Everything is going to be the same with us. I've even bought another plane, bringing it down tomorrow and start giving flying lessons next week. Two customers lined up already. There's a hangar at the field here, so I can keep it handy. For us, particularly." There was a ghost of his former charming smile with the words. "I'll see that you get your license at once—and away we'll go 'into the wild blue yonder,' together again. And—'falling in love again,' " he sang with perfect assurance.

"It's no use, Eric!" Cynthia was divided between resentment at his past duplicity and amazement at his present arrogance. "Let's make this final! I know now that I never loved you."

"I can remember times when you gave a good imitation."

"Then forget them!" Her cheeks burned at similar memories. "I hadn't even begun to grow up then. Call it a schoolgirl crush, a teen-age thrill to be 'going steady.' Now I'm grown up, I think, at least enough to know what I want in a man."

"Something along the lines of Houston? To me he looks like a cold fish. You need somebody with a little fire, Cynthy." Without warning his arm was around her shoulders, drawing her close.

Furiously she twisted free and faced him.

"Don't touch me!" she snapped. Almost she blurted out what she had heard from the porch, but a momentary hesitation allowed him to speak first.

"I'm warning you, Cynthy—come off your high horse and play ball. Or shall I step in and entertain your employer with a few unvarnished truths?"

"You *wouldn't!*"

Eric laughed. "I would prefer not to, believe me; your masquerade suits me, you know. And you prefer it, too? So everybody's happy." He grasped her hands and pulled her toward him. "Or will be in a moment—"

It was not Cynthia who made him drop her hands.

"Eric?" Miss Crane spoke from the doorway, and advanced with the ponderous momentum of a battleship. "Before I retire I should like a nightcap. Get me a small brandy."

"In a minute, Sis—I want to—"

"Right now, Eric!"

For a moment their eyes locked in a battle of wills, and then to Cynthia's amazement he shrugged, winked broadly at her and walked with exaggerated leisure into the hotel. Nothing in his actions up to now had filled her with such dread as this casual postponement of a showdown; he must be supremely confident of success. But there was little time to wonder at him, for his sister faced her with hands on hips and a forbidding scowl.

"Now then, Mrs. Farley, I want a word with you!" Miss

Crane might have been speaking to a scullery maid in her ancestral home. "This pursuit of my brother must stop at once!"

"Pursuit of—?" Cynthia was too dazed to finish, and stared open mouthed at the flushed and angry woman.

"Don't play the wide-eyed innocent with me!" the other raged. "You know exactly what I am talking about! I said nothing the other night, when you dallied in the kitchen with him until even Miss Shaw wondered, and I don't know how often you may have been with him since. But tonight I *saw* you follow him out here with such brazen boldness that I cannot keep silent!"

"Miss Crane!" At last Cynthia managed to interrupt. "You are entirely mistaken. I am not pursuing Eric—if anything it is quite the other way—"

"I wasn't born yesterday. You are making a fool of yourself, Mrs. Farley! If you think that my brother has a fortune you're wrong, and as for his inheriting the title—" She snapped her big fingers loudly, "—*That* for his chances! So you are wasting your time and your charms, my good girl!"

Cynthia's amazement was rapidly turning to anger, but she held it firmly in check, even contriving a tolerant smile.

"You seem to be laboring under a misapprehension, Miss Crane," she said sweetly, "so I will ignore your manner. Let me remind you that I am *Mrs.* Farley, with a perfectly good husband in Japan, and not a designing widow as you imply."

"I don't care what you are, although I have my own idea. You Americans think nothing of divorce, I know, but I assure you *we* have a different view. In any case, Eric would never consider marrying a servant, and that is all you are—"

"Oh, stop it!" Cynthia burst out with wrathful indignation. "You are being ridiculous! I wouldn't marry Eric—I haven't the most remote interest in your brother! I wish that he had never come here!"

"Of course you would say that!" Miss Crane nodded in grim satisfaction. "Borrowed from one of your horrible movies—or the television, no doubt. You aren't fooling me a bit, my girl—"

"If you call me that again I'll—" Cynthia clenched her teeth to smother the threat. This was too fantastic to be real. She was descending to the level of this boorish woman, in another instant she would be snarling too. She saw a couple at a nearby table twisting in their seats to stare, a man leaning against the porch railing had turned his head. She clenched her trembling hands.

"I tell you again, Miss Crane," she said slowly, repression making her voice quiver like a taut wire, "I would prefer to have nothing to do with your brother—or you, and you may believe it or not, as you choose. But I will not listen to your nonsense one minute more. Good night!" She stepped aside to pass.

"You will listen to this!" Miss Crane's heavy hand pulled her back, then shook a finger in her face. "Mrs. Farley, you—"

"Mrs. Farley?" Alex Houston's suave voice echoed the name as he slipped an arm through Cynthia's. "My dance, I think?" He nodded to Miss Crane. "Lovely night, isn't it? Excuse us, that waltz they are playing demands our presence." With the words he led the girl around the sputtering woman and to the door of the ballroom.

There he halted to smile down at Cynthia.

"Crowed in there. Would you rather get a breath of air in my car?" he asked.

His thoughtfulness was almost more than her frayed nerves could bear.

"Much rather," she murmured gratefully and was afraid to say another word lest she burst into tears.

All evening the tension had increased, from her first dance with him, then the meaning plain in his eyes when he quoted, " 'I'll come to thee by moonlight—' " then that soul-shattering discovery of Claire Herbert's identity. And finally the punishing scenes with Eric and Miss Crane.

She shouldn't have come out with Alex—she should have fled to her room for a good cry, she thought distractedly while they crossed the drive to the Annex where his convertible was parked. Now it was too late, they were rolling smoothly out along the shore road toward town.

"A spot of trouble with our English friend back there?" Alex commented gently. "I hope my intervention was welcome."

"Oh, so welcome!" she breathed, and then, as she had dreaded, sobbed convulsively, shivered, and began to cry.

"My dear!" Alex swung the car off onto the turnout for sightseers and killed the motor. "Cynthia, please—get hold of yourself—you'll have hysterics!" He moved over beside her and put his hand on her shoulder. "It can't have been that bad—"

"You don't know!" she gasped between sobs, fumbling in her evening bag for a handkerchief. "I—I'm sorry—I can't seem to—to stop!" Then she was in his arms, crushed against him, feeling the impetuous pressure of his lips on hers, returning it with passionate relief as all her troubles were forgotten.

She made no move to end the embrace. This was happiness that she had never dreamed of, when at a man's kiss the black thunderclouds of a brewing storm thinned to a rosy mist gilded with sunshine. What was there to fear from anyone, from anything in the world, if Alex Houston stood by her side? She had only to tell him of Eric's faithlessness, and his tyrannical pursuit which had driven her to the desperate expedient of pretending to be a married woman to escape him—

A married woman! That thought burst the iridescent bubble of her joy and shocked her to sick despair. Alex, the man she so admired—yes, loved—believed that she was married, yet could deliberately make love to another man's wife. Like a mocking echo in her mind came Miss Shaw's complaisant decree, "Alexander Houston's conduct is always above reproach!" How little that elderly spinster really knew men! The pent-up emotions of the evening flooded to anger.

With a gasp of resentment Cynthia twisted out of his arms, fumbled open the door and jumped from the car. Alex was too surprised to move, and that gave her the opportunity to vent some of her indignation by slamming the door viciously.

"For heaven's sake, Cynthy!" Alex began.

"Don't speak to me!" she snapped. "And don't ever call me 'Cynthy' in that disgustingly tender tone! Don't speak to me at *all!*"

"But Cynthia, I don't understand—"

"Can you understand this?" she raged. "I am not the kind of girl you evidently take me for, the free and easy kind that you must play around with. Your straight-laced Cousin Eva took the trouble to warn me about Mr. Bruce and Dr. Ferguson, it's too bad that she didn't include Cousin Alexander!"

"Cynthia, you're hysterical, you don't make sense." He slid across the seat to open the door.

"Stay where you are! I am not hysterical, I am disgusted! I suppose you are now going to say that you forgot yourself, forgot that I am married! Well, I don't believe it!"

He sat motionless, steady eyes probing deep into hers.

"Aren't we good enough friends to drop that foolishness?" he asked softly.

"Faithfulness is not my idea of foolishness," she retorted, hardly knowing what she said in her agony of disappointment.

"I didn't mean that, and you know it."

"I don't care what you meant!"

"At least be reasonable and listen to me." Impatience roughened his voice.

"Listen? Judging from your actions, anything you say will be an insult!"

"That's enough!" Alex snapped. "If you will act so childish how can I talk to you?"

"I've had quite enough of talk. I'm going back to the hotel —alone." She turned and walked away.

She had not taken a dozen steps before the car purred along at her side and stopped.

"Get in!" Alex ordered sharply. "No girl ever had to walk back from a ride with me, and you're not beginning it."

"I am!"

"Then you are going to attract attention, walking along with a car creeping beside you in low gear. The Harbor House will be agog."

There was too much truth in that suggestion to be ignored. In stony silence Cynthia climbed in. If he had attempted a word she would have either screamed at him—or melted. But he matched her silence as she rode to the door of the hotel with clenched fists and gritted teeth.

"Will you sit here quietly while I try to explain my actions?" Alex asked.

"They need no explanation." She was out of the car in a flash, knowing that the long evening of emotional stress and crushing disappointment in him would take its toll of tears at any moment. "Good night," she gasped.

"Just one observation," Alex said harshly. "In regard to our recent ride. For a girl with your high ideals, didn't it take you rather a long time to remember that you are a married woman?"

He released the brake, stepped on the throttle and sped away toward the Annex, while Cynthia went to her room with burning cheeks and an ache in her heart.

XV

Cynthia came down to breakfast in a mood of black desperation. The hostile world seemed to be closing in on her with irresistible and smothering pressure. Eric had proved that he would use every possible advantage to force himself on her, Claire Herbert's presence was a searing reminder of Cynthia's shame and horror in California, Miss Crane had declared open and savage warfare. And Alex—Alex Houston had shaken her faith in *all* men. "Forget him!" she told herself crossly.

The easiest thing for her to do would be to leave Newbury Harbor, go far away, and this time take care not to attract publicity by any so-called heroic exploit. That last shouldn't be difficult, she wasn't at all the heroine type. She never would have dared to attempt the boys' rescue if Alex hadn't lent his confidence—Alex again! With an effort she channeled her thoughts to a safer track.

Perhaps she could catch the morning train which Mary was to take, even go along when Michael drove her to the station. No, Michael was too loyal to Miss Shaw, he would report her intended flight at once. And that brought Cynthia around to consideration of her own loyalty to her employer, who had come to depend on her not only for secretarial work but for friendship.

In her heart Cynthia knew that the latter would be far more important to Miss Shaw. A secretary she could replace, as she had done a half dozen times. Alex would find one—Cynthia bit her lip as that distasteful name popped up again. Why couldn't she wipe him from her mind? Grimly she determined to do just that, and strode into the dining room as proudly erect as Marie Antoinette going to the guillotine, and feeling almost as desolate.

"Good morning," Miss Shaw said brightly, laying aside her newspaper. "You don't mind my sitting with you, I hope? Mary wanted to prepare my breakfast as usual, but I packed her off. In her state she would have been worse than useless. I wouldn't believe even she could get so addled."

Cynthia rallied to greet her, adding, "You are very chipper this morning. The dance wasn't too long for you?"

"I didn't stay to the bitter end. That may be an accurate description of it, too, judging from the quarrel I did see. I am more sorry than ever that I allowed myself to mix with those English people, quite common it appears, or mad, perhaps. The woman, anyway. No one sane would squall at a girl as she did, accusing her in so many words of pursuing her precious brother."

Cynthia's heart skidded to her toes. "You—you mean that you overheard all that?"

"Why not, when I was practically in the middle of it? Neal had just introduced that Herbert woman to me when Miss Crane swept up and went after her about her brother. I told you that woman has a mother complex where Eric is concerned, but that hardly explains her lack of self-control. Intoxicated, or out of her mind, in my opinion."

"Miss Crane accused *Claire Herbert* of chasing Eric?" Cynthia could not repress a laugh, partly at the coincidence but more in relief that it had not been her altercation which Miss Eva overheard.

"In so many words, my dear! Fantastic—but enthralling. Poor Neal was crimson with embarrassment. And I must say that Miss Herbert surprised me; I thought that she was just theatrical run-of-the-mill, but she gave Miss Crane a lesson in acting like a lady. I will have to admit that for once Neal Bruce selected—I won't say 'picked up'—a thoroughly nice girl."

Miss Shaw leaned back in her chair and frowned at Cynthia.

"Are you looking thoughtful or bored? I know that I am talking too much, but it is so pleasant to have a companion after weeks of solitary breakfasts."

"I'm anything but bored, Miss Shaw," Cynthia assured her with complete truth. "And I love having company, too."

"Then eat your strawberries while I continue to gabble," the other beamed. "There is something that you can do for me this morning, as soon as Michael returns with the car."

"More research into some long-forgotten Shaw?" Cynthia had become expert at that since her first trip with Michael.

"No." Miss Shaw shook her head decidedly. "We will not work on the book today. Did you happen to meet Grace Fenley last night? You didn't? She is a relative, I thought perhaps that Cousin Alexander might have introduced you to some of his North Shore friends. No matter, *I* met her, talked too much as usual, and now find myself scheduled to speak at the Annual Historical Society Tea tomorrow afternoon."

"How exciting! What will you talk about? Your book?"

"Probably. The first one, not the new one; I never believe in discussing my work until it is finished. I might tell of some of the odd happenings during my research for *Off-Beat Yankees*. I never have trouble finding something to talk about, you know," she admitted with a wry smile, "It's the stopping that is difficult. If you see anyone fall asleep you must wave your handkerchief at me."

"I will prod them awake instead," Cynthia promised. "Is the affair held here in the hotel?"

"Certainly not, this is a charity tea to raise money for the Society from local residents, not summer visitors. Ten dollars a ticket. This year it will be at the Fenley house in Magnolia. That is why I wish you to drive there this morning, talk to Grace—Mrs. Fenley—and make certain that she arranges a suitable room for my lecture. Don't allow her to use the ballroom, it is depressingly formal. I should prefer the living room, as it opens onto a large sunporch. Yes, that will be perfect. Insist on it, my dear, and don't let Grace dominate you. She is only a relative by marriage."

After breakfast Miss Shaw commissioned the bell captain to transfer Cynthia's belongings to the Annex, and superintended the operation in person. Hew new room was an immense improvement, Cynthia considered, although she had no complaints of the Harbor House accommodations. But this was Miss Shaw's conception of a guest room, and the subdued sunflower glow of its walls, the straight-hanging white curtains and pineapple fourposter bed with a mellow patchwork quilt folded across its foot, all welcomed with the old-fashioned graciousness of a perfect host.

Cynthia had scarcely stowed away her things when her employer alerted her with a sharp, "Michael is here. Better not keep him waiting."

True to form, however, the erratic lady only gave her time to take her seat in the limousine before calling from a window with an afterthought.

"Don't go!" she ordered. "Michael, wait a minute!"

"Decided she can't trust us not to get lost!" the chauffeur grumbled, switching off the motor. "Coming along with us, I guess."

But it was not Miss Shaw who presently emerged from the Annex. Claire Herbert, clad in canary-yellow sweater, light green slacks and high heeled sandals, descended the steps and approached the car with marked hesitation.

"This looks like awful gall, Mrs. Farley," she said diffidently, "but it isn't my fault. I just stopped in to ask Miss Shaw how to get to the charity tea place and she insisted that I go with you." When Michael hurried around to open the car door she got in. "I hope you don't mind?"

"No indeed." Cynthia did mind, she was revolted at the prospect, but saw no way to avoid the inevitable.

"I just wanted the directions and said that I could get there by myself," Claire apologized, "but she didn't even listen. She's a character, isn't she!"

Cynthia would have agreed with anyone else, but resentment prevented that. Hoping to avoid the girl's company on the trip she suggested, "The tea isn't until tomorrow, you know."

"And I won't be there," Claire said firmly. "That's why I have to go over this morning, to fix things. That North Shore crowd, as they call it, ganged up on me last night. You know this Mrs. Fenley we're going to? Well, somebody—I bet it was Neal—told her to put some *zip* in their show by having me do a number. She fell for it—and how!"

"That's fine," Cynthia said without enthusiasm. "Good for you."

"Not so good for them! Imagine me on a program with Miss Shaw! Huh, they'll expect Shakespeare or something highbrow from an English actress, and they'd get a low comedy music hall turn!"

Cynthia looked her surprise. "Are you English?"

"No, but I played over there a few years and got the background. That's where I ran into that heel—" She bit off the words with an uneasy side-long look, snatched open her purse and added cerise lipstick to a mouth already too liberally adorned. "I called that Fenley dame on the phone this morning to tell her not to count on me, but we might as well have been on different lines, she didn't get it. Thinks I'm trying to get *paid*, as if I wouldn't do a charity turn for free any time!

"I'm not the type for them," she added soberly, "and if I flopped Neal would never hear the last of it, so I'm going to bow out. I'd wring his neck for getting me into it, but he meant well, the old dear."

Cynthia found herself unwillingly liking the girl's honesty and her warm voice. Neither quality seemed to go with the blatant bad taste of her costume and make-up.

"Too bad that you agreed to appear if you feel so strongly," she remarked.

"I know. I missed my cue that time. But I told you they ganged up on me—the Fenley dame and your Miss Shaw and Neal—when I was off balance. I'd just played a torrid scene with Eric's—that Miss Crane—right in front of them, practically. And poor Neal was so mortified that I said anything to square things for him."

"If it is any comfort," Cynthia said with sudden generosity, "Miss Shaw considered that you played that scene just right."

"Thanks, I guess she'd be the one to know. So you heard about it?" Again Claire flashed a look at Cynthia and nodded. "Yes, of course you would." And again she veered away from the subject of Eric Crane. "Well, like I said, I let Neal railroad me into this high-class show, but I'm not going to make a fool of him, so I'm off this morning to show 'em that I'm not what they want for entertainment." She must have dressed to prove it, Cynthia guessed.

When the car rolled up a curving driveway banked with mountain laurel to a long Georgian brick house she could tell that Claire was properly impressed. But the magnificence did not seem to sway her determination; her chin remained defiantly set while the uniformed maid ushered them into a drawing room as vast as a hotel lobby.

They waited there, a strangely assorted pair; beside Cynthia's severely plain tweed suit and tan pumps Claire's garish outfit appeared ludicrous. It might have been that which halted Mrs. Fenley in her tracks when she entered the room.

"I am Mrs. Farley," Cynthia began, "Miss Shaw's secretary and—" She stopped speaking as her companion pushed past her with outstretched hand and swaying hips.

"Hi!" Claire greeted loudly. "Remember me, the dame Old Bruce dragged to the dance last night, and I said I'd be in your show? I guess I was pretty high, huh?" A laugh like shattering glass sent shivers up Cynthia's back and startled Mrs. Fenley.

"Of course I remember you, Miss Herbert, but—"

"Just call me Claire, like Neal does." She made another attempt to grasp Mrs. Fenley's hand and was thwarted. "I've really got an act that will wow the gang!" she shrilled. "Sort of a high-class stripe tease." A second saw-toothed laugh sent pallor into the Fenley cheeks.

"I hardly think that our guests would approve," Mrs. Fenley said with frigid calm. "I am very fond of Mr. Bruce and—"

"Me, too! He's a real doll, ain't he!"

"—And allowed him to persuade me," Mrs. Fenley continued in spite of the interruption. "It was kind of you to offer your services, but I am afraid it might make the program too long. Perhaps another time—?" she trailed the question into silence.

"Sure, that suits me fine. Be seein' you." Claire nodded to Cynthia. "Go ahead now, kid. I'll wait for you in the car." She treated them to another shrill laugh and went out, swaying.

Mrs. Fenley dropped limply into a chair and shook her head.

"I don't know *where* Neal finds such friends," she sighed. "Won't you sit down, Mrs. Farley, and we will discuss the tea."

The interview proceeded much better than Cynthia had expected. Forewarned, she employed all her charm on Mrs. Fenley and found her much less formidable than Miss Shaw had predicted, even on the question of ballroom versus living room. They agreed amicably that the latter was more suitable for the occasion and discussed the arrangement of the folding chairs which the local funeral director would shortly deliver. Then Mrs. Fenley insisted that Cynthia inspect and approve the refreshments already in preparation in the kitchen.

They parted with mutual admiration, Cynthia regretting that she dared not tell the other that Claire Herbert had been putting on an act to get out of her commitment when she was actually very nice. This charitable desire to defend the girl who had wrecked her marriage surprised her, but she knew that the feeling was genuine.

Claire greeted her with anxiety as she entered the car.

"I didn't spoil things for you with Mrs. Fenley, did I?"

"Not at all; she was charming. But did you need to be quite so—so *gauche?*"

"That's a polite word for it! Maybe I pitched it strong, but I *couldn't* do an act there and make Old Neal look like a fool for suggesting me."

"I don't believe—" Cynthia was about to remark that the exhibition which she *had* put on couldn't have helped Mrs. Fenley's opinion of Mr. Bruce, but decided against such frankness. Claire evidently thought highly of him and had done her best to save him from embarrassment. "I am sure that you wouldn't have disgraced him in any case, Miss Herbert," Cynthia encouraged.

"How awfully nice of you to say that, Mrs. Farley!" Claire beamed. "That Miss Shaw sure picked a winner for her secretary."

The casual compliment reminded Cynthia of an errand and she asked Michael to make a stop in Newbury Harbor.

"I am to get a package of copy paper for Miss Shaw," she explained. "Is there a stationery store in town?"

"There's a couple of gift shops that carry writing paper and other things, but I've got paper for Miss Shaw at Eddie Kruger's store. He carries everything."

That statement was no exaggeration Cynthia realized when she entered the Kruger establishment on the main street. A soda fountain on one side faced a display of hardware, guns and canned goods on the other. The space between was so filled with racks of magazines and paper-backs and tables piled with jackets, dungarees and oilskins that progress required all her navigational skill. She set a zigzag course for the corpulent, baldheaded man behind the long counter at the rear of the store.

Before she could ask for copy paper a vividly colorful box distracted her. Its cover presented a series of exciting skin-diving adventures, suggesting that all of them were possible, even likely, with the bright yellow snorkel, or breathing tube, contained in the box. Cynthia instantly thought of Tommy O'Hara, who was saving up for just such an addition to his mask and fins. It would be fun to present him with such a gaudy one.

On second thought, though, would it be wise? she wondered. The O'Haras already felt under obligation to her, any addition to that might be awkward. Wasn't it better to leave well enough alone and let the boy buy it himself. Resolutely she turned away, purchased a package of yellow copy paper, tucked it under her arm, and started for the street.

In the store's entrance she found Scoop Parker, leaning

against the doorway and gazing abstractedly down the street.

"Why, hello, Mrs. Farley," he said eagerly. "Well met, as the poets say. Maybe you can help me." He jerked a thumb in the direction he had been looking. "Remember my asking you what gives with this Crane guy? There he is talking to Fats Mantell. You know who *he* is?"

At a negative shake of the head by Cynthia he explained, "Mantell is a big shot in the rackets in Boston—the gambling syndicate. He's one of the kingpin bookies. The minute I saw them together I remembered what Doc Ferguson told me, about Crane spending so much time in defense plants around here, where there's lots of gambling, in case you don't know it."

Conscious of Eric's secret Cynthia took her time about answering, covering her hesitation by watching the two men. The shorter, dark man beside Eric stirred a memory, but not enough to waken it.

"Why should you assume that Mr. Crane knows this Mantell?" she demanded. "It may be an accidental meeting; he might have stopped Eric to ask a direction, if he's a stranger in town."

"He's a stranger in Newbury Harbor," Scoop growled, "but Mantell knows his way around, if you get me. And they do know each other. Look at that."

The two men climbed into a car at the curb, and as Mantell took the wheel Cynthia's memory flashed clear. She had watched the same men do the same thing in front of the Abbott Hotel in Boston. Eric must have already contacted the gambler then, beginning his work of espionage.

"I remember Eric—Mr. Crane—telling me last night that he was going to Boston to fly his plane down here," she said quickly. "He evidently is getting a ride up there with your—Mantell?"

"Not mine!" Scoop denied with a grin. "Looks like he belongs to Crane. An interesting partnership—that should prove very newsy."

"If you intend to snoop around Mr. Crane," Cynthia said severely, "I ought to warn you—don't." She felt no urge to help Eric, but after all he was assisting her own government. "This is confidential, Mr. Parker, and I was sworn to secrecy, but I feel that I should tell you. You must not interfere with Mr. Crane, he is working on the gambling in the plants—for Uncle Sam."

"You mean for the Treasury Department?" Scoop eyed her sharply.

"Yes, if that is the department which handles such

things. They asked him to help break up the gambling rings.'

"But he's an Englishman, isn't he? He can't be in the Department."

"They are using him because he is famous, and gets along well with the workers. He told me this in strictest confidence."

The reporter pushed back his hat to rub his forehead doubtfully, still studying her through the thick glasses which made his eyes look abnormally large.

"Crane told you—and asked you to keep it dark?"

"Naturally. He couldn't work effectively if it were known."

"You're right on that!" Parker whistled a barely audible tune between his teeth. "Well, thanks for warning me, Mrs. Farley. Many thanks indeed." He tipped his hat and walked away up the street whistling loudly.

Cynthia was suddenly aware that Michael stood holding open the car door only a few feet away, and that Claire Herbert was staring at her from the back seat. She had not intended to broadcast Eric's undercover job, but it was too late to mend matters now. Michael, she felt sure, was thoroughly discreet, and probably Claire already knew all there was to know about Eric Crane.

That idea was strengthened by the girl's first words when the car started.

"Eric goes the whole hog when it comes to being a stinker, doesn't he?" she muttered. Then she darted a look at the chauffeur beyond the glass partition of the limousine. "Can he hear?"

"I don't think so," Cynthia answered.

"I hope not. Because I want to get something off my chest, Mrs. Farley. Maybe you don't know that I'm the Miss Fixit who busted up your wedding rehearsal."

"I know." Cynthia could hardly believe in her own calmness, when once she would have been furious at the woman. Now she felt only friendliness and pity.

"*He* told you?" Contempt roughened Claire's voice. "I guess he also told you what a cheap little chippy I am—"

"Please! You aren't talking to Mrs. Fenley now, so don't put on an act." Cynthia was able to smile warmly. "I much prefer the real Claire Herbert."

The other stared at her. "My God!" she murmured, "you do mean it, don't you! Thanks, but I don't deserve it. I was going to apologize for what I did to you—but I guess I won't. I did you a favor, didn't I? Eric would have ruined your life, too."

"If you know him so well, why do you keep after him?"

"Because—" she stopped, flushing. "Because he owes me something. That's all you need to know, kid—I mean Mrs. Farley—"

"Cynthia."

"Stop it, or you'll have me bawling all over Miss Shaw's old hack." Claire's chin jutted with sudden determination. "Eric owes me something, like I said, and after what we just heard back there, I might surprise you by turning up married to the bum!" She rode the rest of the way in silence, her narrowed eyes fixed straight ahead in what Cynthia felt sure was a malevolent and calculating stare.

She recalled that impression later in the day, when she left the apartment for the beach. She had typed the notes for Miss Eva's speech and then been peremptorily banished while the lady rehearsed. As she went to the elevator she heard Claire's shrill voice coming from the hall of Number Five.

"No, you can't come in! I've said my last word, Eric!"

Crane again, back from his ride with the racketeer and already embroiled in argument. Cynthia decided not to wait for the elevator and went down the stairs as rapidly as possible to avoid overhearing more. But the angry voices carried too well.

"I'm telling you, Eric, you come through for me or I swear I'll spill the beans this time!"

"Rot! Don't try to scare me!"

"I'll *scare* you!" Claire threatened. "If you think I don't know enough to hurt, there's plenty of people to tell me more! Shall I start broadcasting your tie-up with that thug Mantell?"

"Who told you—? Listen, you're asking for trouble!" There was a dangerous snarl in his tone. "Let me in or—"

"I haven't time to argue with you now. Beat it, I've got to dress!"

"That can wait. We'll settle this first!"

"No! I'm late now—they've called rehearsals for every day this week, and the job's too good to risk getting fired. It's up to you, Eric—play ball at last, or see what happens!" The slam of the door of Number Five echoed down the stairwell.

With a relieved gasp Cynthia reached the ground floor and hurried out of the Annex. That five-story stairwell, she thought ruefully, was as good as a party line for eavesdropping on the neighbors.

XVI

THE FENLEY estate seethed with activity on the afternoon of the Annual Historical Society Tea and communicated some of its excitement to the patrons. Officer O'Hara, who had been detailed to the affair, grew hoarse as he strove to keep traffic moving along the curving drive.

Sedans, station wagons and sports cars in dizzying succession disgorged assorted passengers at the front door of the big house and then buzzed away to the parking lot beside the tennis court.

Even Miss Shaw caught the prevailing fever and her habitual self-possession deserted her. She sent Cynthia running to the limousine for the glasses she had left on the seat, and again to dispatch Michael to the Annex for copies of *Off-Beat Yankees* in case some of the guests showed a willingness to purchase them when embellished with her autograph.

Returning from this errand Cynthia cut across the acres of lawn to the front door, only to find herself on the wrong side of the driveway and blocked by streaming cars. While she waited for a break a voice behind her asked casually:

"Is the sabbatical year still going strong?"

She knew without turning that it was Alex; no other voice in the world could affect her so, sending feathery thrills to every nerve. Then her drumming heart skipped a beat and began to ache. How could he so lightly ignore her outraged reaction to his behavior after the dance? Was he used to such scenes? In the habit of making a play for anyone who attracted him, married or not? She crushed the idea, she knew it wasn't true. Not Alex! With an effort she matched his airy greeting as she looked over her shoulder. "Sabbatical? Oh—I remember. Yes, it's been very beneficial."

"Something has all right," he affirmed as he stepped forward. "Never saw you look better, Cynthia. That red dress puts the come-hither in your eyes and—" Alex hastily shifted his ground. "A mere man calls it red, but no doubt it has a more exotic label?"

Cynthia examined her tight bodice and bouffant skirt with satisfaction. "Yes, I believe it's actually *mandarin*."

"Oh, an airmail gift from Alonzo in the Orient?"

They were interrupted by a squeal of brakes in the drive, where O'Hara had flung up his hand with a suddenness that stopped a car in its tracks. He approached Cynthia with a broad grin.

"What are you doing here, so far from home?" she asked.

"Known the Fenleys for years. My day off, so I thought I'd pick up the extra money. Step right across, Mrs. Queen. You, too, Mr. Houston," he added, his brown cheeks flushing. "Glad to see you in person, so I can thank—"

"Skip it, O'Hara!" Alex ordered sharply. "You wrote me a letter of thanks—let's drop it."

"Yes, sir." The officer watched them cross, then waved the waiting car forward.

As they went up the steps Alex observed, "He and his wife sent me a letter about helping their boys that darn near had me in tears. Evidently he feels the same way about you—and no wonder. But what's this 'Mrs. Queen' deal? You seem to have a lot of aliases."

Cynthia's heart missed a beat. Did he suspect her deception? A more likely explanation cheered her.

"Are you thinking of that 'J. Darcy' nom de plume I used when I forwarded your suitcase? This one is not my doing, though. The first time I met O'Hara, after our rescue of the boys, he was so attentive that I remarked he made me feel like visiting royalty, and he promptly christened me 'Mrs. Queen.'"

"I wish that I had his gift for turning an appropriate phrase."

"The Irish are fundamentally poetic, which is not expected of the cold, legally trained Yankee."

"So that's what you think of me?"

It was not a point that Cynthia cared to discuss. She paused at the entrance to the drawing room already filling with guests.

"Excuse me, now," she said. "I must see if Miss Shaw has everything she needs. For once your unruffled cousin is a bundle of nerves, although I showed her my lucky star which I brought along in my glove for her especial benefit. 'Bye!"

"Here!" he protested. "Aren't you going to sit with me? Don't tell me I squandered ten dollars—and no Cynthia!"

"What a pity you only bought *one* ticket, with all the eager single girls you know on the North Shore," she chided, remembering the red-haired Babs in the Portsmouth tavern. "And I do mean *eager!*"

Alex turned the thrust aside with a laugh. "Today I prefer the lure of the unknown." Then he took the offensive. "If you aren't available, how about that attractive blond Miss Herbert we saw at the dance? Is she here today?"

"So you prefer blondes?"

He grinned at her reaction. "A blonde in the hand—"

"How disappointing for you. Claire is studying for rehearsal this afternoon; Neal Bruce invited her to sail and was quite put out when she refused. She's very conscientious about her work, you know. However, I am sure you'll find some congenial soul to sit with in the room. Now I must go."

The annual tea proved an immense success. As Cynthia had hoped, once Miss Shaw was on her feet in front of the audience every trace of nervousness vanished and she was the Cousin Eva known and respected by most of them. Even in a striking dress of flowered blue satin and with a hat which was hardly more than a cluster of blue blossoms clipped atilt on her white hair she was still Proper Boston personified.

In contrast, her rambling account of the thrills and frustrations of research for *Off-Beat Yankees* was constantly enlivened by risqué references to the forbears of well-known families represented at the Tea. All were greeted with bursts of laughter, quite often followed by a loud gasp at some salty revelation of an ancestor's impropriety.

But there could be no lingering resentment, for she ended with the tale of her Great-Great Uncle Barnabas Shaw, who, long after his demise, was found to have left sorrowing windows in Salem, San Francisco and Hong Kong, and was thenceforward referred to as "Solomon" Shaw.

There was no formality about the refreshments which followed the meeting. Cousin Eva had broken the ice with a vengeance, and the dining room became a bedlam of hilarious discussions concerning the long-buried skeletons which she had unearthed, as well as others not mentioned.

Cynthia was in the midst of it, without taking part, because of her duties as substitute hostess. Perhaps Mrs. Fenley had been impressed with her that morning, or perhaps only wanted to be free to join the jovial grave robbers. For whatever reason, she had charged Cynthia with the duty of keeping supplies coming from the kitchen as fast as they were consumed.

It was considered a supervisory job of course, but Cynthia soon found that it required her time and attention to the fullest degree. For although the two Fenley maids in fresh lilac uniforms and the Japanese houseboy in a spotless white coat started skillfully at their tasks, they deteriorated rapidly under the avalanche of hungry guests. Time after time they brought in trays of food as they had picked them up in the kitchen, regardless of whether a fresh supply was needed, and loaded the tables with identical delicacies while plates of other kinds stood empty.

A little more substance in the food, Cynthia thought, would have met with more favor among the men, but they made rapid inroads on the plates of delicate shrimp and anchovy sandwiches and created havoc on the platters of pineapple slices wrapped in ham. There was no evidence of liquor at any table, but punch and tea and coffee flowed in never-ending streams.

Not until the onrush slackened to a mere trickle did Cynthia have time to realize that she was tired and needed a breather. She wandered through the crowded rooms in search of an unoccupied seat and finally found Scoop Parker standing before an empty couch in a corner of the sun porch.

"May I?" she inquired, brushing past him. She sat down, leaned back limply, and closed her eyes. They snapped open a minute later when a hand patted her knee.

"Cynthia, you look positively bushed!" Alex exclaimed as he balanced a plate in one hand and bent over her. "I'll bet you haven't had time to eat a thing!"

"I am and I haven't," she admitted, gratefully accepting a sandwich from the proffered plate. "Are you sure that you have enough for yourself?" she jeered, measuring the heaped plate with outspread fingers. "I've been admiring these sandwiches for what seems hours."

"Is that what these are?" Parker demonstrated the ease with which he could put three at once into his mouth, as he sat down beside her. "I was waiting here for our friend to bring me *food* when you drooped in, and I get these paper-thin pretties," he complained, staring at his heaped plate. "Come down to the press some night when we're getting out the paper, and I'll show you what a sandwich is."

"Stay away from that cave," Alex advised, sitting down on the other side. "You know what reporters are—wolves in—Ha! A wolf in Scoop's clothing," he amended brightly.

The reporter shook his head and groaned.

"Really!" he protested, "I wouldn't even use *that* in my column, and I'm pretty hard pressed at times. Here," he offered, "fill up on some of mine, you look as if you needed sustenance. Why you didn't nibble a bit though, being right at the source, I'll never understand."

"I had no appetite," Cynthia confessed ruefully. "You never heard such ghoulish conversation, or such joy at digging up disreputable ancestors! They made me think of Jerry Cruncher, the dreadful Resurrection Man in *A Tale of Two Cities*."

"We've been doing a little digging ourselves," Alex said gravely. "About one Eric Crane. Maybe you can add to what little we know about him. Scoop was telling me about his hanging around the plants to contact the employees, and your ingenious explanation for it."

Cynthia was annoyed. "Mr. Parker!" she protested, "that was in confidence. You promised not to broadcast it!"

"Correction, please, Mrs. Farley. I *promised* nothing. And I didn't worm the secret out of you. You volunteered it, remember?"

"Just the same!" she argued heatedly, "it wasn't nice of you—"

"I'm not a nice person, Houston just warned you of that."

His grin disarmed her indignation, especially as what he had said about their conversation was true.

"I told you Eric's secret because I didn't want anything to interfere with his work for the government," she pleaded. *"Our* government, remember?"

"Sure, I remember everything you said." Scoop did not seem impressed. "I told Houston because his firm happens to be counsel for several of the defense plants around Newbury. I thought he'd be interested."

"I am," Alex said, "and I'd like to hear everything you know about our Mr. Crane, Cynthia."

Cynthia dreaded further discussion but before she could make up her mind on how to refuse Miss Shaw pounced on her, figuratively at least.

"My dear!" she exclaimed, nodding regally as the two men leaped to their feet, "Because I was selfishly engaged in listening to congratulations on my talk, I just learned that you had entire responsibility for the dining room. The idea of Grace Fenley saddling you with *her* duties! I shall take that up with her! You are pale with fatigue and I insist that you go home and rest!"

"But I loved doing it, Miss Shaw! And I haven't been able to get through your ring of admirers to say how wonderful your speech was."

"Went off very well, didn't it. And I sold all the books—autographed, of course." Miss Shaw indulged in a ladylike version of a guffaw. "Had one or two chances to put in quite a spicy dedication—families I mentioned in my talk, you know. Now Cynthia, Michael must drive you home at once and come back for me."

"Unnecessary waste of gasoline," Alex put in. "My car is at Mrs. Farley's disposal, and I'm ready to leave."

Instant refusal leaped to Cynthia's lips but was repressed while she considered wildly what her employer might think of such an action. But she would not go with Alex—not after what had happened on their last ride together. She trusted neither him nor herself. Scoop Parker unintentionally offered her a way out.

"*My* car is at her disposal, too," he said hopefully. "If you don't mind slumming in such a derelict, ma'am, I'd be delighted to taxi you."

"You are both too kind! Rather than have a duel over who escorts me"—relief made Cynthia's laugh shaky—"I shall play safe with Michael. I will send him back at once, Miss Shaw."

"No hurry about that, I am enjoying myself immensely and won't be ready to go until the last gun is fired."

When Cynthia took her leave she was uncomfortably conscious of Alex Houston's indignant and probing stare following her to the door. Even seated in the security of the car, with the silent and dependable Michael her sole companion, the sense of discomfort and uncertainty rode with her.

Ever since the Cranes and Claire Herbert had arrived in Newbury Harbor, threatening thunderclouds had closed about her with increasing menace. The destruction of her faith in Alex, the loss of his friendship, had left her a rudderless ship in a gathering storm.

She was too honest to blame anyone but herself; if she had not acted the fool over Eric in the beginning none of this would have happened, especially her deception of Miss Shaw, which had only multiplied her troubles. Of course Cynthia had justified it by the grand old lady's need for a secretary, but the truth was that she had done it for her own selfish purpose—to get away from Eric. It was only justice that the dishonesty had recoiled against her.

When the car reached Newbury Harbor she could not bear the dismal thought of sitting in the apartment, rehearsing past mistakes, until Miss Shaw arrived. She had been cooped up at the tea all afternoon, what she needed was fresh air and exercise. Overriding Michael's objections she alighted on the main street, dismissed him summarily, and went down to the shore. Purely on impulse she followed that road beyond town, walking fast and hugging her light coat close to keep out the wind.

This was new country for her, but it could as well have been the familiar route to the hotel, for she was too deep in retrospective thought to notice the beauty of the coast. Not until increasing traffic on the road caught her attention did she think of the time. Her watch said almost half-past five; these cars must be workers returning to their homes. She turned then and started for the hotel, and found the wind in her face suddenly sharp and nipping. Too bad she had come so far, she would be chilled before she ended her walk.

The church bells in the Harbor were jumbling out their individual versions of six o'clock when she turned into the Annex drive. Neal Bruce, coming from the direction of the parking lot, met her and registered concern.

"Mrs. Farley, you look half frozen! What in the world have you been doing?"

"Taking some exercise and regretting it. Was your New England poet kidding when he rhapsodized, 'What is so rare as a day in June?' "

"He didn't mean with an east wind, I guess," Bruce admitted.

"It must have been cold on your sailing trip."

"Would have been, but I gave it up when Claire wouldn't come along. Went for a drive up through Kittery and York instead."

They started toward the Annex and at that moment Eric Crane hailed them from the hotel veranda and came across the drive.

"How did the Great Annual Historical Shindig come off, Cynthia?" he asked.

"A howling success," she said shortly.

"I bought a ticket but couldn't make it." He wiped his forehead wearily. His pale face twitched, Cynthia noticed, he looked almost haggard. "I spent the entire day pretending surprise and attempting to understand and appreciate the work they're doing in a radiation lab, and I feel as though I'd flown eight hours through thunderstorms. Just got back, and was staggering toward the lounge for a drink when I saw you."

"We'd better team up," Bruce proposed with a grin, "for self-preservation. Mrs. Farley's frozen, I'm tired, and you're mentally exhausted. Everybody come up to my apartment for a drink."

"Stout fella!" Eric linked arms with him and Cynthia. " 'Lay on, Macduff.' "

"Include me out, thanks." Cynthia withdrew from his hand under pretense of removing her gloves and opening her purse in search of her door key. "I'm heading double time for a hot bath."

"So are we," Bruce chuckled, "but internally, eh, Crane?" As they entered the hall he moved ahead to the elevator. "Good! The car is here, so there won't be an instant's delay which might prove fatal in our condition." He grinned over his shoulder as he slid open the glass door and the wire door of the car and bowed to Cynthia. "Be my guest."

Her foot was crossing the threshold before she saw the crumpled figure in a corner of the car. A woman. The unexpected sight stopped her short, then the first shock of surprise grew to terror at the crimson stain on the ivory silk jacket and she shrank back with a stifled scream.

Bruce steadied her. "What?—" He looked into the car and let out a startled oath. "A woman—"

"What's the matter?" Crane demanded, pushing Cynthia aside to look in. "Good God! It's—" His voice leaped to a shrill cry, "God, it's *Sis!* Oh, no!" He recoiled from the car, clutched at the doorframe, missed, and collapsed against the girl.

Instinctively she tried to support him and dropped purse and gloves in the effort. But she was too shaken herself to muster enough strength and he slumped through her trembling hands to roll face up on the floor, unconscious. Sick and dizzy she clung to the stair rail to keep from following.

Neal Bruce was stooping in the elevator. "It *is* Miss Crane! She's hurt—must have fallen—" He straightened with a gasping, "No, by God! She's been shot!" He backed out, stumbling over Crane's sprawled legs, gripped Cynthia's arm and shook it. "Don't you faint on me, too!" His own round cheeks were drained of color, sweat beaded his forehead.

"I won't—but—but—is she dead?" Cynthia gasped.

"I don't know, we've got to call a doctor quick. Get on the phone, I'll stand by here. Wait, though!" His hand pulled her away from the stairs. "Try Ferguson! There's his apartment—ring the bell—pound on his door!"

The panic in Bruce's drawn face as much as the strident commands drove her to obey. She circled Eric's body and raced to the door of Number One, beat on the panel with her fist while she searched wildly for the bell. She found the bell, stabbed at it repeatedly. Then in desperation she tried the handle and flung the door open, stepped into the apartment.

"Doctor!" she shouted. "Doctor Ferguson!"

The little man appeared like magic in a doorway, coatless, his gray hair disheveled, a lime-green towel in his hand. Open-mouthed he peered at her while he pulled his glasses from the pocket of his shirt.

"Come quickly, Doctor!" she begged. "An accident!"

Ferguson fumbled the glasses but adjusted them on his nose at last.

"Oh, Mrs. Farley! Accident? Oh dear, not Miss Shaw?" he cried.

"No—out there in the elevator! Please hurry!" Cynthia longed to grab his arm and hasten his measured pace across the room.

"Yes—yes." He went past her to the hall, saw Crane's outstretched form and stopped. "Hmph, Crane, eh? I doubt if he's had an accident, looked like a heart condition to me, first time I saw him."

Bruce had recovered his self-possession. "Not Crane, Doctor, he's only fainted. It's his sister—there in the elevator."

"Oh?" Ferguson tucked the towel into his trousers' pocket and stepped in to bend over the still figure. The examination was brief. He straightened and backed out of the car. "Nothing I can do for her, she is dead. Shot in the chest—probably instantaneous." He glanced from Bruce to Cynthia and then down at Crane. "Who found her?"

Cynthia's dry lips could not have formed a single syllable. She was grateful when Bruce answered.

"We three came in together. I opened the elevator doors—and Crane keeled over when he saw her."

"Not surprising." Dr. Ferguson went down on one knee and felt the unconscious man's pulse while Bruce crouched to watch. "Mrs. Farley, get some cold water from my kitchen, will you? Last door on the right, down the hall."

"I'll do it." Neal Bruce stood up, picked up Cynthia's purse and handed it to her.

"Don't touch anything!" Ferguson snapped.

"But that's hers, she dropped it when Crane passed out."

"Oh—all right. But let her get the water, Bruce. You had better use the phone on my desk to call the police immediately."

"Police?" Cynthia and Bruce gasped in chorus.

"Certainly!" Ferguson looked up impatiently. "Miss Crane was shot, I told you. I saw no gun in the elevator, so I assume it is murder. And since it evidently occurred here in the Annex, if we don't notify the police at once we are apt to be their first choice as suspects. The water, please, Mrs. Farley."

XVII

MINDFUL of Dr. Ferguson's warning that she might be numbered among the suspects of the murder Cynthia spent a worried half hour alone in the apartment. At first she paced the floor, shivering now and then with chill or reaction, dreading the expected summons by the police. Twice cars sped up to the Annex and halted, and from the stair landing drifted an occasional dull echo of heavy footsteps, but she had no desire either to look out the window or the door. The less she knew of what went on the happier she would be.

It was the crime itself which paralyzed her mind rather than the identity of the victim; she had little reason to regret the passing of Miss Margaret Crane. But it was incredible that the energetic, even boisterous woman would no longer stride about the Harbor House issuing curt commands to Eric—and engaging in wholehearted brawls with any girls who seemed to show interest in him.

When the crystal and gold French clock had softly ticked away thirty minutes and no official had rung the bell—or more likely pounded on the door, Cynthia thought gloomily—it began to appear that the doctor was a nervous old fussbudget whose imagination had run wild. After all, there was no sensible reason for the authorities to question Cynthia Farley about the death of a woman she scarcely knew.

Defiantly she retired to indulge in the hot bath to which she had been looking forward so long. Then, in a fresh dress and with hair carefully arranged—any occupation helped to keep her mind from dwelling on that horribly crumpled figure in the elevator—she sat tensely on the edge of the couch and waited—and waited.

It was nearly seven when another car drew up before the Annex and Cynthia thought she recognized the heavy thud of the limousine's door when Michael closed it. She made the window in time to see Miss Shaw mount the steps while Michael picked up a box from the front seat. Hurrying to the hall she opened the entrance door a crack and listened to the commotion on the lower floor.

"Stop repeating that you are a policeman! I have eyes!" Miss Shaw's voice cracked with annoyance. "I have no intention of interfering with your work, but I live upstairs and I wish to go up now."

"You can't until we finish!" growled an angry voice. "You can't touch that elevator."

"Then I shall walk up. Step out of my way!"

"No, stay by the front door, damn it! Excuse me, ma'am, but we can't have you treading on this part of the floor yet. Go on back there!"

Cynthia jerked open the door with every intention of rushing to the aid of her besieged employer, but there was no need. She almost laughed her relief when Michael's bellow sounded.

"What the devil's going on here? Take your hands off her, guy, or I'll flatten you!"

"I didn't touch her—"

"You looked like you might," Michael countered hotly. "Are you off your rocker? This is Miss Shaw!" From his tone it was obvious that he felt nothing more need be said.

"Okay!" the officer shouted. "So it's Miss Shaw—but we've got a murder here, and we're investigating—"

"Murder?" Miss Eva's interruption was one part amazement and three parts interest. "Really? Is it anyone I know?"

Michael brooked no side issues. "Go on with your investigating then, bud, but she's got nothing to do with it. Come 'round by this wall, ma'am, so's you won't tramp on their blasted floor."

"Hold it!" the policeman barked. "You'll get into trouble—"

"Belden! What's going on down there?" The harsh question came from upstairs and brought a momentary hush. Then Officer Belden answered with a relieved shout.

"Lieutenant Hunt! There's a dame and a fresh chauffeur—"

"Who are you calling a dame?" snarled Michael.

"Be quiet, Michael!" Miss Shaw commanded, and raised her voice. "Is that Lieutenant Harry Hunt up there? This is Miss Shaw, Lieutenant, and I wish to go to my apartment."

Again there was silence. Cynthia could picture the group below waiting as breathlessly as she for the decision. All except Miss Shaw, she felt sure; that lady would take permission for granted, no doubt was already coming up the stairs.

"Sorry, Miss Shaw." The lieutenant's apology sounded strained. "You may come up to your room."

"I *am* coming." She paused on the third step to say quietly but definitely, "Put the car away, Michael. I won't need you tonight."

"How about this wise guy, Lieutenant?" demanded Belden hopefully.

"Get on with your job, Belden. Miss Shaw, I'd like to drop in a little later and talk with you."

"Do, Lieutenant. Oh, there you are, with Neal. Yes, please come, I am simply bursting with questions."

She appeared at the head of the stairs and saw Cynthia in the doorway. When Cynthia clasped her hands and shook them in the time-honored gesture of congratulation she allowed herself a complacent smile and nod. Then they were in the apartment with the door safely closed.

"Isn't Michael wonderful!" Cynthia gloated. "I could have hugged him!"

"He would be delighted, I'm sure." Miss Shaw sailed across to the walnut mirror, removed the little flowered hat, stared at it for a moment as though unable to believe that she had worn such a frivolous concoction and laid it beside her purse on the table. Then she sat down, stiffly erect on the long couch. "Now then, my dear, I won't fall on the floor if I faint. Who is murdered?"

"Miss Crane."

"Good Lord!" Miss Shaw's cheeks paled, but she gave no indication of fainting. "I have said a great many mean things about that woman and thought even worse ones. I'm sorry for all I said—but I couldn't stand her!" she ended with characteristic honesty. She glanced about the room absently and sighed. "My, I'm suddenly tired!"

"You must be, after your exciting day," Cynthia sympathized. "Shall I make you a cup of tea?"

The older woman brightened visibly. "That would be wonderful; I was too busy to eat much this afternoon."

Miss Shaw trailed Cynthia to the kitchen and sat primly watching the preparations.

"Wouldn't you know something exciting would happen while I was away, so that I miss it!" she complained. "Now I must wait until the lieutenant comes to hear about it."

"You needn't wait unless you insist," Cynthia told her, forcing a matter-of-fact tone. "I'm afraid your secretary is going to be in the papers again. I found—er—the body."

"Cynthia, you didn't!"

"Well, I was there, with Mr. Bruce and Eri—Mr. Crane." She described the occurrence as briefly as possible, not only because re-creating the scene revived her shock and fright, but to spare her listener any gruesome details. This turned out to be misplaced kindness, for the gruesome details were exactly what Miss Shaw craved.

She followed Cynthia and the tea tray back to the living room firing a barrage of questions. Was there a great deal of blood? Any signs of a struggle? Wasn't Cynthia paralyzed with horror—?

"Sit down and drink your tea," Cynthia suggested in desperation. "I'd rather not undergo a third degree from you at the moment, because your friend Lieutenant Hunt is probably going to give me one as soon as he arrives. You'll hear it all then."

Like a well-timed cue, the promise brought an imperious ring of the bell.

"The law!" Cynthia announced, pretending more assurance than she felt, and went to the door.

A short, thickset, redheaded man in a dark blue suit stood there, hat in hand. He immediately extended a badge and announced, "Lieutenant Hunt, Newbury Police Department. You are Mrs. Farley?"

It was more an asssertion than a question, and so abrupt that Cynthia could only nod as he brushed past her to the living room doorway. Miss Shaw was not similarly affected.

"Come in and sit down, Harry," she invited graciously. "And put away that badge you have in your hand, you are among friends. A cup of tea?"

"No thank you, ma'am. I'm sorry to say this is business and not a social call." Lieutenant Hunt struggled to preserve his official sternness. "I have to ask Mrs. Farley some questions."

"Aren't you going to question me, too?"

"Why, no—that won't be necessary, Miss Shaw." He sat carefully on one of the aged Hitchcock chairs, as though expecting it to collapse. "We know all about you, you see."

"I doubt it," she objected with a grim smile.

"I mean—about this afternoon, ma'am. When you left the tea, and so on," Hunt explained hastily, and turned to Cynthia. His face hardened. "I would have been here sooner, Mrs. Farley, but Mr. Bruce forgot to mention that you were with him when he found Miss Crane's body. *Forgot* until it slipped out, that is. Any idea why he should try to conceal the fact?"

"Why, no—"

Miss Shaw sniffed. "I should think it was obvious, Harry—or perhaps you would prefer that I address you as Lieutenant? Of course Neal didn't want to drag Cynthia into this—and expose her to your third-degree methods!" Her glance at Cynthia was almost a wink. "Her only connection with the murder was being present when it was discovered, and I imagine the two men can give you all the information you need."

"*One* man," corrected Hunt. "Eric Crane isn't available."

"Where is he?" Cynthia demanded. "And how is he?"

The lieutenant shrugged. "Dr Ferguson had him taken to the hospital in Salem—put him under sedatives. We won't be able to question him tonight." Irritation roughened his voice. "For a famous test pilot he seems to have kind of a weak stomach.'"

"It was his sister who was killed!" Cynthia reminded sharply.

"Yeah—that may be it. Now, Mrs. Farley, would you tell me exactly what happened from the time you came into this house? That was about six o'clock, I understand?"

"A few minutes after, because I heard the town clocks striking as I came up the drive. I met Mr. Bruce and Er—Mr. Crane and we talked a moment—"

"This was at six?" Hunt interrupted. "But I understand you left the tea party at Mrs. Fenley's about five, when Miss Shaw's chauffeur drove you home. A fifteen minute run or so. Wouldn't that bring you here at about quarter past five?"

"I didn't come back here with Michael. I got out in town and took a walk along the shore for a while."

"For three-quarters of an hour? Weren't you cold?"

"Yes, but I didn't notice," Cynthia explained. "I was upset, and thinking about—about things."

Hunt suddenly abandoned that subject. "O.K., ma'am. So you met the other two outside, and came in?"

"Yes. Mr. Bruce opened the elevator doors—" A shudder halted her but she recovered and plunged into the story, trying to remember every incident.

Lieutenant Hunt's eyes, fixed unwaveringly on her, gave no assistance. They were brown, with an amber glow of intense concentration, and seemed to dart at every fact she mentioned and file it away securely in his brain. When she described her search for water in Dr. Ferguson's kitchen the eyes narrowed.

"Bruce said *he* got the water," Hunt interposed.

"No, he called the police. I suppose that he had to tell you he went for the water, if he didn't want to mention me." She tried to soften the steady stare with a smile. "It was very kind of him."

"And no end confusing," the lieutenant added dryly. "He tangled himself up so bad that he's lucky he isn't in the jug right now. All right, go on."

"That's all, Lieutenant. Mr. Bruce told me to come up here and I stayed right in my room until I heard Miss Shaw come home."

The red-haired lieutenant relaxed enough to grin. "I guess we all heard that. Too bad you riled Belden, Miss Shaw; this is his first murder, and he's taking it seriously."

"Will you apologize for me, Harry?" Miss Shaw sounded sincere. "I had come from a tiring afternoon and was less patient than usual."

Cynthia noticed that this bland understatement amused Hunt as much as it did her; his covert glance of understanding made him seem more human.

"Now—Lieutenant Hunt," Miss Eva continued with punctilious formality, "if you are through with Cynthia tell us what happened."

"We haven't much dope yet, but Miss Crane was shot while she stood in the elevator. We found the wire door broken where the bullet went through, so someone must have slid open the glass door of the shaft and fired through the inside door. Queer," he said with a sidelong glance at Cynthia, "that the murderer was so sure someone was in the car."

"But he could see her shadow on the frosted glass, Lieutenant," she explained, "from that light on the back wall of the car."

"Yeah?" Hunt stared directly at her now. "It's funny that Mr. Bruce said the same thing. You've noticed that, too, have you?"

"So have I—often!" Miss Shaw said hastily.

"It's true, all right," the officer admitted. "You can see a person's silhouette plainly. O.K., then. The medical examiner reports that she died around five-thirty, his best guess at present. And the bullet was a .38 caliber from a pistol. Now you know all we know."

"You haven't found the gun yet?" Miss Shaw asked wide-eyed.

"Not yet. When we do, tests of it and the bullet will identify it. I'm telling you everything, Miss Shaw, because I hope you'll do the same for me."

"You intend to—er—grill me next?" The prospect appeared to please her.

"Hardly, ma'am. As I said a while ago, we know all we need to about you, and I'll take this chance to say we know what you've done for a lot of hard-luck folks in Newbury Harbor over the years. I don't mean just your contributions to the Red Cross, Welfare Fund and such, either. You've helped plenty of people on the quiet, and we appreciate it—"

"People talk too much! Get on with your questions, Harry."

"I want you help in getting the set-up here sorted out in my mind. You've lived in this house for years, know everything about everybody, and can—"

"I'm a nosy old gossip. That what you mean?"

"No, ma'am!"

"Of course I'm not. But I am interested in people, especially those with whom I come in daily contact, and I like to know about them. But I look for facts, not idle tales. If I have any information that will be useful, you are welcome to it."

"Thanks." Lieutenant Hunt referred to a black notebook. "Let's cover this annex. Dr. Ferguson's on the ground floor?"

"Yes." Miss Eva started to rise and put her empty cup on the tray, but when Cynthia relieved her of it she sank back and resumed her uncompromising pose. Very much the reigning monarch giving an audience to the peasantry, Cynthia thought with amusement.

"Surely you have no doubts about the doctor, Lieutenant?" Miss Shaw demanded.

"He's pretty well known, of course, but we are making some inquiries just the same. Now, you are in Number Two here."

"As you see, with Mrs. Farley who is kindly staying with me while my maid is away. Neal Bruce is in Number Three. Four is empty at the moment; the last tenants left their windows open during a thunderstorm and ruined things. The management is redecorating the entire apartment so there is no one there but painters and workmen. No one at all, this week, I believe, because the new wallpaper hasn't been delivered. It seems literally impossible, these days, to find anyone with interest enough in their business to keep their promises—"

"I know what you mean, Miss Shaw," Hunt interrupted smoothly. "That takes us up to Number Five."

"Yes, the Whiteheads, but they are in the West. At the moment a young woman, Claire Herbert, is staying there. Neal Bruce's friend whom he engaged for his Summer Theater. She is looking after their fish." At the other's bewildered look she smiled. "Tropical fish, in tanks; very expensive and the ultimate in pets, though *why* I can't imagine. So they have to be taken care of; so Neal introduced this friend to nurse them."

The lieutenant consulted his notebook and frowned.

"Bruce didn't mention any Claire Herbert among the people he thought might be in on about this annex today."

Miss Shaw started to speak and checked herself. She clasped her hands in her lap and stared down at them.

"That was careless of him," she admitted.

Cynthia could not refrain from offering an explanation. "Don't you suppose he wanted to shield her from unpleasant questioning, as he tried to do for me? Because Claire wasn't in this house when Miss Crane was shot, so wouldn't know anything about it."

"Oh?" Hunt stared at her. "You *know* that she wasn't here, although you say that you weren't here, either?"

"I say I wasn't, and I wasn't!" Cynthia resented the innuendo. "I know that Miss Herbert had rehearsal every day this week. She goes to town at five for a snack, then to the theater, until all hours, because the show opens so soon."

"And Bruce knew about that, too, and gallantly omitted it? Quite a feller!" Hunt growled. "Miss Shaw, what about this man Bruce? You know him of course?"

"I've known him all his life, he's a relative. A confirmed bachelor with an inherited income who has never done a stroke of work in his life."

Again Cynthia rushed to Neal Bruce's defense. "He puts in

a great deal of time with the theater group. Surely that's worthwhile work!"

"Just a chance to meet pretty girls!" Miss Shaw snapped. "That's how he picked up this Herbert woman."

Hunt rubbed his chin and showed interest.

"A chance acquaintance, then? And he installed her in the apartment upstairs? Hummm!"

"I don't like your insinuations, Harry!" Miss Shaw never permitted outside criticism of her family. "Confine yourself to your job!"

Hunt bristled. "My *job* is finding out all I can about anyone who *might* be connected with this killing, in any way!"

"I should think that we three who found the body would be eliminated as suspects," Cynthia interposed meekly.

"Why?" snapped Hunt. "You yourself were wandering along the beach for three-quarters of an hour on a chilly, blustery afternoon. Bruce went for a ride all afternoon and got back here at six. This Herbert woman was supposed to be at the theater, and Dr. Ferguson left the plant where he works before five and is just home and washing his face and hands at six, although it's less than half an hour's drive. That's four people with good stories, and any one of you could have been here and shot Miss Crane, then ducked out, hung around out of sight, and come back for the unveiling of the crime, innocent as a baby."

"Harry!" Miss Shaw protested, "You can't suspect any of *them* of *murder!*"

The lieutenant nodded and gave her a sour grin.

"I'm suspicious by nature, ma'am. This is our first murder case for a long time, and we're not going to soft-pedal it. I'll check and double check every story, believe me!" His brown eyes stabbed at the girl. "You claim that you walked the beach, upset and thinking? About what?"

"Personal problems, Lieutenant. Nothing to do with—" She intended to say "with Miss Crane," but that would have been far from true. "Nothing to do with this case," she amended.

If Hunt noticed the hesitation he ignored it. "Meet anybody on your walk? Anybody who would remember seeing you there?"

"I didn't notice anyone."

"Too bad." The lieutenant sat back, relaxed. "Strange thing about this killing, Miss Shaw. Done with a .38 caliber gun; pretty big and heavy for a woman to handle, but we found these in a corner of the hall by the elevator." He produced a pair of white gloves and spread them carefully on his knee.

Cynthia leaned forward to stare. "Why, they look like mine!"

"You identify these as your gloves?" Hunt became heavily official.

"What are you talking about?" Miss Shaw broke in impatiently. "Everyone I know has gloves like those. Short, white cotton for afternoon wear. I saw a dozen pairs at the Fenleys!"

"Mrs. Farley thinks they are hers. Maybe this will help her decide." Hunt lifted one glove and shook it gently. A small golden star tumbled into his palm.

"My lucky piece!" Cynthia gasped. "Of course they're mine. Now I remember, I dropped them with my purse when Eric fainted and fell against me. Mr. Bruce gave me the purse, but he didn't notice my gloves, I guess." She extended her hand, but Hunt returned the gloves to his pocket.

"So many things Mr. Bruce forgot, or didn't notice," he said. "Do you mind if I hang onto these for a while, Mrs. Farley? We'd like to run a few tests on them."

"Tests?" she murmured, puzzled. "For what?"

"Powder stains." Hunt's glowing eyes watched her for reaction. "If you don't object?"

"Not at all." Cynthia's clear conscience allowed her to speak calmly, but she felt stirrings of alarm. "Your idea is that I shot Miss Crane, wearing my gloves to avoid finger prints, and then dropped them there for you to find? Rather stupid, wasn't I?"

"Or too panicky to think?" Hunt stood up. "I've got a lot of things to do, Miss Shaw, so I'll run along—for now. You won't mind if I drop in again later?"

"Delighted, Lieutenant. I shall be agog to hear of new developments." She ushered him out with regal courtesy, and returned to eye Cynthia with a worried frown.

"Don't tell me," Cynthia smiled, "that you are becoming suspicious of me, too."

"You know better, my dear. But I can't say I like Harry Hunt's attitude. A nice local boy who has done very well for himself, but he seems a little too officious. The idea of his holding the faintest suspicion of you or Neal! I'm not so sure about that Herbert woman." She paced the floor, shaking clasped hands. "I'm going to call Cousin Alexander, he should be here."

"Oh, *no!*" Cynthia objected.

Miss Shaw stopped pacing and stared at her.

"Why not? That policeman has ideas about you, and you're not going to fight him alone. Alexander is a lawyer—"

"I—I would rather you didn't call on Mr. Houston."

"Nonsense! He's my lawyer, isn't he? I don't know what you and he have been up to, but it's something silly, I'm afraid."

"Why, Miss Shaw!"

"Don't 'Why, Miss Shaw' me! I may be old, but I'm not senile yet. I intended to relieve him of pursuing females by having a married secretary." Her snort of derision was bitter. "All I accomplished was to put the shoe on the other foot, evidently. I should have known better than to hire such an attractive girl, married or single! Of course he'd fall in love with you!"

"You mustn't say such things!" Cynthia protested, conscious of flushing cheeks and pounding heart. "Alex has never mentioned the subject—"

"Nor given any hint?" the other snapped. "You two must think that I am blind. When you and he left the dance in his car—and were back in ten minutes—and you disappeared for the rest of the evening—!" She left the sentence unfinished. "However, that is your affair. This police business, as long as you are in my employ, is *my* affair, and I intend to handle it properly."

She crossed to the telephone and dialed the hotel desk, tapping her foot impatiently until the clerk answered.

"This is Miss Shaw," she said. "Please call Alexander Houston at his home in Boston." She gave the number with careful distinctness. "Simply tell him that I want him down here as soon as possible. Put the call through at once, and keep on calling until you reach him."

XVIII

THE EVENING dragged its hours away at a snail's pace. Cynthia was in wholehearted agreement with Miss Shaw's reluctance to appear in the Harbor House dining room and become the target for a barrage of questions, so together they ransacked the refrigerator of her apartment. The result was a pair of what Miss Eva christened "stuffed-club sandwiches" rather clumsily assembled but delicious when accompanied with steaming coffee. Thereafter they sat numbly before the television set through a succession of programs not one of which Cynthia could have identified afterward.

At ten-thirty the doorbell rang and Miss Shaw groaned.

"Part Two of the Great Interrogation, my dear," she complained. "Let the lieutenant in."

But it was Alex Houston who stood outside, and Cynthia's surprise was mingled with a surging relief so intense that she could not speak, but only extended both hands in eager welcome.

" 'I'll come to thee by moonlight,' " he quoted softly and entered the living room with a cheerful smile for his cousin. "So at last you are up to your neck in murder, Eva; I'm sure you must be very much delighted."

"Delighted to see you, anyway. But I'm not the one who needs your legal assistance. Cynthia is the suspect."

Alex lost some of his nonchalance. "I didn't get that from the hotel operator or I would have burned up the road to get here. You're not serious, I hope?"

"I'm afraid we are," Cynthia admitted, "but perhaps it's nothing to worry about." She sank into a wing chair and found herself smiling. With Alex there her confidence was reborn; he would make short work of Lieutenant Harry Hunt's wild assumptions.

Alex removed a protesting Topaz from the couch and sat down. His concentration on Cynthia while she told what had happened was flattering but unsettling; his eyes never left her face. When she came to the missing pair of gloves he grunted.

"You had the gloves at the tea, I noticed them. Didn't Neal tell the police that you were wearing them when he met you outside the Annex?"

"Apparently he didn't. But remember, he tried to keep me out of it at first."

"Just about the worst thing he could do," Alex growled. When the doorbell rang, he looked questioningly at his cousin. "Visitors at this hour?"

"Lieutenant Hunt—playing a return engagement," Cynthia hazarded with a smile, and admitted the officer who was plainly thrown off stride by Houston's presence, although he shook hands cordially.

"Haven't seen you for some time, Mr. Houston. Glad you came down to help the ladies."

Alex raised his eyebrows. "They need help?" He sounded incredulous. "I've been hearing about the death of Miss Crane, but surely you aren't trying to connect either one of them with it?"

"I'm not *trying* to—just doing my job. You say that you've been given the details. Maybe I can add to your information. We've put in a busy evening—and a productive one." Hunt moved to his former seat on the Hitchcock chair near the window. "We've had to alter some of our ideas."

"Including, I hope," Miss Shaw said with sarcasm, "your suspicion of my secretary."

Hunt ignored that. "Miss Crane was killed by someone on the fourth floor. There is a bullet hole in the glass door there and we found the empty brass shell from a .38 automatic in a corner near the head of the stairs. Because there were no powder marks on the glass, and from the angle of fire, we figure the murderer stood in the doorway of Suite Four and shot as the car came down—or up, we can't tell which."

"Down, I should think," Cynthia suggested, "or the car would have stayed at the top. Unless, of course, the murderer came to the ground floor and pushed the button to bring it down—which seems unlikely."

"Very!" Alex agreed. "Nice figuring, Cynthy."

"Yeah—I should have thought of that," Hunt growled. "Anyway, we're sure of Number Four as the murder scene. And it was a perfect set-up; an empty apartment with the door left unlocked for the workman, and the fire escape to go or come on without being seen in the building. Or from outside, either, because of the tall trees along the back. And there are plenty of recent marks on the fire escape."

Alex spoke from the couch where he lounged carelessly. "Made by the workmen?"

Hunt shook his head. "They say they haven't used it; as they're all local men, we believe them. But someone's used it lately—and left no fingerprints. More proof that the murderer wore gloves." Although he avoided looking at Cynthia his thought was obvious.

Alex must have read his mind for he laughed. "Going to hang on to Mrs. Farley's gloves, even though you found them on the ground floor?"

"Yup—because they were in the corner between the elevator shaft and the stairway—just about where they'd land if someone dropped them over the railing from above."

"Oh, Harry!" Miss Eva protested sharply. "If there's much more of this foolishness I'll lose my mind! I refuse to listen!" She bounced up from the couch and began to gather the teacups and plates from the coffee table with impatient clatterings.

"Let me do that." Cynthia advanced to relieve her of them.

"Stay where you are! I'm perfectly capable of clearing away —and you are not a servant. Besides," with biting sarcasm, "Lieutenant Hunt has further damning evidence against you, I'm sure. Give him a chance to make a complete fool of himself!" She stalked out and they heard her noisily stacking dishes in the kitchen.

Cynthia felt an unwilling sympathy for the officer, whose ruddy face was a deeper crimson. It must be difficult to impress an elderly and opinionated lady who had known him since his boyhood.

"I am perfectly willing to answer any questions, Lieutenant," she encouraged. "But really, do I look like a girl who goes around shooting people?"

"I don't know as there are any distinguishing marks for that, ma'am."

"But we do know, Hunt," Houston said dryly, "that she *is* a girl who will take off in an unfamiliar plane to rescue a couple of boys in danger. The two characters don't seem to fit together, do they?"

"We're still going to test those gloves," Hunt stated doggedly.

Cynthia refused to take him seriously. "If you do find powder stains, they will be face powder. By the way, have you decided on my motive for this murderous attack?"

"On the night of the dance you had a fight with Miss Crane."

At this totally unexpected charge Cynthia's heart stopped and then pounded with apprehension. Where had the officer learned that? How much did he know about it? Of course there had been a number of people within sight and hearing at the time. Naturally the police would question everyone in the Harbor House, and people did enjoy gossip. If Hunt had not already learned the whole story he soon would. Better to co-operate than arouse further suspicion by attempting to conceal it. She sent a silent appeal for guidance to Alex; his sober nod confirmed her own judgment.

"That is true, Lieutenant," she admitted reluctantly. "I had a—an argument—quite a scene, I suppose, with Miss Crane on the hotel porch. She seemed under the impression that I was —well, pursuing her brother." Indignation at the memory overrode caution. "She didn't mince words. According to her I am trying to ensnare Eric, intending to get a divorce so that I can marry him!" With an impatient laugh she added, "She lost her temper—and so did I."

Hunt scratched his chin with the notebook he had withdrawn from his pocket.

"And was there any basis for her charges?"

"None at all! Actually I would have preferred to avoid him completely, but you know that isn't possible at a dance."

"So you don't like him?" Hunt referred to his notes. "The Cranes haven't been here long; wasn't your dislike—and the sister's attitude sort of sudden? Or had you known them before?"

Once again the unlooked-for accusation shook Cynthia, and again she realized that more of her conversation that night might have been overheard.

"Better explain, Cynthy," Houston advised. "It will avoid trouble."

"I did know Eric before—in California. I haven't mentioned it because—because the whole experience was unhappy and I hoped to forget it."

"Sorry, but I'd like to hear about it." Hunt sounded genuinely apologetic. "So you knew the Cranes already?"

"Only Eric. We—we were engaged for a short time and then called it off."

"Did Miss Crane have anything to do with this broken engagement?"

"Oh, no! She was in England then, I imagine. No, it was entirely between Eric and me."

"She could have known of it, written him to break it."

"That wasn't the way it happened." Her voice trembled as she relived the shame of that tragic afternoon.

"Suppose we say that was the explanation, though." Hunt pounded out the words. "Naturally, you were sore. Right? So when you meet here—"

"Hold it, Lieutenant!" Houston ordered sharply. "You're letting this run away with you."

"I'm going to find out what happened!"

"You have been told that, by Mrs. Farley, so stop trying to sell her *your* version of it. This isn't a brain-washing session, so pull in your horns." He walked over to the officer and stood, hands on hips, frowning down at him. "You have only the flimsiest excuse for questioning her at all. A pair of gloves, which she explained."

"And where she was all the time until six o'clock!"

"Let's come back to that point later. You are now attempting to manufacture a motive," Alex challenged, "and I don't like your method. Mrs. Farley is not on the witness stand, remember. We are willing to help you on this case with any pertinent information, but the minute you try to intimidate my client I'll direct her to refuse to answer."

Hunt gaped at him. "You mean you're acting as her lawyer?"

"I didn't come down here at this time of night just for the ride." Houston returned to his seat on the couch. "Now go ahead, but watch your step!"

Visibly shaken, the lieutenant hesitated. "Well, I still think the quarrel is pertinent, Mr. Houston. It shows bad feeling between the women—"

"You are *assuming* again, Hunt—cut it out! The bad feeling was only on Miss Crane's part. I heard the altercation and would testify that any threats were made by her. As to the broken engagement, Mrs. Farley states that the sister had no part in it. On what grounds do you insist that isn't true?"

"I was only suggesting it, Mr. Houston. We've been through the victim's effects at the hotel; she seems to have a pretty flush income from some estate in England. And according to stubs in her checkbook it looks like she's been supporting this brother for quite a while, so maybe she was running his personal life, too."

Miss Shaw entered in time to hear that and put in the acid comment, "She ordered him around like a lackey!"

"Yeah?" Hunt glanced at Cynthia. "Seems like she rode herd on him and his girl friends, too."

"The mother complex," Miss Shaw sniffed. "I noticed it that first night. Remember, Cynthia? I spoke of it—"

Alex intervened with an indulgent smile. "Let's stick to facts, Cousin Eva. The lieutenant just introduced an interesting one. Miss Crane's inherited income. I wonder if it goes to Crane on her death?"

"And he got tired waiting for her to die? You're right on the ball, sir, aren't you!" Hunt made a note in his book. "We can get the dope on that from England, I guess. And we sure will ask Crane some questions the minute the doctor will let us at him. But his fainting spell washes him out as a suspect," the officer admitted with regret. "If he already knew she was dead, why should he pass out like that?"

Houston shook his head. "I can't judge because I didn't see him, but are you sure he wasn't faking?"

"Oh, no!" Cynthia was positive. "It was frightfully real!"

"Dr. Ferguson says the same," Hunt admitted, "and *he* wouldn't be fooled. Any other suggestions for me, Mr. Houston?"

Cynthia almost laughed at the humble question. The leaden apprehension was lifted from her heart by Alex Houston's presence, it had lightened by the minute while he took up her defense until no shadow remained. In this happier mood some quirk of memory recalled a favorite story in which an inept Inspector Gregory respectfully asked Sherlock Holmes, "Is there any other point to which you wish to call my attention?." She darted a glance at Alex and knew from his amused expression that he shared her enjoyment.

"There is something you brought up before, Hunt," he said thoughtfully. "You wonder where Mrs. Farley was at the time of the murder. How about the others?"

"Yeah—how about them! Every one with an alibi. We've been able to check Bruce's. He did drive up the coast, had a flat tire about five, got it fixed in a filling station on Route Seven." Hunt flipped back a page in his book and refreshed his memory from it. "A kid named Oren Hunter did the job, and Bruce slipped him five bucks for it because the boy was supposed to go off duty at five-thirty but stayed on his own time to finish it. He remembered Bruce for that, you can bet."

"Scratch Neal Bruce, then, which is no surprise. He isn't a killer."

"Ferguson's cleared, too, and we're still following up on Miss Herbert—and Mrs. Farley."

"Then hurry up!" Miss Shaw commanded, "so you can forget your asinine assumption that Cynthia left the tea early, climbed a fire escape and shot Miss Crane! She was with me all day until she left the Fenleys, where would she get a pistol? And how did she know that woman would be here in the Annex—where she doesn't live—at any particular time?"

Houston leaned forward, elbows on knees.

"That's a good question, Hunt," he acknowledged. "What *was* Miss Crane doing here? Apparently everyone in the Annex was away then, there was no one for her to call on."

"That's something we ought to find out, all right. She being dead makes it difficult." Hunt thoughtfully tilted back in his chair until it squeaked in protest.

"Harry!" Miss Shaw protested nervously, "sit straight or take another chair! I'm rather fond of that Hitchcock."

"Sorry, ma'am." Abashed he got to his feet and closed his notebook, any further questions driven from his mind by the reprimand. "It looks like we've got plenty of work to do, and I'd better get after it. Good night, ladies, and thanks for your time. You, too, Mr. Houston; I've a hunch that you can be a lot of help to me, if you will."

"Glad to assist, as long as you don't ask me to help you pin the rap on Mrs. Farley." Alex accompanied Hunt to the door. "That wouldn't be consistent with my position as her lawyer, would it?"

When he returned to the living room Cynthia said earnestly, "I want to thank you, Alex, for coming to my defense when the lieutenant tried to confuse me."

"He was way out of line, and he knew it. Hunt's a good man, but not too experienced in as serious a case as this; Newbury Harbor doesn't go in for murders. His preoccupation with your gloves shows how desperate he is for clues. Don't worry about it."

"I'm not a bit worried—since you arrived, you always restore confidence. And I'm very grateful."

Miss Shaw sniffed. "You objected strenuously when I wanted to call Alexander!"

"I—I didn't want to bother him," Cynthia protested with pink cheeks.

"Bother?" Alex laughed. "It's a treat, especially when I find *you* involved. Besides, I enjoy coaching the lieutenant, makes me feel like Sherlock Holmes." He smiled at the girl. "I saw you catch his echoing of Inspector Gregory's appeal to the great detective. So did I. Great minds run in the same channels, they say; we must be soul mates."

"We must *all* be tired out," Miss Shaw broke in. "High time to retire. You are staying at the Harbor House, Alexander?"

"Certainly, until this affair is ironed out. Why don't you turn in, Cousin Eva?" It was a pointed suggestion. "I have a couple of matters to take up with Cynthia."

"As her lawyer?" demanded Miss Shaw suspiciously.

"What else?"

Cynthia had a premonition, or rather a certainty, that legal questions were far from his intention and the light in his eyes frightened her. She was too emotionally worn out to trust herself if he should demonstrate his affection as he had that night in the car. Even his unexpected arrival so late in the evening had betrayed her into a far warmer welcome than she had intended. It was strange how quickly forgotten was her indignation at his philandering with "another man's wife." It required an effort to remind herself of it now and school her voice to calm indifference.

"I really am tired," she apologized. "Could you wait until tomorrow?"

"It won't take long—"

"For heaven's sake!" Miss Eva protested. "Leave the poor girl alone!"

Cynthia caught the flicker of amusement in his eyes as he looked from her to his cousin, and knew from the quirk of his lips that he would not say what he had intended. Instead he shrugged and spread his hands.

"It's merely that I wondered if we shouldn't cable Alonzo Farley about this affair."

"Alonzo?" Cynthia gasped, completely taken aback. "Why in the world tell him?"

Alex studied her amazement with the trace of a smile. "You don't feel that *your husband* should be notified?"

"My goodness!" Miss Shaw sighed. "Perhaps you are right, Alexander. I never gave him a thought!"

Neither had Cynthia, but now she did. A vision of Lon abandoning his trip to speed to her side shocked her speechless. And he would come, she knew; arrive cursing the idiocy of "fool girls" and the jams they got themselves into, but ready as always to move heaven and earth to rescue her, just as he had done that day in California.

He might even, by this time, be back in the States—only a day's flight away! And the endless explanations and apologies entailed by the appearance of a fuming brother instead of a worried husband—! Mentally she quoted, " 'Oh what a tangled web we weave, when first we practice to deceive!' "

Aloud, and as coolly as she could, she scoffed, "How absurd to worry him with this, when it doesn't amount to anything! Does it, Alex?"

"Who knows?" There was nothing comforting in his manner. "The gloves—no; that quarrel with Miss Crane may be awkward."

"What's this?" Miss Eva frowned. "Did *you* quarrel with her, too, Cynthia?"

"Yes. I didn't tell you, it seemed unnecessary, but I had the same scene with her that Claire Herbert did."

"The woman was mad; I suspected it."

"Let me in on this," Alex snapped. "Are you saying that Miss Crane bawled out Claire Herbert as she did you? For the same reason? Do you suppose Hunt knows about that?"

"He seems to have picked up an awful lot of information," Cynthia sighed. "Maybe he does; remember his remark about Miss Crane 'riding herd' on Eric and his girl friends? Plural, you notice."

"Then I hope he's following up that angle, too, and double-checking her alibi. I'll make sure he knows before I turn in."

"I wish you wouldn't mention it," Cynthia disagreed. "I like Claire, and she simply couldn't have had anything to do with it, when she was nowhere near the Annex."

"Then she has nothing to worry about." Alex waved away that subject and returned stubbornly to the previous one. "I repeat, you should let your husband know what's going on."

"But what could he do—six thousand miles away?" Cynthia fervently hoped that he was. "It will only upset him."

"That's a fairly mild word, isn't it?" Alex shrugged. "However, you know best, Mrs. Farley. Well, I'll see you all in the morning."

"Wait." Miss Shaw laid her hand on his arm. "Now it is I who wish to have private words—with my lawyer," she emphasized with a smile for Cynthia. "Run along to your room, my dear; a good night's rest is what you need."

Powerless to object without being discourteous to her

employer Cynthia retired, feeling very much like a small child who has been sent to bed by her parents just when the party promised to become interesting.

XIX

CYNTHIA slept late the next morning, so late that Miss Shaw had gone to breakfast leaving a curt note pinned to her door. The note was on a pale orange index card, a color which Cynthia automatically identified as referring to the Talbot-Whittaker branch of the Shaw family, but it did not concern them.

Couldn't wait, Sleepyhead, the lady had scrawled in evident haste. *Alexander has news. Join us if you are interested.*

What a perfectly fiendish sense of humor she has, Cynthia thought, hurrying to dress. No mention of what the news might be, whether good or bad, and not even the decency to wake me so I could hear it when she does! She flung into a candy-pink cotton dress, pulled a white cashmere sweater around her shoulders, and hurried out of the house and across the drive to the hotel dining room.

The cousins had finished their meal and were waiting for her, Alex smoking a cigarette while he smilingly watched Miss Eva leaf through the morning paper with an angry frown.

"Here you are!" he greeted, rising to draw out a chair for Cynthia. "Fresh from a highly successful beauty sleep, I can see."

"For goodness' sake, Cynthia, sit down!" Miss Shaw commanded. "In another minute I should have burst with impatience!"

"What's the big news?" Cynthia demanded breathlessly.

"I haven't the faintest notion! He impudently refused to tell me until you came!"

"Since it concerns my client," Alex soothed, "I naturally—"

"And haven't *I* been your client?" his cousin snapped, "since you passed the bar examinations?"

"Certainly, but this is the case of the State versus Cynthia Farley, another client."

"Oh, stop it!" Cynthia implored. "Tell me at once—but first, *please,* is it good or bad?"

"Good." With a triumphant flourish Alex drew a pair of white gloves from his pocket and laid them before her. "The police returned your property with proper apologies, but thinly disguised disappointment." Grinning broadly he shook his head. "No powder marks, to their apparent sorrow."

"Who but Harry Hunt would expect to find any!" Miss Shaw scoffed.

"Don't be too hard on him," Alex urged. "He was in a spot—he still is—grabbing at anything to give him a lead. His superiors are bearing down on him, demanding action, and he hasn't a single clue to follow up. Except Cynthia's grudge against Miss Crane, as he sees it."

"I'll make him the laughing stock of Newbury Harbor if he keeps on with that brain storm!" Miss Shaw promised with gleaming eyes.

"Please don't," Cynthia begged. She would be glad to have suspicion against her dismissed, but since she had never considered it serious the relief would be minor. She felt along the fingers of the gloves without success. "Didn't they give back my lucky star, too?"

"Why, yes," Alex admitted after a moment's hesitation. "I have that. I wonder if you would let me keep it—just for a while. Having heard of your success with it, I'd like its power working for me in a certain project I have in mind."

The warmth in the look which accompanied the request sent little shivers of excitement along Cynthia's nerves. It was strong enough to attract the attention of Miss Eva as well.

"A case you are going to try, Cousin Alexander?" she asked archly.

"It has certain legal aspects, to be sure." His eyes never left the girl's face.

"Of course you may borrow it," Cynthia agreed, and to prevent him from pursuing the subject asked, "Aside from a few far-fetched suspicions, am I completely cleared with the police?"

Houston became absorbed in grinding out his cigarette in the glass ash tray.

"There's nothing to worry about," he encouraged. "They will locate someone who saw you walking along the shore." He looked up with a reassuring grin. "Lieutenant Hunt is as sure of that as I am. You needn't have a single worry when we see him at ten o'clock."

"He's coming here?" Cynthia had a recurrence of her nervous tremors.

"No, we go to his office, but it has nothing to do with any suspicion of you, trust me. Something new has come up and Hunt thinks we may be able to help him. You, because of your connection with the Annex, and me"—he laughed deprecatingly—"because he's taken it into his head that I'm Sherlock Holmes. So eat your breakfast, Dr. Watson, and sharpen your wits."

Lieutenant Hunt's office disappointed Cynthia. From the movies and television she expected a spacious room bustling with cigar-chewing detectives and hard-faced patrolmen. But Newbury Harbor was of necessity economy-minded. The red-haired lieutenant occupied a small cubicle partitioned off in a corner of the police station. He looked up from a scrambled pile of papers on his desk as Cynthia and Houston entered, took in the girl's immaculate pink dress and hastily brushed off a chair with his shirtsleeve before offering it to her. "Sit down, ma'am," he invited. "Morning, Mr. Houston. Glad you could come over, maybe you can help—if you want to bother with us, that is."

"Anything I can do, Lieutenant," Alex promised, "but don't expect too much from me, I'm no mastermind. I understand that you've dug up something new."

"I'll say, and it's thrown me for a loop. First, though, I'd better tell you that Crane is out of the picture as a suspect. That was a bright suggestion of yours, Mr. Houston; at least it cleared the air. We've heard from London—all the details we asked for. Miss Crane did have an income from the estate of a distant relative—for as long as she lived. On her death it all goes to a charity foundation in England. Her brother inherits nothing, so he wasn't likely to have anything to do with wiping out the woman who had been contributing regularly to his support."

Alex nodded. "That seems conclusive. Have you been able to talk to him yet?"

"Sure—this morning. He's up and around now, but still shaky. Dr. Ferguson tells me that Crane has been in a highly nervous state as long as the Doc has known him, and his sister's murder naturally didn't help. He's gone to Boston to arrange for shipping the—" Hunt checked himself with an apologetic glance at Cynthia and finished, "—to make the necessary arrangements."

He leaned across his desk to pick up a key from the wire basket. It was of brass, with a brass tag attached, and Cynthia recognized the familiar shape of a Harbor House key. Hunt dangled it by the tag.

"This is the new development I mentioned," he said wearily, as though resigned to a succession of new developments. "Remember nobody could figure out what Miss Crane was doing in the Annex elevator? This key was in her purse. We were careless, we assumed it was for her room at the hotel. We didn't need to use it as the manager let us in there when we examined her things. This morning, for the first time, I really looked at it."

He held up the brass tag for inspection.

"5-A," Cynthia read on it. "Why, that's an Annex key! Number Five is the Whitehead apartment! Where Claire Herbert is staying. But why should Miss Crane have it? They were—were far from friendly."

"This isn't Miss Herbert s key—I mean the one she uses—it's the spare, and Miss Crane got it from the hotel desk."

Alex sat forward. "Why would they hand that over to her? What kind of a story did she give them?"

"No story needed," Hunt sighed. "Miss Crane simply sailed up to the desk while the clerk was in the back office and told the switchboard girl to hand her the key to Number Five in the Annex—and got it! The girl explains that she assumed Miss Crane had left hers in her room and wanted to get back in—and she didn't use her head enough to remember that Miss Crane lived in the main house."

He shrugged. "From the kid's story, the English woman acted so high and mighty that she just jumped to obey her royal command."

"I can believe that," Cynthia nodded. "Miss Crane could be extremely overbearing at times. But why did she want to get into Claire's place?"

"Maybe for another battle?" Hunt nodded at her surprise. "Sure, we know about the one at the dance. Haven't said anything about it to Miss Herbert—yet, and don't you tell her either."

"You intend to spring it on her?" Houston asked with distaste.

"At the proper time."

Alex shrugged. "Not the way I'd handle it, but you're in charge. As to Miss Crane, though, if she thought this Herbert woman was at home, why get the duplicate key?"

"Huh, you're right!" Hunt registered disappointment. "I got off the track again, I guess. Miss Crane must have believed she *wasn't* there."

"Probably she knew it," Cynthia suggested thoughtfully. "I told you that Claire has been going to rehearsals every evening this week, because the play is almost ready to open. The whole Harbor House knows that; everyone is interested in Neal Bruce's Summer Theater venture, and there's a lot of talk about it."

A loud rap at the door was followed by the head of the young patrolman who sat at the desk outside. He jerked a thumb over his shoulder.

"That Herbert dame, Lieutenant," he whispered.

Hunt glared at the discourtesy. "Show *Miss* Herbert in, and get a chair for her!"

Cynthia was glad to see that Claire had taken pains to make a good impression. No tight slacks this time, no absurdly high-heeled slippers. The bold print skirt and short-sleeved cardinal red sweater made no particular display of her figure and her pretty face wore only a touch of makeup.

"I'll bet I know what you dragged me down here for," she charged bluntly, taking the chair which the young officer had wedged into the crowded room. "Did you find something of mine in the elevator, like you picked up Mrs. Farley's gloves and made a Federal case of it?"

"Who told you about the gloves?" Hunt barked.

"For Pete's sake! D'you think *anybody* in this town doesn't know about them? And anything of mine you found, I can explain—if you'll believe me. Which from what I've heard I doubt. I was in a hurry yesterday, when I got in the elevator. I caught my handbag on the door and spilled half the stuff in it. That's God's truth!" she finished breathlessly. "What did you find?"

"Nothing," Hunt said with a grin.

"Oh!" Claire's laugh was strained. "I guess I talk too much. I couldn't imagine what I'd missed, I was on my hands and knees most of the way down, picking up the stuff." She eyed the lieutenant speculatively. "What's the big idea calling me in here, then? Found a hole in my alibi?"

Obviously her directness confused Hunt and annoyed him as well. "As a matter of fact, Miss Herbert, we haven't had much luck with your story. You were at rehearsal all right, but from six-thirty on. Between five o'clock and then, there's a kind of yawning gap. Nobody remembers seeing you."

"That's just dandy, isn't it!" Claire muttered.

"We're in the same boat," Cynthia encouraged. "Nobody noticed me walking along the shore at that time, either."

"You should worry, with plenty of friends around here." Claire rolled her eyes at Alex. "Me, I'm on my own. O.K., Lieutenant, I'll play the record again for you; maybe it will click this time. I left my place a little after five, walked over to that Land's End eating pace, and had a snack before the rehearsal. There were a lot of people there—" She paused and lost some of her nonchalance. "Mostly a busload of sightseers, though, I guess."

Hunt grunted. "So they aren't around now—and wouldn't have known you anyway."

"But the help there should have noticed me! I've been in often, and talked to a lot of them."

"We've checked and not one of them saw you."

"Then they're lying!"

"Not necessarily, Miss Herbert," Alex calmed the brewing storm. "If it was busy, as you say, they might not remember you. Which waitress served you?"

The other bit her lip in an effort to recall. "Sorry—I didn't notice. I was studying my lines, and just ordered English muffins and iced coffee—and ate 'em when they appeared." With grudging honesty she offered, "Guess I'll take back my crack about them lying; I'm not so good on the memory test, am I?"

"Let's hope *somebody* remembers," Hunt grumbled. "But that isn't why I sent for you, Miss Herbert. You didn't return to the Annex until ten-thirty, and knew nothing of the murder until then?"

"That's right."

"When had you last seen Miss Crane?"

"Well, that afternoon, as a matter of fact. She came into the Annex just as I got out of the elevator. But we didn't speak. She glared at me and pushed past me into the car. I guess she went up, but I didn't wait to see. Didn't give a particular damn what she did."

"What time was this?" asked Hunt, making notes.

"A few minutes after five. I was on my way to eat, before the rehearsal, and—"

"Yeah—we've got that. So you didn't know that she was heading for your apartment?"

"*My*—" Claire gulped and her faced paled. "So that's it! Listen! I wasn't going to mention it, because I wasn't sure. When I got back from the theater it looked like someone had rummaged through my things. The way I'm camping in the Whiteheads' place, my stuff is mostly in one bureau drawer and a suitcase, and I'm not too neat. But even so, things seemed kind of stirred around—know what I mean?"

Hunt's grunt was noncommittal, his expression skeptical. "Anything missing?"

"I don't think so, and I wasn't worried, because I don't leave anything worth stealing lying loose. Honest," she smiled, "the first thing I checked was the fish tanks, Neal—Mr. Bruce, made such a to-do about taking care of them that he's got me nervous, too. The fish looked O.K." Suddenly sober she mused, "So that old buzzard was giving my things a going over! What crust!"

"Why would Miss Crane want to do that?" Hunt asked.

"How do I know!" Claire's cheeks had an angry flush. "She's a nosy old witch who'd already bawled me out for chasing her worthless brother!"

Once more Hunt was staggered by her frankness. He sat back and rubbed his chin.

"We know about that quarrel—"

"Why wouldn't you? Half the dance crowd heard it." Caustically she suggested, "Maybe the old fool thought I had Eric hidden in my suitcase!"

Hunt started an angry retort but Alex intervened. "If Miss Herbert isn't sure about it, perhaps her things weren't searched, Lieutenant. Miss Crane might have intended it, but was killed on the way up."

"No, Alex," Cynthia objected quickly. "You thought I was clever to figure out that the car must have been coming down, because we found it on the ground floor."

Houston made a courtly bow. "Right you are, Watson! I forgot about that."

"Watson?" Hunt asked with a puzzled grin. "Oh—I get it. I wish I had a Dr. Watson to remind me of things."

Cynthia noticed that Claire had lost her color again and was fidgeting with her purse, ignoring the humorous interlude.

"Say," Claire exclaimed, wetting her lips, "you mean Miss Crane was shot when she came down from my room—as she went past the fourth floor?" She shivered. "And I'd come down there just before—the same way—! Nice thought, isn't it!" She looked at the lieutenant. "Are you through with me—can I go?"

"Unless you can tell us anything more."

"You know more about it than I do!" She stood up. "By the way—where's Eric—Mr. Crane? Haven't seen him around today."

"He went to Boston, to make arrangements about his sister."

"Oh. Oh, yes, he'd have to, wouldn't he." She licked her lips, her voice was husky. "You sure he'll be coming back?"

"Of course, later today. Why shouldn't he?" Hunt demanded sharply. "He isn't involved in this—he's completely broken up by it."

Claire opened her bag, surveyed herself in the mirror and applied a touch of lipstick. Her fingers trembled.

"I'll bet he is," she muttered. "He's got such a kind heart. Well, so long all!" She went out swinging her purse.

"A tough character," Hunt observed, and Houston agreed with a nod.

"How can you say that!" Cynthia demanded hotly. "She's a nice girl and I like her. She is terribly upset and—"

"What's she upset about?" Hunt demanded incredulously. "Nobody's charging her with anything—yet. That alibi of hers is probably all right—we just haven't hit the right person to okay it"

"*I* find that something to worry about," Cynthia reminded. "I'm going after her and try to cheer her up."

"Go to it," Alex said. "If you have nothing better to do about one o'clock meet me at Land's End and we'll hold a conference over a lobster salad."

"It's a date." Cynthia hurried out of the police station and caught sight of Claire Herbert further down the street. She stood in front of a dress shop window dabbing at her eyes with a handkerchief. She turned with a start when Cynthia came up behind her and spoke.

"These police sessions are upsetting," Cynthia smiled. "I'm having a cup of coffee. Won't you keep me company?"

"That would hit the spot all right." Claire looked up and down the street. "We generally go in the Lobster Claw there, after rehearsals. O.K. with you?" She led the way to a restaurant which consisted of three small tables in front of a short counter and one tiny booth to which they carried their cups.

Claire gulped the black coffee nervously, although Cynthia found it too hot to drink.

"I sure needed something like this," she gasped. "Thanks for trailing me, Mrs. Farley—"

"Cynthia."

"Oh, all right, *Cynthia*. I don't know why you bother with me after what I did to you, though."

Cynthia smiled. "I thought we agreed that you did me a good turn, getting me out of Eric's clutches."

"You can say that again!" The other set down her cup and with a quick look made sure they were alone. "When I think that I was nuts about that guy once, I have to laugh." But there was no amusement in her voice. "I guess I got over it long ago, actually, and have just been stubborn, chasing him the way I have."

She leaned across the table as her voice dropped to a hoarse whisper.

"Look, kid—Cynthia, I mean, you've been awfully decent to me, I'm going to give you the straight dope. Eric Crane and I were married in England a couple of years ago."

"You—?" Cynthia stared at the other sympathetically. "—A divorce, among your other troubles?"

"There was no divorce."

Anger flooded Cynthia. "You mean he was *married,* and yet came to California and asked *me*—?"

"Hold everything!" Claire's smile was grim. "Don't get the wrong idea—he's no bigamist. It was a fake wedding—I found that out when he got sick of me in a few months and walked out. And me thinking I was Mrs. Joe Crandall—that was the name he used. I had a little money and was a perfect sucker. The ceremony was a joke, even the minister was a fake!"

"How awful!" Cynthia breathed.

"That's what I got for playing out of my class over there," Claire continued. "I told you I was with a theatrical troupe then. Lucky I held onto my job—Eric wanted me to, you bet! I knew there was a rich sister in the background that gave him money, and he was always scared she would catch onto us and disown him. I guess worry over that, and my nest egg running out, helped get him fed up with me.

"He disappeared finally, and it was only by luck that I located him again. Funny coincidence—it was his picture in the paper that did it, same as he found you here."

"Then he isn't a famous test pilot at all?" Cynthia asked.

"Yes, he was—pretty famous, I guess. But he had other irons in the fire, and those were what burned him. He was discharged by his company for something to do with gambling in the plant."

"But he's connected with that now!" Cynthia protested. "He's helping to uncover the men who operate it in these plants here."

"Who told you that?"

"He did—but don't mention it, because he's working secretly for our government."

"In your eye!" Claire snorted with withering scorn. "Cynthia, you are too trusting to be let out alone. No wonder that crook snared you in California; he's got a smooth line, don't I know! Listen—"

She paused and then slipped out of the booth as a couple entered the restaurant.

"Let's go outside where we can talk," she whispered. "You need to know the facts of life!"

They paid for the coffee and walked along the main street in the direction of the Harbor House. When they were clear of the town Claire took up her recounting of 'the facts of life.'

"So you think Eric's a G man now?" she sneered. "Listen, dear innocent girl, he was working for gamblers in that Lancaster plant in England when he was caught and fired. He was in with the same sort of crooks in California, too. When I traced him there—I guess you remember *that*—he promised to marry me legally if I gave things time to quiet down. And he gave me the money to live on while I waited. Say!" she stopped in the road and eyed Cynthia closely. "Did he get money from you?"

"Of course not!" Cynthia said indignantly.

Claire sniffed and walked on.

"Don't think I'm slandering him—he would have before long. I know! If he didn't scrounge it off you, then he got it from the gambling syndicate he worked for."

"But I thought his sister gave him money," Cynthia defended.

"Not then, she didn't, because she had an attack of something and was at death's door for months. No, I know Eric got his money from some of the crummy characters I used to see him palling around with. Guys like that Mantell we saw in town the other day; your reporter friend knew *he* was in the rackets, didn't he?"

Claire's sudden laugh was harsh and angry. "You should have seen Eric's face when I mentioned Mantell. Gee, we had a real showdown then!"

Cynthia hesitated, then confessed, "I heard it. I was downstairs in the hall. I'm sorry."

"Who cares? When I threatened to spill the beans about him and the gamblers he got so blazing mad that I locked the door on him. Honest, there was blue murder in his eyes. Don't ever monkey with a crook who's got pals that carry guns—it's too scary!"

"Why don't you forget him, Claire?"

"From now on I do! Lord, the time and tears I wasted on that creep before I found out what a real gentleman is like—too late. Skip it—and curtains for Eric Crane! Let's talk about something pleasant for a change."

XX

MISS SHAW was not in the apartment when Cynthia returned, but she had left a pile of manuscript with a note, this time on a gray file card.

Called to Boston, home late. Please type this, and forget Harry Hunt's nonsense. Eva S.

More easily said than done, Cynthia thought gloomily, dropping her hands from the keys after a few minutes of typing. It seemed impossible to recapture her former interest in the family history of the Shaws. She pushed back from the typewriter and sat staring out the window.

The ocean rolled in as always, unconcerned with human

problems, each wave pounding the rust-brown rocks with a spouting fringe of spray which glistened like jewels in the sunlight, then foaming on into the cove to overrun the sand in emerald beauty.

What a pity that with all this loveliness of nature some people were preoccupied by sordid crime and distrust. Poor Claire, after years of struggle and frustration, now plunged into the very heart of a mystery with which she could have had no connection.

Out in the hall the elevator rumbled its way upward, then stopped with a dull clatter. It had not run long enough to go to the fifth floor, was Cynthia's automatic reaction. Neal Bruce must be using it, for Claire had professed an aversion for that car since the murder details had been aired in Lieutenant Hunt's office. She would walk up the four flights of stairs with pleasure, she averred. No wonder; there had been nothing theatrical in her shudder when she remarked to Hunt, "I'd come down there just before! Nice thought, isn't it!"

Cynthia's heart skipped a beat and began thumping feverishly. Had the horror of yesterday's discovery permanently upset her nerves, conditioned her to only macabre imaginings? She sat gripping the table, unseeing eyes fixed on the ocean, while bits of Claire's rambling story flickered in her mind like threatening sparks, sparks which slowly merged into a smoldering flame of suspicion.

She stood up, shivering with excitement and uncertainty, afraid to pursue her thoughts to a conclusion without the support of a more experienced head. If Miss Shaw were here—but she would not return for hours. With sudden certainty Cynthia knew what she wanted most of all, and that was Alex Houston's reassuring presence; no terror could daunt her if he shared it. And he would be waiting for her at Land's End in—she looked at her watch—in fifteen minutes!

Alex was there as promised, sitting in the almost empty restaurant and chatting with the young Hungarian waitress. Cynthia controlled her impatient eagerness to confide in him until Anna had departed with their orders, only to have Alex take the initiative with a disturbing comment.

"Is there something depressing in the atmosphere today?" he asked. "I just remarked to Anna that she looked rather below par—which unfortunately didn't seem to help her any—and then you appear with a noticeable lack of color." His cheerful tone did not match the concern in his eyes.

"That doesn't help *me*, either," she confessed. "I am upset, because I have to tell you something—and dread it."

Houston put a hand over hers on the table.

He noticed Anna at the serving table behind Cynthia and put a cautioning finger to his lips.

The warning was wasted. The waitress, her cheeks waxen, placed a covered dish on their table and then leaned close to Cynthia.

"You are talking about the—the murder?" she whispered.

"Yes, but forget anything you overheard, Anna."

"I forget that, but please—you have been kind to me—will you help me?" Her big eyes implored them both. "The police came here asking questions—and I was afraid."

"Anna," Alex said earnestly, "don't ever be afraid of our policemen. Their job is to *help* people, and most of them try hard."

"It is not like that in Hungary—"

"Take my word for it, in America it's true. What did they ask you?"

"Not me, the other girls. I hide when they come in." Embarrassment brought color to her face. "I heard them ask about actress woman—Miss Herbert, is it?"

Houston nodded. "They wanted to know if she was here about five-thirty the afternoon of the murder."

"Yes." The whisper shook with apprehension. "She was here, at my table. I should have told?"

"You should have told," Houston said quietly. "But it's all right now, Anna. We'll tell Lieutenant Hunt for you. He may want you to come to the police station to make a statement—"

"Oh, please! No! What will they do to me?"

"Not a thing, honestly," Cynthia encouraged; the girl's fright was pathetic. "Alex, couldn't they send someone *here* to talk to her?"

"Good idea, I'll try and get Hunt to come himself, and I'll come with him."

"Would that be better?" Cynthia asked the girl.

With unexpected courage Anna shook her head. "Thank you, but no. I go to the police when I am off duty. That is the way in America, isn't it?"

"That's the way," Alex nodded. "And cheers for you, Anna. I'll tell them that you are coming."

When she left them he gave a muted whistle of sympathy. "Somehow that made me appreciate what life in her native land must have been; more than I've got from a dozen newspaper stories and films! And there are people who complain about life here in the U.S. I'll see that Hunt handles that girl with kid gloves!"

Near the end of the meal Houston abruptly brought up

another subject. "Are you still against notifying your husband of this matter, Cynthia? The papers are full of it today, and they'll have more with every edition."

"Oh, but Alonzo won't see them," she assured brightly. "And it won't be in any Japanese journals, I'm positive."

"Then he isn't back in this country yet? A while ago you gave the impression that your 'sabbatical year' would last only a few more weeks."

"Did I?" She wracked her brain to recall anything she might have said on the subject. She had better not commit herself now, against his memory which she had learned was razor sharp. She would avoid the issue if possible. "He knows that I'm all right," she smiled. "I've written him several times."

Houston set down his iced coffee with a clatter to stare at her quizzically.

"Have you indeed?" he murmured. "Written to your loved one *'several times'*! What splendid devotion!"

"Well, oftener than that, really." She gave all her attention to the last of her sherbet to avoid meeting his eyes. "I didn't want you to consider me a silly, lovesick bride who deluges her adored mate with letters."

"Shall I tell you what I do consider you?"

The restrained tenderness of the question warned Cynthia of his meaning and sent her pulse into a quickstep. But against every inclination she postponed a showdown. It would be inevitable, but not yet—not until she could devote her whole heart and soul to his appeal. At the moment too many conflicting ideas and questions swirled in her mind.

Taking that for a cue she answered slowly, "I—I think this is not the time or place for personalities, Alex. There are more important matters."

"As you wish." He stared silently at the tablecloth for a moment. "You refer to the Crane murder, of course. Very important, isn't it, since you are involved. Now, speaking as your lawyer, Cynthia, are there any facts I should be told before you get in any deeper?"

"I'm not going to get in any deeper!"

"That hardly answers my question."

"The answer is no." She snatched desperately for another topic of conversation. "Shouldn't you hurry over and tell Lieutenant Hunt about my theory of the murder?"

"I surrender," Alex laughed. "Obviously it's useless to try to interest you in any other subject until your brainchild has been presented to the authorities. I'll drive you to the Annex and then go to headquarters." He looked at his watch.

"Crane's supposed to see Hunt this afternoon and I want to be there when he does."

"Then never mind me. The walk back along the shore will blow the murder cobwebs out of my brain before I have to tackle the Saga of the Shaws."

Cynthia made a valiant effort to lose herself in Miss Eva's latest chapter, but too many times some facet of the Crane case and her own proposed solution of it caused her fingers to stumble on the keys. Too often she came out of a brown study to find that the fresh sheet of paper, inserted in the typewriter five minutes before, was still unmarked by a single word.

Alex would have told the lieutenant of her wild surmise by now; were they laughing at her untrammeled imagination? And by now Eric must have returned to Newbury; how would they broach the matter to him—if they considered it serious enough for that?

At half-past four she abandoned the futile struggle, changed into a swimsuit and robe, and fled to the sunshine outside.

Neal Bruce, who sat on the Annex steps with chin propped on clenched fists, moved aside to let her pass but his desolate expression made her pause. He nodded back toward the doorway.

"Is Claire still in there?"

"I don't know," Cynthia said. "Are you waiting for her?"

"I am, but I guess it's no use; she won't talk to me." He looked up hopefully. "Cynthia, she likes you, you could get her to listen to me. I might as well tell you—I've tried to convince her—I've fallen for her—No! That's no way to say it. I love her!"

Cynthia dropped down beside him on the step.

"Why, that's wonderful, Neal! But why the gloom? Don't tell me she turned you down?"

"Flat! At first I thought she might have the wrong idea—you know what I mean. But when I came right out and asked her to marry me she burst into tears and slammed the door in my face." He sighed. "Damn, what beastly luck! I've played the field for years, and when I find someone who suits me—curtains! She's such fun, ready for anything, but she can be serious when I want to be—and she's so pretty—beautiful, I think. Why did she have to turn me down?"

"Perhaps," Cynthia suggested cautiously, thinking of Claire's past history, "she doesn't want to involve you in—in any troubles she may have."

"You mean the phony wedding that was pulled on her? Forget it! She told me the story and it makes no difference —I still want to marry her!"

His devotion warmed Cynthia's heart. "It may be this murder she's been dragged into. But a waitress at Land's End has cleared her now, Neal. Tell her and try again. She may feel differently." With that encouragement and a heartening smile she left him to his problem.

She walked quickly beyond the hotel beach, deserted as usual, but as usual under the watchful gaze of a line of idling guests on the porch. Today she craved something different to take her mind off her problems. The cove where Tommy O'Hara had initiated her into the joys of skin-diving beckoned invitingly. But she had explored that until she felt she knew every inch of sand and ledges, above water and below.

She walked on to where the road swung close to the rocks with the gravel turnout for sightseers. Here the shore dropped steeply in brown and green boulders tumbled together like pebbles piled by a giant's hand, with intriguing crevices and dark caverns inviting exploration.

Mindful of Alex Houston's warning Cynthia climbed down to the water and swam about for a few moments, diving under to survey the bottom. It was clear sand all around, no dangerous ledges in sight. Reassured, she mounted to an overhanging rock a dozen feet up and enjoyed a succession of exhilarating dives which helped to wash her mind clear of anxiety and confusion. Then she came out to sun herself, removing her cap and fluffing her hair where it was damp.

It was annoying that heavy clouds began to mask the sun at once; to keep warm she must keep moving. Nearby, two tilted boulders formed a small cave whose sides were white with barnacles and still dripped moisture left by the receding tide. She crouched at the entrance, trying to make out details in the dark interior, but it was disappointingly bare. One small jellyfish flattened on the seaweed in the bottom, and one or two large periwinkles clinging to the wet rock.

At the top of the bank a car whirred in from the blacktop road and came to a crunching stop on the gravel of the lookout. Could it be Alex? she wondered. He seemed adept at arriving unexpectedly whenever she took a dip. Before she could move a man appeared at the edge, sending her heart into a tailspin of disappointment. It was not Alex, but Eric Crane.

There was no one on earth whom she had less desire to encounter at the moment, and she froze against the rock lest some movement might attract his eye. Perhaps only her dark hair would be visible from where he stood, and that might blend into the discolored stone around her.

Fortunately Eric was not studying the slope below, but stood, hands in the pockets of his sport coat while he looked up and down the shore road. Then he withdrew his right hand, swung it back, and with an underhand toss sent something flying out into the water. Without even waiting to see it splash he whirled back to his car. The door slammed and spinning wheels flung rattling gravel over the edge as he gunned the throttle and shot away.

Cynthia straightened from her cramped position with a gasp. The whirling suspicions were back, churning madly in her brain, making her knees quiver as she climbed the rocks. It had been something black and solid that Eric had thrown away. Suppose it was a pistol! That had been her impression as it soared in a slow arc and plunged from sight with a spout of foam.

With a thrill she realized how well this incident might fit into her suggested solution of Miss Crane's death. If Eric had hired some racketeer to get rid of Claire, something Alex and Hunt said could well have warned him of their suspicion and he would lose no time in putting the murder weapon where they could never find it. It might even be Eric's own pistol, supplied to the killer and then returned, an awkward thing to have in his possession if the police questioned him further. Well, they would never find it now.

With the thought came another which caught at her breath and started her heart thudding with mingled determination and apprehension. If that was a pistol that had been tossed there *she* might be able to salvage it. She turned to stare at the place where it had disappeared, gauging the angle and distance from her rocky point, fixing them in her mind.

It should be a simple task with her lately acquired knowledge. Not so pleasant as exploring the sunlit cove with Tommy; the clouds covered most of the sky now, darkening the water to cold blue steel. But there must be still light enough below the surface provided the water was not awfully deep. She slipped into shoes and robe and hurried down the road to the next cove and the O'Hara cottage.

There was no one in sight so she knocked on the screen door, waited, and then rapped harder. In her tense state she jumped when a voice behind her said, "Hi!"

A small boy, his tanned body bare except for grubby brown shorts, stood surveying her with calm blue eyes.

"Hello!" Cynthia smiled. "I'm looking for Tommy O'Hara, is he here?"

"Nope. He went fishing with the gang." The child scowled. "They wouldn't take me along, darn 'em!"

"Will he be home soon?"

"Shouldn't wonder." He cocked an eye at the sullen clouds. "Or they'll get soaked. You want to wait? Come in—I'm Sammy."

"Oh, of course—Tommy's brother." She too cast an anxious look at the ever darkening sky. "I'm in a hurry—I hope he comes soon. I wanted to borrow his mask and flippers to—to do a little diving. Tommy showed me how; I am Mrs. Farley."

"Yeah?" Sammy honored her with a gap-toothed grin and a fervent, "Say, you *are* pretty, like they said! Sure, you can have the stuff!" He darted into the house and came out with the equipment.

"I'd go with you only I'm not allowed away for another day, on account of that rotten old raft! You be careful, won't you? Gramp says nobody'd ought to go diving alone."

"I'll be very careful. And thank you, Sammy."

Back at the lookout point Cynthia climbed down to the water and strapped on the fins. It was annoying that her teeth chattered, and it was not the wind which made her shiver. The sea looked dark and forbidding. Clenching her teeth to repress her nervousness she took a final bearing on the supposed position of whatever Eric had thrown, fitted the mask, and slid under the surface.

It was even more eerie under the water; the possible consequences of what ever she might find chilled every nerve. What had before seemed lovely swaying garlands of seaweed now showed like writhing arms brushing her shoulders and hips, clutching to halt her and bind her fast forever. When she glided to the bottom, peering right and left through the mask, her hand touched a muddy patch which instantly sprang alive, whipped past her face in a swirl of dirty water, and sent her up in a panicky rush to grasp for air. Only a flounder, she told herself, disgusted with such timidity, and dived again with grim determination.

If there had been rocks and ledges here her search might have been endless, but the bottom was a smooth slope of sand and mud between the clumps of kelp and weed. On her third dive she came down almost on top of the black automatic pistol which lay at an angle, its muzzle tilted up at her face like a waiting snake. She slipped her fingers around the butt and surfaced with a frantic kick of the flippers, then swam ashore.

She stood on the rocks a moment, holding the gun, wondering if it was safe to handle—and what she should do with it. If only Alex were there—

"Don't be childish!" she advised herself impatiently. "You needn't lean on him for everything! Take it to the police at once, and let *them* carry on."

But it wouldn't do to appear in Newbury in a dripping swimsuit, and carrying a pistol. She took off the fins and laid them on a rock with the mask; better to return them to Tommy later—it might scare little Sam if she came back armed to the teeth.

She wrapped the gun in her bathing cap and tucked it into the pocket of the robe, but it bulged too noticeably and threatened to fall out. Finally she bundled it with the diving equipment into the robe and hurried to the Annex, feeling like Eliza crossing the ice with a precious baby in her arms.

XXI

IT WAS an unpleasant thrill, when Cynthia entered Miss Shaw's apartment, to hear muffled stirring somewhere in the back rooms. It wasn't likely that Miss Eva had returned unexpectedly, because her morning mail had been in the box downstairs.

"Who's there?" she called with assumed bravery.

"It's me, ma'am!" Mary the maid appeared, in uniform and pinning on her little white cap. She goggled at the bundle in Cynthia's arms. "Sweet Mother of the Angels—what have you got there? A—a body?"

"It's just some things done up in my robe, Mary. Did your sister have her baby all right?"

"Not yet—she'll have to get along without me! I never should have left Miss Shaw. I said so, too! Look at her now, mixed up in a murder case the minute I turn my back!"

"She isn't involved," Cynthia laughed. "She's enjoying it immensely."

"It ain't over yet!" Mary warned gloomily. "Once them police get after her, she'll know no peace. The minute I heard about it on the TV I knew my place was here. Someone has to take care of the poor old dear."

"That 'poor old dear' could give us pointers on taking care," Cynthia said impatiently. "Anyway, I was here with her."

"And you without sense enough to stay out of the water

on a raw afternoon like this! Look at you shivering and covered with goose flesh!"

"I'll go and dress, if you'll stop worrying me about Miss Shaw." Cynthia went past her as haughtily as the clumsy bundle permitted and took refuge in her room.

A racing car slammed to a stop in the driveway below, but she took no notice of it. She had dressed and was emptying her handbag so that it would hold the pistol when the door bell rang repeatedly. She heard Mary open the door, and then the maid's angry voice.

"Who are you shoving? Get back where you belong!"

An equally wrathful male voice barked, "Police business! Let me in—I want to see Mrs. Farley! Is she here?"

"You'll not get in by pushing, police or not. I'll scream!"

Cynthia hurried to the living room doorway. Lieutenant Hunt, his face an apoplectic purple, swept Mary aside and advanced with extended hand.

"All right, Mrs. Farley—let's have that gun!"

"It's all right, Mary," Cynthia said calmly, and smiled at the maid's look of horror when she produced the pistol from her bag. "Certainly, Lieutenant. How did you know? I was just dressing to deliver it to you."

Hunt eyed her suspiciously, weighing the weapon in his hand.

"Heard you had it," he growled, "and thought I'd better come over before you used it again."

His implied accusation caught her unprepared, and while she hesitated the half-open door was flung wide.

"Watch what you say, Hunt!" Alex Houston warned as he stepped in. "You have a bad habit of jumping to conclusions."

"Keep out of this, Houston! I'm running things now!"

"Then I certainly should be here to protect my client's rights," he pointed out calmly. "Mary, you'd better get on with your work; you aren't involved in this."

The maid bristled like a gaunt bulldog.

"I'm not leaving the likes of him loose in here!"

Houston laughed. "Trust me to protect Miss Shaw's property, Mary. He really is a policeman, so it's all right. Better run along while we sit down and talk this over."

"Well, then—!" With a final glare at Hunt Mary stalked away to the kitchen, the slam of a door registering her feelings beyond the possibility of misunderstanding.

It was so dark now that Cynthia switched on the lamp beside the couch and found that the cheerful glow improved her state of mind, especially when it made Alex's comforting smile more visible.

"Now, Mrs. Farley," he said, leaning on the back of a

chair and dropping his light manner for his courtroom tone, "if you wish to make a statement to the lieutenant you may do so. If not, say nothing."

"Of course I want to!" Cynthia had moved to shut the outside door, but turned to stare at Hunt while she considered how to begin. Somewhere above the elevator clanked to a stop and a man's harsh voice echoed down the stairway.

"Going out, huh? No, you're not! I'm coming in!"

"Beat it—I'm through with you!" Claire Herbert's angry retort was easily identified.

Cynthia promptly closed the door; she had no desire to overhear another Eric–Claire battle. She came back to face the two men.

"I've only been trying to help," she protested. "I was swimming at the lookout point beyond the hotel when Eric Crane drove up and threw the pistol into the water—"

"And you caught it in your teeth?" Hunt sneered. *"You* threw it in and—"

Houston shot out a long arm and jerked the officer around.

"I'm a patient man, Hunt," he said with ominous calm, "but if you don't stop these wild accusations I'm liable to forget myself and slug you!"

"Listen, you! I'm a police officer!"

"Then act like one! From the brawling I heard as I came upstairs anyone would take you for a thug. Cool off, man—be your age. Let Mrs. Farley explain."

Cynthia looked her gratitude and was encouraged by a smile in return.

"I believed Eric must be trying to get rid of evidence which would show who killed his sister," she said, "and thought I could recover it."

"Never thought of notifying us, I suppose?" Hunt demanded.

"It would have been impossible for me to show you the right place afterward, Lieutenant. With the tide at a different height everything would have looked different."

She went on with the sequence of borrowing Tommy's equipment, recovering the gun and returning to the Annex. The story progressed slowly because of Hunt's interrupting questions until Alex persuaded him to let Cynthia tell it in her own way.

"It seemed better to dress before I went to you with it," she ended, "and then you burst in. That's all."

"It isn't enough for me!" Hunt grumbled.

"Why not?" Alex demanded impatiently. "Use your head, man!" He turned to the girl. "At what time did this happen?"

"I left here about four-thirty, and swam a while—it must

have been around five o'clock when he appeared. I went after the gun as soon as I could, because clouds were making it so dark I was afraid I wouldn't be able to see under water."

Alex nodded. "Does that time suggest anything, Hunt? Crane left us in your office about five and drove off in his car. He was still badly shaken by his sister's death, wasn't he?"

"Why ask me? You saw him—but yeah, he acted pretty nervous."

"Especially," Houston queried, "after you mentioned the new angle I'd given you—we didn't bring Mrs. Farley into it—the possibility that the murderer shot the wrong woman?"

"You talked about that more than I did, kept coming back to it."

"I did, because his reaction was interesting. He grew more and more restless, he was sweating."

The lieutenant sat down, hands on knees, and stared at Houston.

"I didn't catch that," he admitted. "You don't miss much, do you. He did leave us pretty suddenly, when you kept firing questions." With grudging admiration he added, "I'd hate to be on the stand with you examining me."

To Cynthia it seemed that he *was* on the stand, with Alex guiding his thoughts. She was grateful for such a competent defender.

"This is an unofficial conference, so rest easy," Houston smiled. "Now I'll ask you what we call a leading question—one which any judge would order stricken from the record. Does it occur to you that Crane was most upset by the idea that the police might start hunting for someone who wanted to kill *Claire Herbert*—not Miss Margaret Crane?"

Hunt slapped his knee. "You mean he was so in the clear for his sister's death that we never questioned him—he's been coasting along without a care—but now things don't look so good!"

"They look so bad for him, that he leaves us and gets rid of the gun just as fast as he can."

Cynthia could not repress a question. "Then you think he did hire someone—a gunman—to kill—?"

"Nuts!" Hunt snorted. "That's the only part of your theory I can't buy, Mrs. Farley. I want to question Crane—and fast. We'll round him up now!"

"A few minutes ago," Cynthia offered with reluctance, "I heard Claire Herbert upstairs telling some man he couldn't come in her apartment—and it sounded like Eric."

"Damn!" Hunt left his chair with a rush. "I hope she

doesn't try to pressure him again—if it was Crane." He shut the outside door quietly behind him.

The increasing evidence against Eric gave Cynthia a sickly feeling, wracked her emotions with the many indications of his character which she had seen and ignored or weakly excused. What a fool she had been about him from the first! Now the very thought of him was a black cloud closing in on her, darker than the threatening sky outside.

If Alex hadn't taken her part, stood at her side so steadfastly—! But why imagine dangers which had never come to pass—Alex *had* stood by her, as he would for the rest of their lives, she was sure, if she gave the word. Not yet, though, not until this nightmare was completely ended.

"Thank you again, Alex," she whispered, as if she expected that someone might be listening, "for coming to my rescue. Lieutenant Hunt was so menacing that he frightened me. How did he know I had the pistol?"

"From one of your faithful O'Hara slaves. Tommy came home and heard that you'd gone diving alone—apparently the cardinal sin in that sport. He went to look after you, saw you come up with an automatic pistol, and wisely decided that it was the wrong plaything for a pretty girl. So he ran to town and told Lieutenant Hunt."

"And where did you hear of it, to arrive in the nick of time?"

"At the police station; I returned there with some more news for Hunt and promptly trailed him. If he hadn't been in such a hurry to gather you in his attitude might have been different. I left a man at the station eagerly supporting your alibi for the murder afternoon. Someone connected with the police saw you walking along the shore."

"But I don't know any policemen, except O'Hara, and he was at the Fenley tea."

"I said *connected* with the police." His smile was tantalizing, but then he took pity on her evident bewilderment. "One John O'Hara, grandfather to Tommy and Sam."

"The ex-lifeguard who was watching us skin-dive the other day!"

"Right. And you would have been flattered by his testimony. When his son mentioned your connection with the case Grandpa remembered seeing you." Alex rolled his eyes dramatically. "'It was her all right, in a dress like flame, and striding against the wind like a goddess!' was O'Hara's description. As you said once, the Irish are fundamentally poetic, but even a frigid Yankee can agree with that picture."

The conversation was taking a turn which could lead to

the showdown Cynthia hoped to postpone and she seized his last words to make a diversion.

"Speaking of ice-cold Yankees, your cousin is a rock to cling to in my troubles. Since the first news of the murder she hasn't turned a hair at any development, no matter how frightening."

Alex laughed. "Cousin Eva reminds me of what Thackeray wrote in his verse about Werther's death—

> "Charlotte, having seen his body
> Borne before her on a shutter,
> Like a well-conducted person,
> Went on cutting bread and butter."

He checked any further words to tilt his head toward the hall. Cynthia, too, heard the feet pounding up the first flight of stairs and she walked expectantly toward the door. But the pounding passed and began the second flight. She looked out in time to see a bellboy from the Harbor House disappear on the run.

"Do you suppose Lieutenant Hunt sent for help?" she asked over her shoulder.

"Who was that?" Houston joined her at the door.

"One of the bellboys. I'm sure he went to Five."

Alex snapped his fingers. "I should have gone along with Hunt; maybe there's trouble." He crossed the landing and punched the elevator button.

From above a boyish voice yelled, "Leave the car alone —the lieutenant wants it here! It won't run anyway, I've got the door open!"

Without a word Alex dashed for the stairs and Cynthia followed. If there was to be any excitement up in Number Five she meant to see it. But it was a punishing climb and Alex easily outdistanced her. She was panting from exertion and excitement when she reached the top.

"What's happened?" she asked the bellboy between gasps for breath.

"I dunno! The Lieutenant called the desk from Four— for a passkey to here in a hurry. And I brought it!" he said proudly.

Cynthia went into the apartment. Alex and the lieutenant were at a window, looking down the fire escape. The room was in disorder, a chair overturned, a crumpled towel on the floor showed ominous red stains. In the adjoining room a bed trailed blankets and torn sheets on the floor. With pounding heart Cynthia crossed to the window. Another smear of red on the white sill.

"Is—is that blood?" she whispered.

"Looks like it." Hunt leaned out the window, swore under his breath and came back in, beating a fist on the sill. "It must have been Crane—gone clean crazy. Knocked out the Herbert woman, tied her up and lugged her down the fire escape. You can see tire marks down there in the grass—his car!"

"Never mind that!" Houston snapped. "Let's get busy!"

"I have; called the station first thing from here. They'll throw roadblocks all over the point. He won't get away if he hasn't too much of a start."

He sent a rapid, searching glance around the room, then motioned them to go out.

"What a mess; she must have put up quite a fight. There's nothing to do here now, I'm going back to the station."

"Is she—do you think she's dead?" Cynthia gasped.

"How do I know? Why the devil did she go and rile him again, after what he tried last time? And all the while I'm sitting downstairs, gabbing with you!" Hunt snarled. "All right, out of here—I want to lock up."

He herded them out of the apartment, tried the door to be sure that it had locked, and brushed the boy away from the elevator.

"We'll get him!" he promised grimly, stepping into the car and closing the doors. His shadow loomed on the glass like an avenging demon dropping slowly into the depths.

Cynthia and Houston went down the stairs, too full of thoughts to speak. At the door of Miss Shaw's apartment the girl murmured, "Nothing to do but wait, now, and I can't say I look forward to it!"

"You're not going to wait here," Alex corrected gently. "Let's get away from all this for a while. Be my guest, Mrs. Sherlock Holmes, for dinner at Land's End."

"Please don't call me that! I'd like to forget my part in this dreadful business—but how can I!"

"For a start, come on to dinner. I promise to talk of nothing but the latest plays and books, the prospects of a World Series in Boston—in short, be the perfect escort. My car awaits below." His hand turned her toward the stairs.

Helping her into the convertible, he paused to scan the leaden sky.

"Still threatens rain, but I think it's a false alarm. However, if you'd like the top up—?"

"No, the more wind blowing through my weary brain the better," Cynthia decided. "Could we ride around for a few minutes before dinner? It might help get me back in the groove."

"I could use a little orienting myself."

Alex drove along the road to Newbury Harbor, skirted the town by a back street, and headed for open country. At once a police car darted out of a side road and pulled alongside. Officer O'Hara leaned from a window, recognized them with a grin, and waved them on as his car dropped back.

Houston was passing another side road lined with trees when he slowed to a crawl and pointed to it.

"Road to the air field, Cynthy—remember? What a lot has happened since we went up there that afternoon!" His warm smile was on her as he said softly, "A little heroine!"

"Careful!" she admonished half-seriously. "The perfect escort, please."

"Excuse the slip." Alex turned his head. "Sounds like a plane warming up on the field. Only a maniac would fly in this weather."

Cynthia jerked erect when his words penetrated, her fingers clenched. In a blinding flash that dizzied her she guessed what might be happening.

"Eric!" It was almost a scream, and startled Alex into jamming his foot on the brake. "It's Eric! He has a plane at that field—and he's getting away!"

Houston reacted with a speed which stunned her. The car backed almost into the ditch and then leaped ahead in a whirling turn that snapped her head back. He went far over the other shoulder of the road, skidded, pulled out of the skid, straightened until they reached the airfield lane and took that turn in a screaming slide.

The tree-lined narrow road was so dark that Alex switched on the headlights, and in their yellow glare Cynthia watched the elm trunks flicker past with terrifying speed. The wind brought tears to her eyes, she clutched the side of the car as it careened on the rough surface of the road. When the lighter stretch of the open field showed ahead Houston shut off the lights. The car rocked across the uneven ground toward the hangar.

Cynthia saw the small plane beyond, its propeller spinning, but Alex's motor drowned out its sound. Then the wing flaps moved, the rudder swung over and the wheels began to roll through the grass.

"He's getting away, Alex!" she cried.

As though the plane could see them approaching its motor roared and the wheels rolled faster. Houston tramped on the throttle, careless of the rough ground, and raced for the plane. It swerved away and he followed, bounding across the field in front of it.

At the last instant the pilot cut his motor to avoid a crash, the roaring died, the wheels locked and the spinning propeller slowed and stopped. A dark figure dropped from the cabin and ran headlong toward a car beside the hangar. When Alex set the emergency brake and jumped out to intercept him, the running man changed course and disappeared among the trees.

"Let the police gather him in," Alex said, as he opened the door on Cynthia's side "If Claire's alive she needs our help."

They found her in the plane, slumped on the seat, strips of torn sheet wound tight around arms and legs and a nylon stocking gag pulling her mouth into a ghastly grimace. There was blood on the stocking from her bruised nose, and a bluish lump on one temple, but her eyes were open, glaring at them as they lifted her from the plane.

Cynthia tried to be gentle as she worked at the tightly knotted gag.

"Everything's all right, Claire!" she soothed, regretting the tremor in her voice. Her hands were shaking. "I can't untie this, Alex!"

He dropped the strip of sheet he was unwinding from Claire's arms, ran his fingers under the nylon on her cheeks, and worked the gag carefully down under her chin.

Claire gulped and choked, shaking her head drunkenly.

"Thanks!" she mumbled, and then laughed so unexpectedly that Alex, who was unwinding her again, stopped and leaned back.

"Easy does it, Claire," he cautioned. "No hysterics, please!"

"Never had 'em in my life!" she protested, the color coming back in her cheeks. "It just struck me funny to be saying 'Thanks,' as if you'd lit a cigarette for me. I'll try to do better than that when I get my breath."

She kicked loose the last twist of sheet and stood up. Then she swayed dizzily and clutched at Cynthia.

"Sit down!" Cynthia urged. "Better lie down!"

"Not me. I never played a fainting female—I'm not the type." Claire set her teeth and straightened her shoulders. "Where did that rat go?" she demanded, peering into the plane.

"He took off," Alex assured her. "But he won't get far. It was Crane, of course?"

Her laugh mingled scorn and relief. "Who else? I could tell I was in for trouble when he barged into the apartment, but I never expected this!" She shook a clenched fist. "I gave him a couple of good ones until he knocked me down —punched me in the—"

She stopped with a gasp, lifted a hand toward her face and then dropped it.

"Is my nose broken?" she wailed. "I'm scared to feel of it! Gee, is it awful?" A sob choked her but she gulped and muttered, "Neal won't want to look at me—!" She shut her lips on that revealing statement.

"Your nose is as pretty as ever." Cynthia patted her shoulder "And if Neal Bruce doesn't know that you've got a lot more than good looks, he's plain stupid!"

"Which nobody ever said of Neal," Alex encouraged. "I take off my hat to you, Miss Herbert, for an exhibition of plain old-fashioned courage! Beaten up, tied up and almost abducted—but you come out of it laughing!"

"I didn't do any laughing in the plane, I can tell you that!" she confessed with a shudder. "And this was no eager lover-boy snatch, believe me! He meant to get rid of me for good this time!"

"Eric was going to kill you *himself?*" Cynthia gasped.

"Nothing else but! He said he was going to dump me when we got over the ocean—and don't try to tell me he wouldn't have done it!" Claire tugged at her wrinkled jacket and hitched at her skirt. She gave Houston a shaky smile.

"Sometime I'll try to thank you properly, Mr. Houston, but right now—could you run me down to town—or the Harbor House? I think I could use a drink."

XXII

BREAKFAST the next morning was served by Mary in Miss Shaw's living room to a select company consisting of that lady, Cynthia and Alex. It was Cousin Eva's idea, to avoid annoying interruptions from curious hotel guests while the other two brought her up to date on the exciting developments which she had missed—to her abiding regret.

Mary had set a gateleg table near the window where she plied them with omelet and bacon, hot biscuits light as puffs of cloud, and coffee so strong that it made Cynthia blink. The pleasure of serving her mistress with her own cooking, in place of what Mary called "that hotel grub!" acted as a tonic on the usually dour maid, and she smiled continually.

Cynthia, too, felt the happier mood of the day. The storm clouds of the night before had vanished and the sea glittered with ten thousand diamonds in the sunlight. Her own storm clouds were gone as well, now that any danger of interference by Eric Crane was permanently removed. She still faced the prospect of a cards-on-the-table session with Alex, which was becoming more inevitable by the moment, and she had consciously prepared for it by putting on her most becoming dress, a creamy Shantung which—she hoped—increased the glowing golden tan of her skin and the dark luster of her hair.

Now she could only wait for his opening move, and in the meantime enjoy his detailed—and often flattering—account to Miss Shaw of what he entitled, "The Case of the Misguided Marksman."

Cousin Eva listened with her habitual calm, but her eyes sparkled with enjoyment. When he described Cynthia's inspired theory of mistaken identity she beamed on the girl.

"I knew that I was getting a prize secretary," she announced proudly. "I am never mistaken in my estimate of character."

Cynthia caught a speculative glance from Alex and felt uncomfortable. Could he possibly be aware of her deception? Inwardly laughing at his cousin's mistaken faith? If he was, he covered it quickly with a laughing compliment.

"Cynthia out-Neroed Nero Wolfe and Perry Mason and all the rest of the fictional sleuths," he chuckled. "She guessed every step of Crane's plot to rid himself of the bothersome Claire—even to his reason for not taking a shot at the elevator when it was on the way up.

"He ducked out of sight because it *might* have been someone who would get off at the fourth floor—a workman, for instance. But when it came down later he knew it must be Claire; because he had heard her use her key when she went up."

Alex smiled at Cynthia. "The single item you went astray on, my dear—Cynthia—" he added the name hastily when his cousin frowned, "—was the existence of an imported gunman—your obsession that Crane hired someone else to do the shooting."

"I still can't believe that *Eric* could do such a thing!" she protested.

"A hold-over from the period when he was the one and only man in your life?"

"I suppose that must be it," she admitted, flushing at his steady stare. "I have always refused to believe rumors about friends, or anyone I know well."

Miss Shaw had pricked up her ears. "What's this about your one and—umm! Refusing to believe gossip is a very commendable trait, Cynthia," she approved hastily and turned again to Houston. "You say that the police caught

Crane soon after he ran from the plane? Harry Hunt must be more efficient than he appears!"

"A thoroughly efficient police officer, Cousin Eva, but not a detective. I know you thought he was foolish to waste so much suspicion on Cynthia, but remember that he had nothing to go on aside from her quarrel with Miss Crane—always a possible motive—and her lack of alibi; and the same set-up for Miss Herbert. So when the waitress, Anna, came through so bravely to establish the Herbert alibi, it left him with no one but Cynthia."

Miss Shaw was staring out the window. "This Anna interests me," she murmured. "The girl seems to have character; that is a commodity in great demand these days, and difficult to find. I must make her acquaintance," she announced decisively.

Alex grinned at Cynthia. "Anna's fortune is made!"

"Rubbish!" his cousin snapped. "Get back to your story. Did Crane confirm all Cynthia's theories when he was captured? Did he talk?"

"He babbled like a mountain brook," Alex nodded, "when they first questioned him. He was too overwrought to watch his tongue. I believe that Dr. Ferguson is right, Crane has been teetering on the brink of a nervous breakdown—or worse—for some time. His first failure to kill Claire Herbert and then our sudden switch to suspecting him threw him over the edge—drove him berserk. I'm sure he did intend to drop her out of the plane, although when he pulled himself together he tried to deny it. But I think a jury would believe Miss Herbert."

Cynthia shivered. "Will it come to a trial if Eric isn't in his right mind?"

"Frankly, I won't attempt to guess what is going to happen. As I said, at first he talked a blue streak, obviously unbalanced and uncontrolled, but then he seemed to realize what a case he was making against himself. Gradually he cooled off and finally refused to say another word until he had a lawyer."

"Did he ask you to act for him?" Miss Shaw demanded. "He couldn't do better!"

"That from *you*, Cousin Eva?" Alex laughed. "I thought you considered me incapable of even drawing up a simple lease without your guidance. No, Crane didn't need me, I'm glad to say. He made the one phone call—always allowed a suspect—to his pal, Mantell, and that estimable character had a lawyer on the way from Boston at supersonic speed. A sharp man, too, although his reputation isn't lily white.

It was an education to watch him go to work when he got there."

"How can they get around Eric's confession, though?" Cynthia asked.

"Confession?" Alex arched his eyebrows in mock astonishment. "The lawyer took care of that before you could snap your fingers! And I quote; 'An oral confession—while he was in a state of shock at being seized by the brutal police—a confession made under duress, in fear of bodily harm from those same Cossacks!' End quote. Remember how Claire boasted that she socked Crane a couple of times, Cynthia? The lawyer had a field day with those bruises. Obviously inflicted during the police grilling! Nazi Germany all over again!"

"You can't mean that he'll get Crane off?" Miss Shaw protested.

"Oh no, he's in for it, but it will be a nightmare of a trial with *that* lawyer defending him. I'm glad I'm not the prosecuting attorney." Alex leaned back and lit a cigarette. "You see, that shyster succeeded in messing up the case for sure. He even had an excuse for Crane beating up Claire. According to him that was nothing but a family quarrel."

Alex adopted a nasal whine as he mimicked, "She's practically his wife, ain't she? Who says the marriage was a fake besides the dame, and she'd say anything!"

"How dreadful!" Cynthia protested. "I believe Claire!"

"No question of that; I'm only telling you how tough the defense will be. Was that what Claire has been putting pressure on Crane for—the fake marriage, I mean?" When Cynthia nodded he shrugged. "Another count against him, as if there weren't enough!"

Miss Shaw finished her coffee and sat back.

"At any rate, we're through with the unpleasantness now, and I can get back to writing my book." She cast an anxious look at Cynthia. "I hope all this hasn't made you feel that you want to shake the dust of Newbury Point from your feet forever, my dear. Because I don't know what I would do without you!"

"You can count on me," Cynthia assured. "Until the last Shaw is duly chronicled, I promise to stand by at the typewriter. Every one of them is too fascinating to abandon."

Houston blew a smoke ring toward the ceiling.

"I'm a Shaw, too, you know."

"A remote connection!" his cousin snapped before Cynthia could think of a suitable retort, and immediately suggested, "Could we do some work this morning. Cynthia?

We have wasted a great deal of time on detecting and post-mortems."

"Hardly wasted." Houston stood up. "I take it that my presence is disturbing to authorship, so I'll disappear—when we've taken care of one final matter in 'The Case of the Misguided Marksman.' Lieutenant Hunt asked me to bring Mrs. Farley over this morning to sign a statement of how and where she recovered Crane's pistol."

He smiled at Cynthia. He had produced her lucky piece from his pocket and was tossing it in the air and catching it. The little gold star winked and glittered.

"Then," he said softly, "after a few words with her I will return her to you, Cousin Eva, and go where my fate and luck direct me."

As they went downstairs to his car Cynthia waited with fast beating heart for him to bring up the subject she expected—and waited in vain. On the porch he pointed to a couple walking along the hotel beach, hand in hand.

"Fade out to a happy ending?" he suggested. "That looks like Neal and Claire."

"It is, and they seem to be very chummy, don't they? I'm so glad. Isn't it nice that Neal finally found someone who suits him?"

"It's always nice when a man finds a girl who suits him," Alex agreed soberly. "If he suits the girl, that's the nicest of all." He closed the car door and stood looking at her. "Then their road leads straight to happiness."

"Our road," Cynthia reminded, "leads to the police station." The look of disappointment on his face made her regret the unfeeling remark, but she cheered herself with the thought that after their visit to the police, when he tried again, she would not rebuff him.

A flame of anticipation ran through every nerve at the thought. The time had come to confess her deception, no matter how it might anger him—or Miss Shaw. That latter consideration chilled her a little. Not that she feared an outburst from the controlled Miss Eva—but disappointment, surely. A look of reproach in those level eyes for a girl whom she had grown to love and trust. Well, it was something that must be done, and lived down afterward, if earnest endeavor could accomplish that.

The conference with Hunt took only a few minutes; he had her statement already typewritten from his own notes, and after she had read it she signed it. Before she realized if they were back at the car, Alex standing ready to help her in. He was tossing the gold star again, looking up and down the main street with evident indecision.

"This is no place to talk," he muttered. "Will you ride out the shore road with me? I have something to say which can't wait."

"Anywhere you like," Cynthia agreed a trifle breathlessly.

A piercing whistle and a screech of brakes made them both whirl toward the cross street in time to see a yellow sports car slide to a bouncing stop. Beside it towered Officer O'Hara, white gloved hands spread wide, the whistle chain dangling from his lips. He snatched it away.

"Oh, you didn't see me?" he roared, his brown face darkening by degrees. "In a pig's eye, you didn't!"

"Don't yell at me, you hick cop!" the driver of the car answered with equal heat. "I was watching for my turn!"

Cynthia's heart leaped to her throat. That was the voice of a Farley! She would recognize it even though it came echoing down from the stratosphere. Alonzo had arrived!

"Don't give me that, you crazy hotrodder!" O'Hara's temper boiled over at the unfortunate adjective 'hick.' "You came around that corner like a bat out of hell; no wonder you couldn't stop! Why don't you take lessons, before you kill someone!"

"Oh, shut up!" Alonzo jerked on the emergency brake and began to pry his big frame out of the cramping seat. "I don't like being yelled at!"

Cynthia sprang from the curb and ran toward the car. "Please, God," she prayed silently, "let me get there before Lon hits him!" Her brother slid out onto the street, straightened to face O'Hara, and was drawing breath for another blast when she clutched his arm. "Lon!" she cried wildly.

He turned reluctantly from the policeman. "Hi, Cynthy! How are you? You look fine!" He kissed her heartily. "Wait a second, will you?" And he swung back to O'Hara. "Listen, you!" he growled.

"No, Lon, don't!" she implored. "Please, Mr. O'Hara—let him go!" she gasped. "He didn't mean anything. He—he's my husband, and he's been away—in Japan for so long he's forgotten our rules!" What a lot of little lies it takes, she thought desperately, to keep the first big lie afloat!

The officer looked from her to the blustering Alonzo and his lip curled.

"For you, Mrs. Queen, I'll let him off this time." His anger seemed to have been replaced by sorrow, for he shook his head pityingly. "If you're married to the likes of *him*, ma'am, you've got trouble enough coming to you without me adding any." He turned and strode away swinging his whistle.

"You're too flip for your own good!" Alonzo called hotly.

"I'll—!" Cynthia's heel came down on his foot with a force that cut off any further words for the moment. "What's the idea, Cynthy?" he gasped, with a grimace of pain as he shook his foot.

"Must you begin a brawl with the police the minute you arrive, Lon?" she reproved. "You could have ended up in jail!"

"I can take care of myself, thanks! But what about you, and why the devil are you still here? I wrote you to quit this fool job!" With a sudden scowl he glared over her shoulder. "What do *you* want?"

Cynthia turned and met the stony eyes of Alex Houston, whom she had completely forgotten in her excitement. His face was colorless, strained to an expression of cold indifference as he held out her gold star.

"I won't be needing this after all, Mrs. Farley," he said quietly, and dropped it into her hand. "It doesn't work for me." With a slight bow and the barest nod to Lon he swung on his heel and went quickly back to his car.

"Who's that wooden Indian, and why did he high-hat me?" Alonzo demanded.

"He's not a wooden Indian!"

"Then he needs a blood transfusion!"

"Oh, don't make life so hard!" Cynthia moaned, struggling against an almost irresistible impulse to call to Alex, even race after him. *Don't let him go,* her heart counseled eagerly, but a timorous voice advised against such precipitate action. Suppose he didn't wait, but drove away and left her in vain pursuit, a ridiculous picture of frustration? *No matter,* her heart argued fiercely, *don't let him go out of your life—*

"Quit mooning!" Alonzo ordered, and his heavy hand urged her toward his car. "Get in!"

It was as though she had been piloting a plane through rough weather and suddenly crashed head on into an invisible barrier. Automatically she obeyed, with passive acceptance of that masculine Farley habit of ordering her life for her, let the chips fall where they may! And before she recovered enough to assert her independence the chance was lost; Alex had driven off without a backward glance.

"All set?" Lon released the brake, sublimely ignorant of any disaster caused by his interference. "I've taken a room at the hotel in Salem, we'll have lunch there—and talk. You sure can get yourself into the damndest jams, Cynthy, but I'll straighten you out—if it's still possible. This time, though, it looks rough!"

With Alex deserting her and exposure to Miss Shaw imminent, if she knew Alonzo's impetuous nature, Cynthia could think of nothing to offer but the threadbare promise, "I can explain everything."

XXIII

HOW MUCH easier to make that promise than to make' the explanation, Cynthia thought, an hour later while she still battled with her headstrong brother in his hotel room. He had ordered luncheon served there to ensure privacy, endeavored to soften her stubborn resistance by presenting a meal chosen with the lavish hand for which all Farleys were famous, and showered her with gifts from the Orient which took her breath away. But for once she stood up to his commands and blandishments with equal bravery.

"You've got me beat, Cynthy," he admitted at last. "You've changed so! When you pulled that bloomer with Crane in California you let me take charge—and I cleaned up the mess, didn't I? I can do it this time, if you'll let me."

"If I've changed it's because I've grown up. And I'm *not* in any trouble that you can help me with now. The murder case is finished as far as I'm concerned. It's past history. As for pretending to be married, I'm glad I did it because I met Miss Shaw and—and Alex—"

"Yeah, this guy Houston—what about him? You've gone overboard again, huh?"

"Don't say that, Lon, as though I were a child. After that fiasco with Eric Crane I promised myself to be *sure* the next time; to wait until I found a man I could respect as well as love." Her voice trembled at the thought of Alex but she steadied it. "I found him; someone who makes me know that life won't be worth living unless it is shared with him."

Alonzo studied her with brotherly affection. "This is the man who made love to you even though you were married?"

"That hurt unbearably, Lon—but perhaps it should encourage me. If he cared enough to do that—"

"Glad you can see it that way, Sis." He still probed her pleading eyes, and slowly nodded. "You think this is *it*, don't you."

"I know it!"

"O.K." He stood up in smiling surrender. "I only want your happiness, Cynthy, so anything I can do to help—"

"Oh, Lon, please don't do *anything!*" she implored, with a frightening vision of his heavy-handed methods. "I appreciate the offer, but—but *please* stay out of this!"

Perhaps I made a mistake in declining Lon's offer of help, Cynthia mused, as she stood at the window of Miss Shaw's living room and stared unseeingly at the pale violet shades of twilight creeping across the sea. A wonderful brother, deep down below his front of Farley omnipotence; could he have advised her on how to resume friendly relations with Alex without appearing to pursue?

Lon would surely have tried; in spite of his professed scorn for 'fool girls' he would do anything for her. At her throat sparkled the exquisite string of crystals he'd brought her from Japan, on her arm glittered the matching bracelet, and her fingers caressed the silken beauty of the fabulous mandarin coat which completed his array of gifts. Perhaps Lon's generous heart might have concocted some scheme to bring her another chance with the man she loved, something more practical than she could devise.

"That wouldn't be difficult," she said aloud. "*I* certainly have made a mess of things!"

"You have indeed," agreed a husky voice from the doorway where Alex stood with hands thrust hard into his pockets and tormented eyes riveted on her. He must have noticed the sudden dazzling glow of joy at his arrival, although he misinterpreted it.

"You are lovelier each time we meet," he growled, "or could it be those glamorous adornments from the Orient which become you so? Gifts from Alonzo, the ever-loving but absent husband? You and he must have enjoyed a hearty laugh over my blindness—" he muttered, and then with a quick change to decisive action asked, "may I come in—since you left the door partly open?"

"Why did you come here, Alex?"

"Not to pursue you further, so don't look so frightened. I dropped in to confess to Cousin Eva that she was right—as usual—and that I've made a fool of myself. You actually are married, and all the suspicions I retailed to her so trustingly were completely unfounded."

He towered over her, lips drawn to a hard thin line in his white face, and nodded slowly.

"Unfounded suspicions!" he repeated bitterly, "born of hope, I admit, but that doesn't excuse me. Do you remember that night after Hunt left us, and she insisted on a private conference with me? She knew how I felt and tried to save me—but I was too far gone then, too deeply in love to listen. So I've come here to admit that she was right. Where is she?"

"I—I don't know, there was no one here when I came

in," Cynthia whispered, wondering if he heard the words above the pounding of her heart.

"Too bad she isn't here, I could save time by telling you both at once." His voice was iced, his eyes held hers hypnotically. "You know what I wanted to say to you today—have wanted to say many times. That I'm in love with you—everything about you, Cynthia—your laugh, your eyes, your gallant spirit. They hit me like an avalanche that first day I drove you down here—no, before that—one night on a wrecked train. Remember that?"

She tried to smile, offer a bright and casual, "Of course I remember!" and could only choke and nod silently.

Alex put out a hand to grasp hers, then snatched it back and strode away to a safer distance.

"You think I shouldn't be saying this to a married woman? But I must—I've got to square myself with you, Cynthia. All those thoughts I had about you were honest love, because I never believed that you were married! I knew you weren't, couldn't be! You are so young and—and ardent and innocent." He struck a table impatiently with clenched fist. "Good God, do you suppose I would have talked the way I did—behaved as I did—to another man's wife? *Do you?*"

Cynthia's world was spinning with relief and hope as he tore away the only doubt of him she had ever had.

"No!" she said eagerly.

"I may be modern," he muttered, "but not modern enough for wife-stealing! Cynthy, you believe me, don't you? From the first I was sure you pretended to be married to get the job with Cousin Eva. Good Lord, little Miss Ober was enough to give the show away by herself. Did you think she fooled me, when I've been cross-examining witnesses for years? She was scared stiff, and lying her head off!

"You were, too, clumsily—tying your slick story into knots whenever you forgot your part for a moment—or so I thought. Married a few weeks, engaged to Eric Crane just before that—you weren't sure when! And another thing. That night on the train, you weren't wearing a wedding ring."

"How did you happen to notice *that?*" she asked faintly.

"*Happen* to? Your left hand was clutching my arm in a death grip and it was an automatic masculine reaction to check on the third finger while I carried a lovely girl out of there. Can't you see how everything I learned about you from the very first was evidence that you weren't married, if I wanted to take it that way? And Lord knows I did! I think I had almost convinced Eva, much as she hated to admit that *you* could deceive her."

"Miss Shaw didn't quite lose faith in me, then?"

Alex shook his head. "She's steadfast as a rock where friends are concerned, although my theories did worry her. But I was sure of myself," he muttered, fumbling in his coat pocket, "so sure I could force you to confess today that I went prepared. Why, even that ring you wear looked phony—not at all the sort any man would choose for a girl like you!"

Involuntarily Cynthia's eyes dropped to her inexpensive band of thin gold, and from habit she defended, "It isn't the cost that counts, it's the thought—"

"I was going to ask you to exchange it for mine," Alex interrupted. He extended his open hand. " 'With this ring I thee wed!' " he quoted bitterly.

Fascinated, she stared at the glittering circlet of diamonds on his palm, but before she could speak he thrust the ring savagely back into his pocket and laughed harshly.

"And then," he muttered, "out of nowhere appears a husband after all—that cocky, blustering Alonzo with his possessive airs! Curtains for Houston! It has been a comedy for you, hasn't it, a hilarious comedy!" He turned away with an impatient, "Why did you come back here tonight, anyway?"

" 'Thrift, thrift, Horatio!' as Hamlet said," Cynthia announced with fast-beating heart, hoping the obscure answer would turn his scowling eyes back to her. When it did her lips curved in a smile which made him catch his breath and frown more angrily. "Even if I'm not a New Englander like you and cousin Eva—I'm thrifty. I have a room here, so why put Brother Alonzo to the expense of hiring another—"

"Brother?" Alex glared for an amazed instant before understanding flamed in his eyes. "So that's who 'Lon' is—and I was right after all!" His hands were reaching for her when he stopped and the scowl returned. "But you told O'Hara he was your husband!"

"The maternal instinct, I suppose; a throwback to Mother's way of edging in between the Fighting Farleys when they lined up for battle. I was terrified of what O'Hara might do, because Lon *was* unbearable, wasn't he! And I thought a plea from a mere sister wouldn't impress the wrathful cop. But as a wife—"

Then at last his strong hands did close tenderly on her shoulders to draw her close, and as his lips brushed her cheek he murmured:

"As a wife, dearest? Yes, let's talk about that!"